Th

A

COUSIN

Cousin Suzanne

MYRNA BLYTH

AVON
PUBLISHERS OF BARD, CAMELOT, DISCUS, EQUINOX AND FLARE BOOKS

"The White Cliffs of Dover" by Alice Duer Miller, reprinted by permission of Coward, McCann & Geoghegan, Inc. Copyright 1940 by Alice Duer Miller. Copyright renewed 1967 by Dennig Miller.

AVON BOOKS
A division of
The Hearst Corporation
959 Eighth Avenue
New York, New York 10019

First Avon Printing, July, 1976

AVON TRADEMARK REG. U.S. PAT. OFF. AND
FOREIGN COUNTRIES, REGISTERED TRADEMARK—
MARCA REGISTRADA, HECHO EN CHICAGO, U.S.A.

Printed in the U.S.A.

For Jeffrey
And with thanks to my
editor, Nancy Davis

The Fates assigned to Aphrodite one divine duty only: to make love. But one day Athene caught her surreptitiously at work at a loom and complained to the other gods that her prerogatives had been infringed. She even threatened to abandon them completely. Aphrodite, in tears, apologized profusely for her indiscretion and since then has never done a hand's turn of work.

Hesiod, *Theogony*

Sally Says

. . . I just love London weddings, don't you? And yesterday's was a dilly. Greek shipping tycoon Nicho Anapoulis who Fortune Magazine says is one of the twenty richest men in the world—I always believe *them*—married Miss Suzanne Felice Goldfarb of Hewlett Bay Park, Long Island.

After the surprise wedding in a London registrar's office, Suzanne's mum hosted a luncheon at the Savoy where the champagne flowed, well, like champagne. Suzanne, who's a real looker, was wearing a cream-colored Dior gown in a billowing tent shape which is just as well. Suzanne, the sweetie, is a tiny bit *enceinte* which in case you don't know is *francais* for preggers. Oh, you *naughty* Nicho. Who else tells you these things?

1

SUPER SECRETS OF
THE SUPERSTARS

I am the I of this story but not its most important character. I am about midway in importance between most and least, a position I have often assumed. I am confidante and chorus, friend and reporter, advisor and explicator, part of the scene but at the frazzled far end of the picture.

Personally, I have trouble taking center stage.

Reading poetry in college, I had an immediate gut reaction to Eliot. "No! I am not Prince Hamlet, nor was meant to be—" Exactly.

So call me Emilia, Bianca, Lady MacDuff. Hell, call me Ishmael if you want to. That's another of my characteristics, I like to make a good first impression and I try very hard to please.

No, the star of this little production is my Cousin Suzanne. *The* Suzanne Felice nee Goldfarb briefly Poparossa now Anapoulis who has recently become well known to even the most casual readers of gossip columns, the social pages of the *New York Times,* *Cosmopolitan* magazine, the large circulation British Sundays and/or the Hewlett Bay Park Hadassah Newsletter. "Married: Daughter of our Israel Bond Chairwoman—"

Suzanne's recent courtship, wedding, and her current extended honeymoon on her very own Greek isle have enthralled the several million who are enthralled by such things. But then Suzanne and Nicho, especially together, combining brains and beauty, hard cash and photogenic allure peppered over nicely with the stimulating flavor of illicit hanky-panky are enthrallers, superstars. While we—and I certainly include myself smack in the middle—are the onlookers, the fans, yes, and I admit it, the *groupies.*

"Everyone's someone's groupie, luv," the fat-lipped, spaced-out leader of a rock group once told me. And since it was the only coherent sentence he uttered during our two-hour interview his words had a certain depressing validity.

Until recently—about four weeks ago, in fact—I was the managing editor of a magazine for teenage girls. And so I know a fair amount about the basic common-denominator groupie scene. For seven long years I sat at a typewriter churning it out daily for the readers of *Modern Teen, the With-It Magazine,* writing everything from astrology columns (with me, last month's forecast for Pisces was this month's forecast for Aries) to what was laughingly referred to around the office as "think pieces." They changed over the years from "No Date for the Prom: How Big a Crisis?" to "Busted on a Drug Rap: How Big a Crisis?" (a capsule history of the American adolescent, 1966-1973).

But I confess I was almost as nervous and awed as a groupie contemplating the blue jeans of a top-of-the-charter when I arrived on the island and knew I was going to spend weeks and weeks with Nicho. "The Modern Odysseus who found the Golden Fleece," thundered one magazine profile I read about him. The writer of that highly flavored example of mixed metaphor also called him "Horatio Alger, Aegean Style." For Nicho has gone the whole rags-to-riches route from peasant boy to mercantile prince.

Now his tankers carry a quarter of the world's oil sup-
ply from the Persian Gulf to the markets of the West.
He owns shipyards in Japan and Ireland, steel works
in the Ruhr, diamond mines in West Africa, an international airline, all of London's taxis, and, I don't
know why, most of downtown Manila. Even a partial
list of his holdings gives one a touch of goose pimples.
He is a man in a TV news documentary, worldly
success personified. Old King Midas whose wit, not
his touch, has turned the seas to gold.

But my Cousin Suzanne is never mesmerized, never
impressed. Not even by Nicho, that Horatio Alger,
Aegean-style. Not by other famous men she has
known. And there was, I seem to recall, a TV talk-
show host, an internationally known heart surgeon, an
Undersecretary of State.

No, she is the dazzler always, who draws others
into her net. Not, I must hasten to add, that she re-
mains untouched by her victims. Afterwards, but only
afterwards, Suzanne can be hurt, mistreated, cracked
in her perfectly straightened white-on-white teeth.
Maybe it is the enchantress who always suffers the
most from the spells she casts. We just have never
heard her side of the story. Think of Circe. (I've been
rereading a lot of Greek mythology lately. It goes
with the local atmosphere.) Wicked Circe, Super
Siren, turned men into swine. So beware, all foolish
sailors. But poor Circe, after turning her trick, was
left with dozens of men at her feet acting more like
beasts than usual. And who else but Circe was around
to slop the pigs?

My Cousin Suzanne—how to describe her? Think of
the last beautiful girl you saw on a magazine cover or
in a TV commercial. It may have been Suzanne. If
not, it was a reasonable facsimile. A yard of blonde
hair, a perfect face, a figureless figure. (Recently

Suzanne has gained twenty-seven pounds.) Men looked at Suzanne and fell in love. One fast look. Shazam! Believe me. I've been there and seen it happen.

Another portrait: Suzanne running. When the going gets tough, complicated, even a little sticky, Suzanne runs. She doesn't say anything. She doesn't say much in general. She just goes thataway.

At age six she ran away from home without giving any explanation. Twelve hours later the Nassau County police found her crying with vexation because the cars on the Long Island Expressway wouldn't stop to let her cross. She tried again at seven. At nine she got as far as Pennsylvania Station. During her teens she left her house more often by the second-story window—a graceful climb down a convenient rose trellis—than by the front door. She ran away with her first husband, Johnny Poparossa, a Mafioso soldier, and three days later, after learning how to load and unload his Colt .45, ran away from him. She ran away from the nice Jewish doctor she was supposed to marry. Three hundred guests were already assembled in the Imperial Suite at the Plaza Hotel, munching pigs-in-blankets and egg rolls. She even ran away from Nicho once, sort of an involuntary fear-and-flee reflex. At the moment, though, her opportunities are rather limited. We are on a small island and she is rather heavy on her feet.

D-for-Delivery day. Three days ago. *This is the day they give babies away with half a pound of tea.* Though Suzanne snarled as we all watched her very carefully, expecting her to crack open like an ostrich egg: "I've never been on time for anything in my life, so why the hell should I be on time for this?" It was not her most interesting remark of the day.

I awoke midmorning but the exact time I never knew. There are no clocks in my charmingly decorated bedroom. (Shiny green-and-white lattice wallpaper, white wicker furniture, quilts.) There are no clocks anywhere in the villa except in Nicho's office where there are six in a row set on New York, London, Zurich, Kuwait, Buenos Aires, and Tokyo time. Nicho wears two Piaget wristwatches, one on each wrist, set for London and Kuwait time. Nobody is supposed to care about the time here.

Iphigenia knocked on my door softly and then padded in when I gave a shout. Her bare feet made a soft flip-flop on the imported terracotta tiles.

"Good morning, Miss Lady," she said brightly. "You sleep nize?"

She smiled as she opened the shutters and let the Mediterranean sun, which never stops blazing, blaze in. She smiled as she propped up my pillows, smiled as she went out and then came back in with my breakfast tray. I, used to New York City cleaning women, am not all that comfortable around little round Iphigenia. I still have the feeling that somehow she is putting me on.

Iphigenia smiled at me while I wolfed down the omelette fines herbes, my fresh, flaky croissant. Enjoy, enjoy. Nicho has imported the second chef from Lapérouse to take charge of the kitchen. I have been on the island three weeks and gained five pounds. And it is Suzanne who is in her ninth month.

"Anyone up yet?" I asked.

Iphigenia grinned happily in reply.

"Madame?"

She shook her glossy head. After a moment she managed: "Da—Boss—ees—work—"

Constantly. By now I know Nicho's never-changing, seven-day-a-week routine. Up every morning about 6:30 to make his Persian Gulf phone calls. A chat with the Sheik. A little buzz-buzz with the Emir. He works till noon and then takes a break for an Americano and a light lunch. During the afternoon he makes his Western Hemisphere phone calls, sends messages on his Telex, dictates letters. Every day a secretary and an assistant are ferried from Cyprus to the island by helicopter. Occasionally, at night when Suzanne has gone to bed, he returns to his office for a couple of hours more.

"You're working hard," I said to him the other day after a meal which ended nicely, I thought, with a soufflé Grand Marnier. Suzanne had gone for a nap, the others had scattered, and we were alone. I am terribly shy around Nicho and have trouble making anything more scintillating than toneless polite conversation.

"Oh no," he said, lighting up a Churchillian-sized Havana. He buys the entire output of one of Castro's factories to stock the humidors in his various offices and homes. "This is a vacation, a rest, waiting for the child. No, I am not working much at all."

He speaks English well, even subtly, with a nice dusting of a medium-thick international accent. He speaks five languages perfectly, including a bubbling Arabic. One day on the beach Nicho was fielding phone calls, switching casually from Portuguese to Italian to Greek.

"But how did you learn them all?" Suzanne asked afterwards, sounding petulant. I remember when she had mucho trouble with second-year Spanish at Hewlett High.

"When I was a sailor, my darling. I was a very young man then. So in different ports a sailor finds there are girls to teach him many things."

"Sorry, darling," she drawled, "I don't know Yiddish myself."

He threw back his head and laughed. She makes

him laugh, too, once in a while. Not that it matters.

"Mmmmmm, well, how hard do you usually work?" I asked during our awkward little after-lunch conversation. It sounded dumb. I even gave a dumb little giggle for emphasis.

He looked at me, taking in the giggle. He looked away. He blew out a puff of aromatic blue-gray smoke. His eyes are small and there are discolored pouches beneath them. But they are an unusually sparkling dark, dark brown and quite beautiful I think. Nicho has the eyes of a gentle man, which may be merely a clever disguise.

"I like to work," he said. "When I was a boy in my village there was no work. The men sat outside their houses in the sun for weeks and months, sometimes for years. Can you imagine such a thing? No, it is not possible that you could. But for me work is a pleasure." He stood up abruptly and went down the path to the sea. I felt we knew each other no better.

At dinner that night I felt even more awkward than usual but he was charming and gay, teasing Suzanne just a little, making even dour Dr. Lavelle, the resident ob/gyn crack a vague smile.

Nicho had arranged for a print of a new movie that had opened in New York that week to be sent to the island. After dinner a screen was set up on the terrace and we conveniently "flicked out." Suzanne and Nicho sat next to each other on large wicker throne-like chairs, holding hands. Her famous engagement ring, blue-white, pear-shaped, 22 carats, looked like a fallen star in the velvet darkness. Halfway through the movie, which was interesting, he kissed the palm of her hand and departed. Back to the pleasures of work.

In another article I read about him—I did my research—Nicho's fortune was estimated at nearly a hundred million. A hundred million. It is almost inconceivable. I was going to ask Suzanne—I like to get my facts straight—but how does one ask? Such questions are too impersonally personal. Strangers can gossip with impunity about the things good friends don't discuss. Only groupies know everything and nothing.

"Ai—leen." A pebble hit my balcony.

I pulled on a shirt and a pair of pants.

Suzanne stood on the patio wearing one of the mini-tents which she claims Yves St. Laurent stitched up for her with his own little hands. Funny, but an Yves St. Laurent maternity dress looks exactly like every other maternity dress.

"Today's D-Day, kiddo."

She made as ugly a face as possible.

"How was your night?"

"Bloody awful. I keep getting these bloody foot cramps." Four months in England enriched Suzanne's vocabulary immensely.

"And I'm no longer comfortable in any position. If I'm on my side my back aches. If I'm on my back my legs hurt. And the bloody thing keeps jabbing at me—" She touched her lump gingerly. "I know it's going to be the kind that sleeps all day and screams bloody murder all night—"

When I first arrived Suzanne was all dewy-eyed and mother-earthish, weaving garlands *à la Primavera* out of the flowers that Nicho had delivered to her daily from Cyprus, reading Guttmacher and Spock, ordering a copy of *The Magic Years* in Greek to make sure Nicho understood and took to heart every little psychological word. But as she continued to swell and swell and swell her enthusiasm dampened. Lately we have taken to calling her belly Moby Dick.

"Come and have a cup of coffee with me. . . ." She shuffled off, a battleship, prow forward, sluggishly cutting through the waves. From the back, Suzanne doesn't look pregnant. Her legs and arms have remained model-thin. She reminds me sometimes of a drawing by a six-year-old of the mommy he secretly hates. Little head, long pole-like arms and legs, and a big swollen menacing female body.

I joined her on the patio. While I watched she started and finished her breakfast in two fast gulps. A half-scoop of cottage cheese.

"I'm hungry." A whine.

Dr. Lavelle had cut her calories again. She gets three vitamin pills and a token offering of protein three times a day.

"I'm hungry," she said a little louder. "I'M HUNGRY, DAMN IT!" Her wail brought three excited maids rushing out of the house. They thought the main event had begun. I waved them back and poured Suzanne a cup of skimmed milk café au lait, sweetened delicately with saccharine. Suzanne's diet frustrates the chef too. She is down to the real nitty-gritty, a hard-boiled egg, three ounces of roast beef, six shrimp artfully arranged to look like seven.

"You've starved before. Hell, all the years you modeled—what did you live on then? Yoghurt and prunes?"

"I know. I know. I thought it was all over."

"It's not going to last forever—"

"I know but. . . ." She stopped and sipped her coffee. "Forgive me, Eileen, for being so bloody again. I guess I'm tired." There were faint smudges under her blue-green eyes. "Look—" she stretched out her arms. She wore two new bracelets, gold, intricately carved. They extended from her wrists halfway up her pale, lightly freckled arms.

Each morning when she wakes up there is a little gift on the pillow for Suzanne. Oh, it may be something small and thoughtful—a rare Nile Valley orchid flown by jet fifteen hundred miles across steamy Africa. Perhaps a copy of this week's *New York* magazine so she can keep in touch. (Cost of publication, 75¢; cost of air freight from JFK, $97.) It may be something big and vulgar—a Bulgari evening bag, shaped like an elephant, 14-carat gold, studded here and there with pearls and sapphires, a set of Gucci luggage, a mummy case. I am not kidding; there is a very well-preserved New Kingdom mummy case—without mummy, thank goodness—in the hall off the patio.

The carved gold bracelets glittered in the sunlight. "From Nicho?"

Who else?

"Mmmmm. They're Minoan. From Crete. Very rare." She traced the carving with a long pink nail. "Fertility symbols."

"It's a little late—"

Happy birthday every day but Christmas. Personally I'd find it a little wearing. Oh, yes, I would. Suzanne delivers her kisses and her thanks like a good girl before lunch each day. It must be the thought that counts because Suzanne is not that devoted to *things*. Sure, she used to be a normally acquisitive girl who half-wanted anything Bloomingdale's was pushing in their windows that week. But she never cried a whole lot for the moon.

Now my Aunt Bea, Suzanne's mother, is a ten-to-four, five-days-a-week, light-heavyweight shopper. Bea is an advocate of the Noah's Ark school of purchasing power. If you like it in one color, so why not take it in two?

Nicho gives everyone lavish gifts. I've already received books, perfume, a Zolotas bracelet, an Olivetti. He is a generous man, I suppose, but his gift-giving may be calculated and done for its effect. One does not look the giver of a gift horse in the mouth or even in the gentle eyes. In London he employs, full time, a former buyer from Harrods who does the buying for him. In one of those magazine profiles it reported that Nicho always manages to come up with a thoughtful and appropriate gift for every business associate, including the writer of that profile.

"Good morning, Madame Anapoulis, Miss Walker." Dr. Lavelle, tall, lean, and dignified in conservative, slightly baggy, bathing trunks, was on his way to the beach.

"Doctor, I'm hungry—" a semi-whine.

"Madame, a swim might be a good idea. Yes, I suggest a little light exercise after breakfast."

"I'm too weak from hunger—"

"A walk perhaps, *chère* Madame."

"My knees keep banging into my stomach—"

Dr. Lavelle ambled on, his expression bland, refusing to react.

"I'm just going to sit here until lunch—" She poured herself another cup of coffee. She yawned. This is the rhythm of our days. "I guess I'll read the papers—" We have daily helicopter drops of the *Wall Street Journal*, the *New York Times*, the *Journal of Commerce*, and, Allah be praised, the *Abu Dhabi Gazette*, the English-language voice of the Persian Gulf.

"Well, since you're no fun at all, I guess I'll put on my bathing suit and have a swim."

"Good idea. I think he likes you."

I scoffed: "He is not my type. He is too uptight. My God, he'd rather look you in the vagina than straight in the eye—"

"So? Is that such a bad place to start?" said Mother Earth and yawned.

Upstairs I pulled on one of my new bathing suits. I

bought three in the wild melee that is Saks' end-of-summer sale, when I decided to leave my job and New York and come here to help Suzanne wait out this last long month. I looked at myself in the mirror carefully. To make it clear right now, I have thought about it a great deal over the years, and no, I am not unduly jealous of Cousin Suzanne's great and unusual beauty. I look okay. I will not bore myself with a copywriter's description of my own "brown hair with glints, etc." Let it suffice: men have always found something or other to admire either above or below my neck when circumstances made it absolutely necessary.

Still—and this I do admit—I may be secretly delighted in some dark and dank subconscious cranny of my psyche that for once I look a helluva lot better than Suzanne does in a bathing suit. When she takes one of her infrequent dips, she wears a tank suit, the world's stretchiest, or a droopy Lady Madonna bikini. "Bellies are beautiful," she says very grimly.

If Nicho is around she makes sure she is prettily covered up, neck to knee in a cascade of ruffles. But Nicho, I can tell, is enchanted by her ever-burgeoning proportions. His first wife died about two years ago. They were married for thirty years and were childless. Suzanne has told me that, desperate for a child, an heir, they did it like crazy every time her temperature rose. At the right time of month he'd even leave business meetings. Above their connubial bed hung a giant Seurat. For three decades Nicho did his manly duty with dots before his eyes. The picture was being sold at Sotheby's the day he met Suzanne. An omen.

The other afternoon from my balcony I watched Suzanne and Nicho together on the beach. She lay on a chaise lounge, looking at the pictures in a French

Vogue. He sat next to her, going over reports as usual, smoking his big, black cigar. Suddenly he was down on his knees, kissing her face and hands and breast. Then he rested his head against her stomach for a long time, listening for the dim fetal heartbeat. I turned away and went inside. There was an ache in my throat. When I looked again, they had gone.

Sur la plage. Our exclusive Mediterranean beach which doesn't rightly deserve the name. A strip of gritty pebbles which become slightly finer pebbles which drop abruptly into the wine-dark sea.

Nicho is planning the creation of a proper TV-commercial-type beach. The Sheik of Kuwait has offered the sand. Imagine their conversation:

"Nicho, you need sand? Fellah, have I got sand. Old sand, new sand. White sand, beige sand. This season, believe me boychik, we are cutting sand."

One of Nicho's tankers will bring us our beach. A modern Odysseus can rearrange the sands of time.

"Hello-o-o," I called.

Dr. Lavelle performed a vigorous Australian crawl. I plunged in. It doesn't take much courage. The Med is a warm bath.

Suzanne and I were raised on the South Shore of Long Island. Every summer her parents rented a cabana at the Shore Point Beach Club, and I was a regular guest. The mid-Atlantic, even when its shores are dotted with card tables, is never a sybarite's pond. The ladies playing canasta at the shoreline, the chicken salad plates, and the bottles of Bain de Soleil cannot temper that gray, mirthless ocean. On a rough day, breakers fall like judgment on the heads of unwary swimmers and iced-tea pitchers and beach bags are swept out to sea. I used to lie on the beach and try to imagine England two thousand miles across the ocean. While Suzanne danced to the jukebox: *"Earth Angel, Earth Angel will you be mine. . . ."* I recited corny English poetry to myself.

> I have loved England, dearly and deeply
> Since that first evening shining and pure
> The white cliffs of Dover, I saw rising steeply
> Out of the sea that once made her secure.

That's the kind of kid I was. What's more, my geography was lousy. Strange as it may seem, it is these small Mediterranean islands that are on the same latitude as New York.

I swam to the doctor. He swam to me.

"Very ni—"

"So, you are—"

Disaster. We both spoke at the same time.

I smiled.

He smiled.

"I was just going in—" he said.

Underwater I hid my disappointment. A school of tiny silvery fishes swam through my legs. They tickled. When I surfaced, he was still there.

"Miss Walker—"

"Call me Aileen."

"Ai-leen"—my hard-edged name did not sit comfortably on his *Suisse-française* pronunciation—"I wonder if you would do me a service—"

"Of course." Ask, just ask.

"I wish very much that you would convince Madame to take a bit more exercise."

Oh, that. "I try but she finds it so difficult to get around now. And you know she's not in the best of spirits—"

He nodded. "Her prepartum depression is not unusual. You see, there is a significant hormonal change during the last days of the gestation period. Personally I believe it is nature's way of signaling that the end of the pregnancy is near. We have been doing some interesting studies at the hospital. . . ." He tread water smoothly as he talked.

Dr. Lavelle heads a maternity hospital in Geneva. Infertile women seek him like a shrine. A sexy French actress who couldn't and couldn't and finally did (have the baby, that is) because of Dr. Lavelle's care. I read about every little pang in the *Ladies' Home Journal*.

I and Aunt Bea and even Nicho, I guess, thought Suzanne would want to have her baby in New York. But during one of our transatlantic phone calls last spring, Suzanne shrieked: "Are you out of your bloody mind? I am not having this baby at bloody Mount Sinai where my bloody mother and her bloody friends will be around to drive me bloody crazy—" Okay, okay.

She had other sensible choices—London, Paris. She could have gone to Lavelle's own Clinique Maternité. But no. Another direct quote: "Having a baby is a *natural* experience. I don't want to have my baby in a cold, impersonal hospital. I don't want to have my baby in an ugly, polluted city."

Fortunately Nicho had just bought this island, a little wedding present for Suzanne, along with the ring, the emerald earrings, the Renoir. The architect said it would take six months to complete the villa. Nicho imported forty Greek laborers and forty Turkish laborers from Cyprus who tried to outwork each other. The villa was built in two months. A small, separate, fully equipped hospital unit was constructed near the house.

Luring the great Lavelle to the island to act as personal physician during the last six weeks took considerable effort, too. Suzanne insisted on him, only him, because he is a believer in natural childbirth. Last spring she asked me to send her by air freight *Thank You, Dr. Lamaze* and *The Womanly Art of Breast Feeding*.

Nicho finally persuaded Lavelle to leave his other patients and concentrate exclusively on Suzanne by giving a hefty donation to his birth defects research institute. Soon Lavelle's hospital near Geneva will begin to construct a Suzanne Goldfarb Anapoulis wing for charity cases.

Lavelle was listing hormones, lots of hormones.

"Well, that certainly is very interesting, doctor—"

I smiled. He stopped and smiled shyly. He has a nice smile. "I get too technical, perhaps?" He is rather shy for such an eminent man.

"Oh no. Fas-ci-na-ting!"

"Well, I go in now—"

I splashed away discreetly. But I noticed that though Lavelle dried himself thoroughly—even his ears—he did not go back to the villa. He sat down rather gingerly on the edge of a chaise lounge and gave me a little beckoning wave.

I kept swimming for a moment or two before heading for shore.

Lavelle is rather comfortably handsome. Even features, dark hair flecked with gray, bright blue eyes. Most of the time he wears a pair of round hornrims with lightly tinted lenses. I have always liked men with glasses. "Gee, he's cute," I've said about dozens of bespectacled toads.

I dried myself off, sat down on the next chaise lounge, applied some suntan cream, and leaned back. For the first time ever, I have acquired a smooth, even, light-apricot tan. Usually I burn, peel, and spend the rest of the summer huddled under a soggy terrycloth cover-up. These last weeks I have learned that a tan has to be cultivated slowly, like an exotic flower. That's why superstars always seem to have the correct shade of flattering tan. They have the time, energy, and self-interest to devote to the tonality of the pigment of their skins.

"This is very nice," I said, ever-so-pleasant.

"Ye-e-e-s, though I must admit, mademoiselle, that this case is rather like a holiday for me. When I wake up in the morning I feel a little guilty—and I think now, perhaps it is not always so easy to be so very, very rich."

"The great American philosopher Sophie Tucker once said, 'I've been poor and I've been rich and rich is better.'"

He laughed politely. "You are Madame Anapoulis' school chum?"

"We're cousins." And I've always been glad of that. If Suzanne were my sister I would have been forced by circumstances to hate her. Nobody wants the Homecoming Queen as her sibling rival. If we were friends, even close friends, our paths would have strayed by now. But cousins are a nice untraumatic combination of family and friend.

"Madame Anapoulis was a mannequin?"

"Yes, she was a very successful model."

"Are you a model too?"

Are you kidding? I looked at him out of the corner of my eye; but no, there wasn't the slightest hint of a subliminal smirk. "I am—uh—I was the editor of a magazine." The Managing Editor. Even there, though I did all the work, made most of the decisions, I couldn't take star billing. (Who else dreams of coming in *second*?)

The editor was a Southern lady who had been with the magazine for twenty-five years, right from the

start. She still wore hats, arrived at 10:30 every morning, and first thing filled the water pitcher on her
desk with Smirnoff vodka. She also spent several
hours a day locked in her private john. Once in a
while she came out and wrote a memo to the staff:

> It has come to my attention that the extra rolls
> of toilet tissues are often removed from the rest
> rooms late on Friday afternoons. I believe that
> those of us who are fortunate enough to have our
> own weekend retreats are fortunate enough to
> purchase our own toilet tissue.
>
> Furthermore, the toilet tissue in the rest rooms
> is white, of poor quality, and most inappropriate
> in a personal decorating scheme.

"It's a magazine for teenagers," I said.

"Teenagers?"

"*Jeunes filles*—" I translated imprecisely. But could
the girls who read the magazine or the ones we wrote
about be considered *jeunes filles*?

Once I interviewed the original Lydia Plaster-Cast-
er, a frizzy-haired supergroupie from Duluth with a
strange and magnificent obsession. Little Lydia would
go back to the hotel with a rock group after their
concert. Quick as a wink she would mix up a special,
fast-drying batch of plaster of paris. While the group
lolled around drinking wine, smoking pot, saying
"Wow" and "Man" and "Too much" to each other in
place of human speech, Lydia, like a little elf, would
be busy at her craft. Since then, whenever I hear the
expression "A member of a rock group," I think of
little Lydia.

"It must be interesting work for you," Paul said after a moment.

"Mmmmm. Well, yes, sometimes—"

I started on the magazine right after college, as assistant in the articles department. Suzanne, who was modeling for the magazine at the time, helped me get the job. Working myself up slowly, being made Managing Editor two years ago, did briefly give me that big achievement flash. But lately I was getting sick of sitting at editorial meetings and asking with a growing desperation: "But do we really know what kids are like today?" Did I really care? My adolescence was receding, like the light across the water, a little further away each year. Always before I had thought, secretly, of myself as sixteen under the skin. Now at almost thirty, God knows, I may be immature, but I'm not a Modern Teen.

"American women are all so efficient, so organized and hard-working. Truly—I admire them so much."

That's not always so, I wanted to say. I've known lots of disorganized, inefficient—take my secretary, for instance. "Is your wife like an American woman?" I asked flatfootedly, to change the subject. The doctor wears a wide gold band but on his right hand. Maybe it's some kind of odd but significant Swiss-French marriage custom.

"I was married a long time ago. When I was a student. I am not married now." A long pause. "I am a widower, mademoiselle."

"Oh," in a tiny, sympathy voice. Suddenly the sun was too burning hot. I stood up. "Well, I better go and change for lunch."

"Yes, time goes so quickly here ... when one is doing so very little."

"Parkinson's Law. Work expands to fill the time allotted."

He laughed politely again. "That is very funny, Aileen."

I got a million of them, doc.

Walking up the rocky path that leads from the beach to the house, I stumbled, twisted my foot, and nearly fell backwards. He grabbed and held tight.

My heart was beating very quickly. It would have been a long, rocky fall. "Thank you, doctor. But you might have had another patient. Give you something to do."

"Can you walk?"

"Sure." I stepped down and it hurt, stepped again and the pain began to fade a little. "Really, it's all right."

"Please," he said, "my name is Paul. Call me Paul, Ai-leen." He held my elbow tightly the rest of the way down the path.

Belly up, Suzanne lay on a Porthault quilt on the terrace. Nicho, stooped over, held a stopwatch in his hand. Sister Hardcastle, pacing back and forth, was in charge. Sister is the fourth member of our little island family. She is matron at Dr. Lavelle's hospital. Around fifty, she is square: square-shouldered, square-breasted, square-bottomed, with the kind of legs Steinway made famous. Both a nurse and physiotherapist, she is an expert on the Psychoprophylactic Method of Childbirth. She studied with Dick-Read in London, labored, so to speak, at the right hand of Lamaze in Paris.

"Madame Anapoulis, you forgot your cleansing breath again," she chided. "It is important, dear *gel*. Shall we begin again? Now we are doing the breathing for the transitional stage. And we won't forget our important cleansing breath now will we, Madame?"

Suzanne nodded. Nicho looked at the stopwatch. "Begin . . ." he said softly.

Suzanne drew in a deep breath, then expelled it. She began to pant, mouth open, like a dog on a summer day.

"Thirty seconds," Nicho said, looking at the watch instead of Suzanne, "forty-five seconds."

As she panted, Suzanne massaged her medicine ball belly gently with a circular motion.

"Cleansing breath," Sister Hardcastle interjected.

Suzanne took another deep, slow breath.

"Sixty seconds," Nicho said and snapped off the watch. He was sweating.

"Veddy, veddy good. . . ."

Iphigenia darted forward and whispered something in Nicho's ear.

"Darling, I must take this call. It's the shipyards in Kobe. I've been trying to talk with the designer for the past thirty-six hours."

Suzanne gave a little wifely grimace. He walked away briskly, lighting a cigar, happy to escape from ward duty.

"Now shall we try again?" Sister clicked the watch briskly. "Be-gin!"

The night I arrived on the island we saw an educational movie showing a baby being born by the psychoprophylactic, or natural childbirth, method. The movie was French. The baby was delivered rather casually in a small bedroom where a flowering plant was growing on the window sill. The plant looked like it was about to burst into bloom. I like the symbolism. At the end, after the baby was born, the mother got up and casually walked away in her floppy bedroom slippers, like an actress who had done her bit and was now going home to a good supper. Suzanne was enraptured. Nicho called for a double brandy—and damned *fast.* Watching a baby being born, even when everyone is smiling and panting and chatting each other up in polite second-person French, can be fairly devastating.

In Europe, papa doesn't seem to be part of the procedure. But the American way is to have daddy right there, rubbing the back or tummy, offering the brave little woman a suck on a lemon lollipop to keep her throat from getting dry after all that panting. Daddy can even take home movies of the blessed event. I've been to some later screenings.

> *"Hey, before dinner, want to see the movie of Andrew's birth?"*
>
> *Gulp. "Sure." A game grin.*
>
> *"See there's the top of his head. It comes out and goes in again."*
>
> *Gulp. "Wow."*
>
> *"That's the episiotomy. I didn't want to have one but that dumb doctor insisted—"*
>
> *"Here he comes. Just like a football. That's you, young fellah—"*
>
> *"It was such a beautiful experience."*
>
> *"Next time we're going to do it at home. Better lighting."*
>
> *"Hey, where are you going, Aileen? You're go-.. ing to miss the placenta and that's really fascinating—"*

At least Suzanne hadn't insisted on hiring a technical crew from MGM. She just wants Nicho there to share every beautiful physical moment.

"Veddy, veddy good," said Sister Hardcastle. "Now shall we try our pushing?"

At this point even I had to turn away. Suzanne lay down, opened her legs wide and gave a hard groaning push. Her face turned red and the tendons in her neck stood out. She looked like she was going to explode in small pieces. Iphigenia, watching, groaned in sympathy and crossed herself. Suzanne pushed down again. *Gr-roan-n-n.* Then she breathed out, lay flat on her back and rubbed her hand gently up and down across the hard bulge.

"A veddy, veddy good practice session, dear *gel*," said Hardcastle briskly.

"How does it feel, I mean, inside?" I've asked Suzanne.

Sometimes she gets this intense withdrawn expression and I know she's feeling the baby move.

"Sometimes it hurts a little but most of the time it feels like a bubble or a butterfly or—well—gas."

She stood up and yawned. "It is going to be all right, isn't it, Sister?" she asked and rubbed her hard belly one more time. "I want everything to be all right. No, that's not enough. That's not nearly enough. I want everything to be absolutely beautiful for my baby."

After lunch there's a rest period for us all, just like sleep-away camp. Upstairs in my room I turned on the air conditioner full blast and thumbed through the papers. The *Abu Dhabi Gazette* has a four-color car advertisement on every other page. In the oil countries, Nicho says the sheiks don't replace car parts; they replace cars. A stalled car is laid to rest in the desert like a horse with a broken leg. The happiest Syrian in town is the one with the Cadillac dealership.

There were three letters on my bedside table. Mail is delivered daily by helicopter, too. The top letter was from the art director at the magazine. He is a funny, occasionally lethal fag who thinks he is my

friend. On the flap of the envelope he had written
"S.W.A.K." Fashions come and go, but "Fire and Ice"
is still Gene's favorite color. The stationery was navy
blue, the ink white:

Lassie come home! You bitch! I am having my
nineteenth nervous breakdown without you. All
hell breaks loose five times a day since you
abandoned ship. And, eat your heart out, our
little Miss Dipsy is trying to become all-powerful
again. The other day she even had the balls to
call a staff meeting. It was quite a shock to some
of the assistants. They didn't think M.J. was a person. Just a couple of initials at the bottom of the
stop-dropping-Kotex-down-the-can memos.

Nothing much else. New York is Dullsville.
That sweet little old lady next door whose Art
Deco collection I'm hoping to inherit got mugged
in the elevator. She's at Beekman Downtown and
I'm taking care of her poodle who hates my Chou
En-lai. Talk about your cat-and-dog fights.

Why don't you introduce me to your rich
friends?

Love and hot, wet
kisses,
G.

I crumpled the letter and threw it in the wastebasket. Gene is so New York that the air in the room
suddenly seemed heavy with pollution and hostility.
A couple of years after we started working together,
Gene said to me late one Friday afternoon: "Listen,
hon, if you're ever up about three and can't sleep and
have the moody blues, just give me a call. I mean it,
Aileen—"

I nodded and he gave me a kiss on the cheek. Our friendship, he thought, was sealed. But his little loving gesture headed me into a two-day downer. I don't want to be the kind of female who has to call the fag she works with for solace at 3:00 A.M. Hell, do I look *that* lonely?

When I can't sleep at three in the morning, and there are times when I can't sleep, I listen to the crazies on the all-night radio shows, a lullaby.

> *"I have been to Venus three times, twice during the rainy season. The people are pale green, very intelligent, and have little pointed heads."*
>
> *"Absolutely ridiculous."*
>
> *"You disagree, sir?"*
>
> *"Yes, Long John. This man is obviously a fraud. Everyone knows the population of Venus is made up of beautiful, love-starved women."*

Just like the population of Manhattan.

At three in the morning I also read the children's books I have always loved, *The Wind in the Willows* and *Charlotte's Web* and *Daddy Long Legs*, which is really very sexy. And, I confess, I confess, I run dirty picture shows in my head. My erotic fantasies, doctor, were deeply influenced by the Saturday afternoon matinees I saw when I was under ten. Fun in the dark. Yvonne De Carlo was a harem slave girl. Maureen O'Hara in low-cut green satin with a beauty mark on her swelling bosom, captured by ruthless pirates. Somehow I just knew that those pirates weren't only going to make Maureen walk the plank.

The second letter, another letter I didn't want to read. From Aunt Bea. Once, walking with Gene on Fifth Avenue, I met Aunt Bea coming out of Bonwit

Teller's. She had just bought six pairs of shoes, killing time before a matinee.

She called me the next day. "He's very attractive. Is he married, dear?" My mother doesn't worry about me. Aunt Bea worries about me.

"Aunt Bea," I laughed, "he's a homosexual."

"I didn't ask you that," she snapped. "I asked you if he was *married*."

Suzanne's London wedding reception (not to be confused with her New York wedding without reception or her New York reception without wedding) was a study in contrasts. The family (Nicho had thoughtfully sent a jet for us and, to be honest, both Aunt Bea and I were thrilled) was on one side; the Arab ambassadors, the French and English bankers were on the other. The Arab contingent's intelligence squad thought at one point that Suzanne was possibly an Israeli Mata Hari out to sabotage the flow of their oil shipments. But her belly seemed to convince them that even if she was, at least she was the one who had been caught.

I ripped open the envelope.

Dear Aileen,

How are you? How is Suzanne? I haven't heard from her in over three weeks. I'm not complaining because I'm sure she's very busy. Though I can't imagine what she's doing. Still, whatever it is, it must be more important than writing her mother a postcard.

Please tell her, when she has a free minute, I have picked out the complete layette for the baby at Saks' Baby Boutique. I will send it through Nicholas' New York office on one of his planes as soon as I'm told that my grandchild is born.

Please also tell her I will be happy to fly there
at a moment's notice. Most girls want to have
their mothers with them when they have their
first child. But then I have learned, through some
bitter experiences—do I have to tell you, of all
people—that Suzanne doesn't usually want what
other normal healthy girls want. . . .

Once Aunt Bea took a New School course on "The
Jewish Matriarch: Studies in Modern American Literature." "Interesting," she said about the books she
read. "Different."

I made a paper airplane out of the pale pink monogrammed Tiffany stationery and sent it winging
toward the wastebasket.

The third envelope was typewritten. My name, office address, PRIVATE, CONFIDENTIAL, PLEASE FORWARD.
I wondered—and then I knew. The man I left in New
York along with my job, my rent-controlled apartment
(oh lucky, lucky me), my career-girl style of life.

His name is Michael, a nice name. A nice man, too.
When we first met, those first few weeks, I walked
around smiling at myself in ladies' room mirrors, singing old songs from the fifties: *"Your eyes are the eyes
of a woman in lo-o-ove. . . ."*

We met at a party. Not a glamorous New York
shall-we-have-drinks-on-the-terrace party. Who goes
to such parties? Nobody I know except Suzanne, of
course. Suzanne even gives them. With me helping,
getting the cheese at Zabar's and the glasses, making
sure there would be enough ice. The party at which I
met Michael was typical of parties I've been to all my
life, since those first teenage gatherings where the
girls whispered to each other and teased each other's
hair in one corner while the boys threw potato chips
heavy with onion-soup-sour-cream dip on the rug.

The hostess was a friend, an editor at the magazine, who had just ended an affair that had drifted and drifted but gone nowhere. Now she was trying bravely to get back into circulation, following the advice she must have read in *Modern Teen* twenty years before:

> *"If his eye is caught by another femme, don't pout, don't play the waiting game. Get back into circulation, girl. Give an informal Saturday night get-together in the family rumpus room."*

We don't tell them to give parties anymore. Hell, no, nowadays a party could turn into a drug bust or a revolution.

I came early and the hostess was nervous and already half-tight. Would enough boys—uh—I mean, men show up? Would there be someone, please God, who was decent. We began to talk over the bowl of shrimp chips. He told me he was a vice-president of CBS. "But don't be impressed—there are forty-seven others."

"I am impressed. There are only forty-eight."

"Hey," he said, "that was nice." His glasses were square hornrims that sparkled, my very favorite. We stopped eating the shrimp chips and went out for a hamburger. We discovered that night and on a date a week later and on a dozen other dates that we like the same books, movies, politicians.

After four dates, we made love on his couch. "Was it good for you, too, Aileen?"

"Oh, yes, yes-s-s-s. . . ." Sharing a cigarette and coughing like hell because I hardly ever smoke.

After that I cooked lamb chops for him one night and he cooked steak for me the next. We both worked hard on creating interesting salads. I tried raw mushrooms. He tried beets. There was no current wife, ex-wife, no kiddies, no kinky little turn-ons. Truly, Michael, VP at CBS, was a Manhattan original.

Yet in a couple of months things seemed too easy and cool and complacent. At night in his apartment, he sat in one Mies van der Rohe armchair and I sat in the other. We drank good wine, listened to music, looked up from our books, papers, magazines to smile at each other. A small problem: at the office, I remembered the shape of his glasses but not exactly what he looked like.

He took me to a family party. I introduced him to my parents. His sister began calling me. In the fall, surely, he was going to Pop the Big Question, she said. Her name was Bernice and she told me she was rooting for me.

I became irritable though I never showed my irritation to him: (*This is the Watchbird watching a Bitch. Were you a Bitch this month? Nobody marries a Bitch. So wait—*) I told myself that this was life, real life (not to be confused with any of your flashy imitations) and I should be happy and content. But little things kept bothering me.

An example? He drank too much milk. At night before we went to bed, before we did it, he had to have two Oreos and a glass of milk. In a French restaurant, after the *coq au vin* and Beaujolais, he ordered milk and poured some on the chocolate mousse.

"It annoys me," I told my friend at whose party we had met. "I don't know why. Why should it annoy me? It's his cholesterol count, right? Right?" We were in the ladies' room at the magazine, and she was trying to restick her false eyelashes.

"Milk? Did I hear you right? Are you coming through clearly, Aileen? You don't like it because Michael drinks too much milk? Are you out of your

skull? Last night I went out with a guy who wanted
me to wear a Merry Widow brasalette and a pair of
spiked heels to bed. What's the matter with you,
Aileen?"

A fair question.

"Aileen, I think I love you," Michael told me
solemnly in bed the week I went away. Suzanne had
called one evening, and for once the overseas call
didn't sound right around the corner but five thousand miles away. "Couldn't you take a vacation?
Couldn't you spend some time with me? Aileen, I'm
getting a little nervous and—well—a little lonely. Gee,
Aileen, do you know you're the only friend I've ever
had."

All right, I'd come. I'd arrange it. And, of course, I
wanted to be with Suzanne, too, when she had her
baby, to know Nicho better, and, I admit it, to get
away, to change my life, to live even briefly the beautiful people's beautiful life.

I sent Michael a note on a Hallmark friendship
card and mailed it at the airport. *Called Away.
Emergency. Will Write.* I never have. I don't know
what to say.

There was a knock on the door. I pushed the letter
into my night table drawer.

"Come in—" Suzanne, in flowing caftan. "Hi,
sweetie, can't you sleep?"

"No, not today."

When Suzanne hasn't been able to nap, we have
long girl-to-girl talks through the long hot afternoons.
We have a lot of catching up to do; we haven't had
much chance to talk in the last nine months, not since
she left so unexpectedly for Europe. Maybe I was
copying Suzanne's own problem-solving method in
the way I dealt with Michael. When in doubt, just
run like hell.

Suzanne tried to sit on the edge of the bed but couldn't quite make it. She doesn't have a lap anymore. She lay back, her stomach a mountain on a plateau.

Her eyes were red and puffy. She looked like she had been crying a lot. "Suzanne—"

"Can I tell you something, Aileen?"

"Sure, what?"

She lit a cigarette and took a deep puff that even the baby must have inhaled. Finally she blew out the smoke.

"I'm not absolutely sure the baby is Nicho's—"

"WHAT?"

"I'm not absolutely sure the baby is Nicho's," she repeated in a dead voice.

"Oh, shit."

"Yeah," she agreed, "shit, shit, SHIT!"

What else was there to say?

2

*Have you heard the one about the pajama
manufacturer's daughter who was always
ending up in bed? Well, you're going to.*

Suzanne and I, always cousins, became friends when
we were about eleven. Back in the never-never land
of childhood, my family lived in the Bronx, hers on
Long Island. Occasionally I, the poor relation, was
sent Suzanne's outgrown Saks Fifth Avenue party
dresses.

The only trouble was, we were the same size and
grew at the same rate. My mother, who likes a bargain, tried to stuff me into Suzanne's velvets and laces
which were hardly worn, very stylish, and left my underpants exposed.

I have a brother five years older than I. In our
cramped four-room Grand Concourse apartment we
shared a bedroom, a circumstance that began to
worry my parents. It didn't bother us. Our beds were
a couple of feet apart but my brother, who devoted
most of his life to stickball, was as much a stranger to
me when I was a child as he is now. He lives in California and dates go-go dancers. When I think of him
I imagine him wearing a cabana set, a brush-cut tou-
pee, dangling his feet into someone important's kid-
ney-shaped swimming pool. He sells real estate in Los
Angeles and dreams of really scoring, of making some
ultimate, breathtaking *big deal*. On weekends he flies
to Las Vegas and sends me picture postcards of differ-

ent hotels: the Sands, the Desert Inn, Caesar's Palace. Does he think I keep a scrapbook?

Last Christmas he came to New York. Watching TV in my apartment—we couldn't keep up a conversation beyond dinner—he said: "Hey, there's Dino. He really is keeping off the sauce," and "Jeez, but Cher is getting thin—why the last time I saw her—"

During the eleven o'clock news I said dryly: "Hey, look, there's Henry and Nancy. I swear that girl is still growing." No reaction. Just before he left he told me, smirking, that he was dating a chick who once balled Burt Reynolds. Wow! (*We are all groupies.*) Then he asked to borrow $500. I loaned him $200. He is planning a nationwide chain of take-out health food stands. It is still in the planning stage. Veg-a-burgers at the sign of the big V. Who knows?

When I was eleven we moved so that my brother and I could have separate but equal bedrooms and would no longer see each other's underpants and therefore would grow up normal. We bought five miles from where Cousin Suzanne and her family lived but there were still differences. They were in Hewlett Bay Park, while we were across Peninsula Boulevard in Woodhampton Park. Ours was a ranch house in a raw development where the lawns were put down daily in squares like outdoor-indoor carpeting. Suzanne's family had an estate—rolling lawns, a motorboat tied up at the dock behind the house, and a live-in maid who wore a pink uniform that matched the formica on their kitchen cabinets.

Within two weeks my family had turned our seven-room house back into a cramped Bronx apartment. The living room and dining room were just for show. My father was a traveling salesman away from home four days a week. When he was out of town my mother sat at the kitchen table and worked determinedly on her handicrafts. She is skillful with her hands. Perhaps she was always working out her frustrations and loneliness but my mother, ever busy, sewed and knit, embroidered and crocheted, wrapped raffia around bowls, stuck little shells on little boxes. In the corner of our kitchen a shapeless lump of papier-mache was always drying.

When my father was home, my mother, to be companionable, would reluctantly tear herself away from her current project—bead rings, dried flowers under glass, converting lunch boxes into sequined evening bags—and the two of them would huddle in what the builder had called the "family room." They sat on the couch opposite the TV as if warming themselves in front of a crackling fire. My parents watched television from seven to eleven each evening with total uncritical concentration as if they were going to be given a quiz the next morning on the previous evening's shows.

Question: Who appeared on the Ed Sullivan Show and in what order?

Answer: Señor Wences, the Ko-Ko Brothers, Myron Cohen, Connie Stevens and The Little Italian Mouse.

My Aunt Bea and Uncle Morris were much more social and, I thought at the time, heaps more sophisticated. My uncle was an extremely successful pajama manufacturer whom my father always called, half-mockingly, half-admiringly, The Pajama King.

"Bea wants us to go to the Hadassah dinner with them."

"No thanks. Let him go. Let him give. The Pajama King."

"As their guests."

"I said, no thanks." My mother, chastised, returned to the kitchen. She was weaving potholders.

Uncle Morris *was* a giver. He liked to get up at a dinner for the United Jewish Appeal or the Federation of Jewish Philanthropies and make impressive donations to the accompaniment of gasps followed by appreciative applause. A grove in Israel was named for his mother. A kidney machine at Hadassah Hospital he gave in Aunt Bea's name.

Since we were now neighbors, both my parents and aunt and uncle wanted Suzanne and me to become better friends. We were in the seventh grade at the same local school but in different classes. That first week after we moved I was invited to lunch at her house.

I remember we were to meet that day in the school yard. When I went outside, Suzanne was in a corner by the fence surrounded by a group of boys. The boys weren't talking to her, just shoving each other hard out of the way in front of her. She wore a yellow sweater, a red-and-yellow plaid skirt, a white dickey, blue suede loafers with pennies tucked in the front flap. She looked exactly right, the cover of that month's *Senior Prom*, which I read assiduously and practically committed to memory. Her smooth blonde hair was held back with a twisted metal band which I was sure was pure gold. She watched the boys and smiled her approval.

When she saw me she waved. As I approached, she reached out and took my hand. "This is my cousin," she said softly to the boys who had stopped and were listening to her. "You can't like me if you don't like her." So *there*.

"Come on," she said to me. "It's a long stinky walk. I hate to walk."

We didn't say much as we wended our way deeper

into Hewlett Bay Park. I had only seen Suzanne a few times before at family parties and at our mutual grandmother's funeral. On that occasion I had tried so hard to feel something deep and significant or even a little spooky—there's a dead body in there, I kept telling myself as I viewed the coffin, trying to raise goose pimples—that I had hardly glanced at my pretty cousin.

"These houses are nice," I said as we walked.

She shrugged.

The houses grew bigger and bigger and bigger with each passing street. But their sprawling size, sweeping lawns, and figures of small black jockeys, arm extended, were the only things they had in common. There were many overblown architectural styles: California Modern, Spanish Hacienda, Mock Tudor in the Cardinal Wolsey Spoils Tradition.

"Here we are," Suzanne said and pointed to a white portico and four tall columns. With one glance at the house you knew for sure that they hadn't burned Tara: it had been bought by a carpetbagger and shipped north to the Five Towns.

"Gee," I said.

Suzanne shrugged again.

Aunt Bea wasn't home that day. I learned later that she was never home. Either she was buying evening dresses on Manhasset's Miracle Mile or in the city studying Pre-Adolescent Psychology at the New School ("I have only one daughter. The least I can do is try to understand her, right?") or looking at upholstery samples at Schumacher's for her constant redecorating schemes.

"Do you want egg salad or chicken salad or shrimp salad? Annie will make you whatever you want." Suzanne said.

We sat in the white-and-gold French Provincial

dining room. Annie brought in an assortment of little sandwiches on both white and brown bread. There was a dish of carrots and celery sticks and radish roses. We drank chocolate frosteds whipped up in a blender.

"Is Aunt Bea here at three when you come home?" I asked.

My mother was always at home, working grimly on one or another of her projects: curtains, slipcovers, clothes. Once she attempted a suit for my father. He wouldn't wear it.

"I don't come home at three," Suzanne said and patted her mouth delicately with the linen napkin, a gesture I longed to imitate. I had already finished my four quarters. Annie came in, gave me a dirty look, and brought me four more.

"These are so *good. . . .*"

"On Monday I have a stinky dancing class and on Tuesday I have a stinky riding lesson and on Wednesday there's the stinky orthodontist. . . ." Suzanne had a delicate silver wire encircling her teeth. I went to a dentist in the Bronx because he was cheap. He was an orthodontist who supplemented his income by giving shows in the public schools, combining a lecture on dental care with magic tricks. There was always a white rabbit in a cage in his bathroom that smelled very funny. Maybe he was a better magician than a dentist because I wore braces for five years and my front teeth still stick out.

Suzanne continued: "And on Thursday there's the Sub-Debs. It's a sort of club."

I'd already heard about them. A strange mole-like girl had accosted me in the school yard that morning. "You're new here, aren't you? Well if you want to be *popular* you have to be a member of the Sub-Debs."

Clearly Suzanne *was* popular. I thought of the boys

who had clustered around her. In the Bronx in the seventh grade you came right home from school and did your homework. In the Bronx, only Joe DiMaggio was popular.

"On Friday I have a friend over or go to a slumber party."

"Oh."

Walking back to school, Suzanne grew a little friendlier. "In the Bronx what do they call *it?*"

"The curse?" I guessed.

"Yeah—"

"Well, the curse," I repeated lamely.

"Oh. One of the girls who moved here from New Jersey says that there they say: 'I have a visit from my aunt in Red Bank.' Isn't that cute?"

"Yeah—cute."

"Do you have it?"

"No-o-o-o-o. Do you?"

"No."

"Do you wear a bra?" I didn't but I should have.

Suzanne shook her head. "Do you know how people do it?"

"Sure," I said.

"My mother gave me a book. It shows chickens doing it."

"Chickens?" I said and began to giggle. "CHICKENS?"

"Want to hear a dirty joke?" Suzanne asked. She was a little flushed.

"Yeah. Sure." Chortle. Giggle. Sputter.

Doctor: Lady, I want to take your temperature.

Lady: But, doctor, that's not where you're supposed to take my temperature.

Doctor: Lady, that's not my thermometer.

I screamed with shocked laughter. It really was a nasty little joke. I would still probably scream with shocked laughter. Suzanne collapsed on the nearest lawn. We rolled gasping, my laughter fueling her laughter.

"Chic-kens," I gasped. Suddenly she sat up. "I wet my pants," she said. There was a dark splotch on her plaid skirt. "I do it all the time. I better go home and change. It's okay. Annie'll give me a note."

I got up. My legs were weak.

"On Friday I'm having a slumber party. Aunt Ethel will let you come, won't she?"

I nodded.

"I'll show you the pictures of the chickens."

"Stop—" I ran away from her, laughing.

Coming of age in Hewlett Bay Park in the late fifties. The boredom, the stultifying, never-ending boredom. We and the Russkies were in a space race and the teachers at Hewlett Bay High acted as if it was our personal responsibility to get it up first. We didn't. The post-Sputnik kids right after us were treated even worse.

Tragedy was not being accepted by the college of your choice. We had four or five hours of homework every night. I was one of the obedient ones, easily conned, churning out anemic editorials for the school paper on the noise level in the cafeteria or the lack of school spirit. (There was plenty of school spirit. Too damn much school spirit.)

Suzanne, unlike the rest of us, was too vague to be conned, too disinterested to be obedient. She ignored the teachers and guidance counselors at school who were always clucking that she wasn't living up to her potential. While I and the others like me were rushing forward, practically standing in line, to become apprentice drones, the Queen Bee waited for her future in her ruffled canopy bed.

For her sixteenth birthday she got her own car, a powder-blue T-bird. In the afternoons she drove around, smoking, listening to the music on the radio, stopping at Shor's for greasy Shorburgers and at Novi's across the tracks for pizza and a sip of someone's beer. She was barely passing most courses and failing Spanish, a disgrace. If all those dumb Puerto Ricans could speak Spanish then nice Jewish boys and girls should be able to speak Spanish even better was the prevalent attitude around Hewlett High. Aunt Bea paid me to tutor her.

"I'll help you, Suzanne," Miss Drone said. "I'll explain the rules to you, but you've got to learn the vocabulary yourself. I mean I can't learn the vocabulary for you—" Suzanne didn't reply. She was looking at herself in the mirror. She usually was looking at herself in the mirror, those days, setting her hair, rolling it up on the new sausage-shaped roller, then rolling it down, staring into the mirror at the blonde rolls on her head. One spring Suzanne devoted herself entirely to plucking her legs until they were smooth as marble. Even in class she plucked, bent over in her seat, her tweezer cupped in her hands as the rest of us chanted irregular verbs.

Once in a while, she roused herself to have a raging fight with Aunt Bea. Afterwards she would climb out her bedroom window, usually come to visit me, climbing in my bedroom window. While I dutifully broke my brain over trigonometry or third year Latin—Suzanne had given me a pony which I was too pious to use—she would lie across my bed, chainsmoke her Marlboros, and hum softly to herself: "*Sha-boom, sha-boom, dadio, dadio, dadio, dadio, sha-boom, sha-boom. . . .*"

"Suzanne, what are you thinking about?"

"I'm counting the barfy flowers on your barfy wall-paper pattern. There are thirty-seven bunches of barfy violets on that wall and twenty-four petals on every barfy bunch and—"

"Suzanne, you are *nuts.*"

"Come on." She tossed the car keys up and down in her hand seductively. "Come on, I'll take you for a little drive, ba-by. Come on—"

And so we drove back and forth to the beach, around the newly laid roads of half-built housing developments, through the villages of Woodmere, Cedarhurst, Hewlett that were streets of hairdressers and dress shops and paint and wallpaper stores. That's all. Like Aunt Bea, most of the women of the area had two abiding concerns: decorating themselves, decorating their homes.

Suzanne loved to drive, the wind blowing through her hair, her hands clenched tight on the steering wheel, singing with the radio's latest rock and roll. Her best grade ever was in driver education.

In the car, I—perpetual, compulsive, greasy grind—studied my history notes, chanted dates to myself to Paul Anka's rhythms. We studied all of world history in one year, gobbling decades week by week. I memorized the immediate, the near-immediate, the underlying cause of *everything*, the fall of the Roman Empire, the rise of Napoleon, the Russion Revolution. Hewlett Bay High gave me a sense of history: tidy.

A nightmare I have to this day: it is the night before the end of the school year and I am preparing for bed. I feel good. All my work is done, I think. And then I remember a history assignment that must be handed in the next morning at 8:30. An assignment I should have been working on throughout the whole nine months of school: *Write the history of the world in your own words.* I glance at the clock. It is 2:30. I begin to sob uncontrollably. Still I sit down, crying, and pick up my pen.

Waking from this dream I have to calm myself, reassure myself that I graduated from Hewlett Bay High years and years ago, that I don't have to do things like that anymore. But usually I can't go back to sleep for an hour. I keep wondering—how would I begin the goddamn assignment?

Life was all work and no fun. Most of the girls (including me, of course) never dated. We kept our page boys or ponytails squeaky clean and shiny, we carried toothbrushes in our handbags to brush after every meal. We were always surreptitiously smelling our underarms (place nose as casually as possible at shoulder level and sniff), always trying to develop our personalities and our bustlines. The boys ignored us.

They would only date the five or six girls in each class who were publicly acknowledged to be beautiful or "cute and a lotta fun" and the one or two others who were rumored to be willing. (Neither then nor now do I fit into any of the above-mentioned categories.)

Suzanne, a beauty, went out on dates every Friday and Saturday nights. Her romances followed as ritualized a pattern as the mating dance of the grasshopper. On her first date she and her latest went to the movies at the Cedarhurst Central and afterwards went out for a hamburger. A hasty fumbling kiss was exchanged at the front door. On the second date, after a cheeseburger (slightly more expensive), they parked on one of the marshy tracts of land that were being turned into Hampton Court or Buckingham Park, ranch houses and split levels, $27,500. By the fifth date his hands were under her cashmere sweater, and she was wearing his identification bracelet, which meant they were engaged to be engaged to be engaged. (Engaged to be engaged was a fraternity pin.) On the twelfth or fourteenth date they broke up without emotion. They had done everything they could possibly think of doing except *it*. And a nice girl like Suzanne wasn't expected to do *it*. The next weekend Suzanne would start dating someone else.

She was a cheerleader of course. Cool and blonde and disinterested but the star of the squad. The other cheerleaders were cute, scrappy little girls with curvy bosoms and fleshy thighs who cried when our boys lost a home game. While the other girls screamed and smiled at the crowd, Suzanne with a blank stare and a whispery voice recited the cheers half a beat behind the others:

> "Rah Rah Rah
> > *Rah*
> Hewlett Bay High School
> > *School*
> Sis Boom Bah
> > *Bah!*"

She told me years later that during the games she imagined the winning team would get to pick one cheerleader. And while the rooting section cheered them on, the boys would reap a pleasant practical reward for their victory.

Every morning Suzanne drove me to school. Because I insisted, she was usually on time. One morning, I watched the clock, gnawing my cuticle in panic. I would be late; I would get a detention. Five detentions meant a demerit. Two demerits would go in my college record. I needed a scholarship. God-

damn her, she was ruining my future. I called
Suzanne in a panic. Aunt Bea answered: "I was just
coming to pick you up."

"What's the matter with Suzanne?"

"The doctor's with her now. He's giving her a sedative. Frankly, I'm the one who needs the sedative—"

"But is she sick?"

"No. Only a little crazy."

"What's wrong, Aunt Bea?"

"She thinks her nose grew overnight. My daughter
Pinocchio. Stay there. I'm coming to pick you up."

"Aunt Bea, it's so late—"

"You're not going to school. You're coming here. It's
an emergency. Can you wait on the corner, darling?"

Aunt Bea never had a thing to say to my mother
except, "Ethel, darling, did you make that yourself?
Isn't that wonderful. It looks like you made it."

Suzanne was in her canopy bed, her face swollen
and red from crying. "I thought you were my friend,"
she said to me accusingly, when I walked into the
room.

"I am your friend."

"Then why didn't you tell me I was *grotesque?*"

"Well—because you're not."

"I AM SO!" She began to cry, great breaking sobs.
Aunt Bea groaned theatrically.

"Suzanne, for God's sake, what happened?"

Hiccupping, she finally explained. The night before,
when she should have been studying her vocabulary
lists, she thought it would be more fun to observe her
oval face from a new and different angle. So she set
up a new combination of mirrors—her closet mirror,
Aunt Bea's standing mirror, a magnifying hand mirror, held approximately at nose level. She was quite
content with what she saw as usual until she caught
an unexpected glimpse of her profile. Then with

mounting horror she noticed for the first time ever, the sixteenth-of-an-inch mound of flesh that separated the pert nostrils of her nose. A dip, I think it's called, a slight excess of flesh, barely noticeable. In Suzanne's case it was a family characteristic. Aunt Bea had a slight dip at the end of her nose. My father's nose was quite fleshy.

"I never had a nose like this before," Suzanne cried out and a cowering Aunt Bea held her hand protectively over her own blemished nostrils.

"Of course you have. That's your nose," I said firmly. Suzanne was being so colossally dumb.

"It's just grown there—" she insisted, beginning to sob again. I wonder: is every Jewish beauty haunted by the fear of a time-bomb nose that will suddenly start growing unexpectedly and will ruin the neatsiest combination of glossy golden hair and round blue eyes?

"It's the nose God gave you," said Aunt Bea.

"The hell with *that*," said Suzanne. She pulled a pack of cigarettes out of her night table drawer. She wasn't allowed to smoke. She lit a cigarette and blew the smoke out through her nostrils as if to emphasize a point. Aunt Bea didn't say a word.

"So you'll have it fixed," Aunt Bea said after a moment.

"I'm not going to Sobel. He's a butcher."

Dr. Sobel was the local plastic surgeon with a flourishing practice. After every Christmas or Easter vacation girls returned to high school with two black eyes and Band-Aids over the bridges of their lumps of newly bobbed noses. Dr. Sobel's dream girl, I realize now, must have been Doris Day. Give him a girl—any girl, tall or short, round-faced or square-jawed—and she came back with a Doris Day deluxe pug, four-cornered, right smack in the middle of her kisser. "I can't place the face but the nose looks familiar," was a joke that had swept the sophomore class the year before, after Easter recess.

"All right. We'll ask Stewart. He'll know someone good." An older cousin, he was the head of dermatology at Mount Sinai and a fount of wisdom where doctors were concerned. "Darling, I promise we'll find the biggest nose man in New York—"

Nobody laughed.

The recommended plastic surgeon was named Dr. Frank Revere. I went with Suzanne to his office in the city. She wouldn't let Aunt Bea go with us. The office was in one of those fortress-like buildings on Park Avenue that have two or three doormen to spare. His waiting room was elegant, pale blue and rose, and silky. On a gilded table were a couple of art books with reproductions of Renaissance paintings. It was a room cleverly calculated to make you too want to be beautiful.

"Miss Goldfarb?" the receptionist asked when we entered. She looked straight at me.

"Nope."

"I'm the patient," Suzanne said.

"Oh," the receptionist tried to smooth away the surprised look on her little face. "All right. You're our last patient this afternoon. Go right in. The doctor will see you now." Suzanne disappeared down a peach-colored hall.

She was gone for three quarters of an hour. I looked at the reproductions in the book, then studied the receptionist's tight little face. Had her nose been shortened, her chin lengthened, her ears sewn back? Though her hair was drawn into a bun, I could hardly see the outlines of her ears, they hugged her head so tightly. Were they there at all? She looked like one of those plastic dolls whose arms and legs could be removed with a sharp pop and whose upper and lower torso could be unscrewed one from the other. When I was little, I had one of those dolls; my brother liked to dismantle it and re-create it into horrible, grotesque deformities and then threaten to do the same to me.

Suzanne returned, looking serious and sober. The intercom buzzed. "Yes, doctor," the receptionist said. "But doctor—of course, doctor—if you say so, sir." She snapped it off and looked at Suzanne. "Do you know that you're a very lucky girl? Do you know that? Doctor Revere's schedule is so tight that he usually can't get to a patient for *months*. But he has a few spare hours on February eighteenth and he has decided to give them to *you*." Her voice was husky with emotion.

"Thank you," Suzanne said. "Thank you."

It was about two weeks away. Suddenly I remembered—"February eighteenth—but that's the start of midterms, Suzanne."

She didn't even look at me. The receptionist went on. "I'll call you a few days before to tell you what to bring to the clinic—"

"Thank you," Suzanne said. "Thank you. And I *am* grateful."

"I hope so," said the receptionist.

As we chugged home on the Long Island Railroad, Suzanne told me: "He said I was taking a chance. He said I was a pretty girl now. With this little imperfection removed I could be characterless, uninteresting—"

"Suzanne, you don't need a nose job. The whole thing is totally ridiculous." Suddenly she was making me very angry and Suzanne had never made me angry before.

"But he said he thought I could be beautiful. That

he'd like to try and make me perfectly beautiful—"
She was smiling at her reflection in the grimy window
of the train.

"Suzanne—" I began forcibly but I really had nothing to say. I had this funny feeling that Suzanne had
some weird dialogue going on with herself that I
would never know anything about. She smiled at her
reflection again. Her finger went to her nose. She explored it. Gingerly she touched the controversial tip.

"He said that beautiful women, really beautiful
women were like a shrine to be worshipped. He said
that's what he sincerely believed and that he'd based
his whole life on this belief. Do you think what he
said is true?" She turned from the window and looked
at me. She was glowing.

"Well—uh—maybe." And I turned away.

Dr. Revere kept his patients in bed at his private
clinic for at least three or four days. The patients remained perfectly still while ice packs were applied so
that the swelling of the nostrils and upper lip would
be reduced as soon as possible and blood would not
congeal in dark under-eye patches.

I didn't visit Suzanne for the first couple of days. I
called Aunt Bea who told me dramatically that the
doctor had said the operation was a total success.

"It was on her *nose*, Aunt Bea. Not her *brain*—"

"Thank God."

Suzanne couldn't talk on the phone and I was too
busy cramming every spare fact about pre-1500 world
history into my head to call her anyway. On Friday
afternoon, with three exams finished, I finally went
into the city to see her.

Dr. Revere's clinic, which hugged the East River
Drive, was small but modern. Directly opposite was a
cat and dog hospital about the same size. Suzanne's

room faced the river and was very bright. There was yellow-flowered wallpaper and yellow sheets. It didn't look like a hospital room.

"Hello—"

She turned towards me. Her nose was heavily bandaged and her eyes were a startling rabbit pink. The rest of her looked shrunken in her baby-doll pajamas.

"Hello, Aileen," she said quietly.

"You look—uh—fine."

"I look shitty. They won't even let you look in a goddamn mirror till you leave. I guess they're afraid you'll break it."

"But I bet you'll look just terrific in a couple of weeks."

"Well, it really takes about three months for the swelling to go down completely."

There was a long pause. I wondered if she was sorry she had it done.

"The exams were—"

"Aileen, can I tell you something?"

"Sure. What?"

"It's more than my nose that's different."

"What do you mean?" I didn't understand.

She sat up in bed. "I DID IT! I DID IT!" She gave a wicked giggle.

"You're *kidding!*"

"I am not. Last night, in the middle of the night. One-twenty-four to be exact. I was watching the clock."

We both began to giggle madly. Suddenly I wondered: "Who with?"

"Shut the door." I did as I was told.

"*Him*, dummy. Dr. Revere. I mean—Frank."

"I don't believe it."

"Believe it." She had stopped giggling and was cool and distant again.

"Did you like it?"

"Not bad. Maybe when my nose stops hurting so much. Did you bring me any cigarettes?"

"Yes." I handed her a pack.

"We're not supposed to smoke." She lit one and blew the smoke through her bandages. "Want to hear about it?"

I nodded. I could hardly wait.

She was half-asleep, half-awake at midnight, with ice bags on her lids and her new sleeker nose throbbing hotly. She had a painkiller injection in her bottom, topped off by a couple of sleeping pills. So she thought she was dreaming when he first came into the room. He had been to a party, he said, and was stopping by on his way home to make sure all his patients were resting comfortably. He sat on her bed, removed the ice bags, smoothed her brow. Her pink eyes fluttered open. No, she wasn't dreaming. "How's my little girl?" he asked. "How's my sleeping beauty all ready to be awakened with a little kiss?"

She felt the pressure on her nose and gasped. "I better examine you," he said thickly. She decided he was a little drunk because he smelled like her father after his pajama manufacturers' testimonial dinner. He unbuttoned her dotted Swiss baby-dolls and placed the stethoscope on her breast. "Very good," he said. Then he touched her nipple, then he kissed her nipple. Then he kissed her there and there and *there*. Suzanne pointed down her body as if she was pointing out the state capitals on a map of the East Coast. He had kissed her *there*.

"Suzanne!" I was very shocked. I had always assumed that grown-up sex was accomplished with the equipment provided in our nether regions. At sixteen I wasn't sure hands were allowed, let alone mouths, noses, tongues.

"But what did you do while all this was going on?"

"Well, nothing. I was kind of sleepy from the sleeping pills."

"Did he just hop on?" I was interested in facts.

"Well, he said something about darling, darling your body is so damn beautiful, and then he pulled down my pajama bottoms. They sort of got stuck around my knees. I had to kick 'em off. Then he—I mean, we did it. It only takes a few minutes. It's no big deal. Afterwards he asked if it hurt."

"Did it?"

"My nose hurt so much that I didn't notice anything else. But I was bleeding. He thought that was terrific. He went out and got me a Kotex. I guess he must have told the nurse I had my period."

"How do you feel now?" I asked.

She didn't reply. "Do you have a compact with you?"

I hesitated. "Are you sure you *want* to look?"

"Yes." I handed her my pressed powder. "Oh boy," she said, "oh boy, oh boy, I do look different. Shitty. My eyes look *rusted*."

"Are you coming home Sunday?"

"Dr. Revere, I-mean-Frank, wants me to stay until Tuesday or Wednesday. He says it's better."

A nurse knocked on the door. Suzanne threw me the compact.

"Your tray will be here in a few minutes. You'd better tell your little friend it's time to go."

I nodded and went to the door. "See you in a few days, Suzanne." After the nurse had gone I asked in a whisper, "Are you going to do it again?"

"Are you nutty? What the hell for?"

Comic aside: Shall I tell you how I lost my maidenhead to a Super Tampax?

Super Tampax?

Inspired by Suzanne's daring, the next time I had my period I decided not to use a smelly old Kotex that had to be wrapped up in toilet paper and disposed of secretly in the garbage pail outside. Instead I'd be all grown up and use one of my mother's Tampax, which she hid in her top bureau drawer. However, since I knew less about my anatomy than I did about the underlying causes of the Hundred Years' War and since I wasn't too good about following directions that were written on the package, I had a little trouble. I managed to stuff the Tampax up without removing the hard cardboard tube in which it was encased.

OUCH!

I pulled it out, my knees weak, tried again but still didn't press the plunger in at the right moment.

OUCH!

I went back to Kotex.

Four years later when I finally did it with a Columbia junior, he said afterwards: "I knew you weren't really a virgin." I gave him my woman-of-mystery smile. Who else has ever surrendered her honor to Tampax, Inc.?

Suzanne's first affair continued for six months. Every Saturday afternoon we went into the city. She told Aunt Bea we were both going to free art history lectures at the Metropolitan Museum. And that's how I learned to identify New Kingdom mummy cases.

After Revere had seen his Saturday morning patients, he and Suzanne would copulate on the examining table.

"How romantic."

"Well, he plays WPAT on the radio. . . ."

"Swell."

The romance ended rather abruptly when the receptionist returned unexpectedly to the office, took a good look, and the next day threatened to tell all to Revere's socialite wife. Revere offered to remodel another part of the receptionist's anatomy to keep her quiet, but since the receptionist was running out of spare parts, the next week he bid Suzanne a tearful farewell. "And if you ever need anything fixed, think of me."

That was the end of Suzanne's first little escapade, but there were lots more to come. That summer she seduced/was seduced by (free choice) the Good Humor man. He was a philosophy major at Brandeis in the winter. They used the back of his ice cream truck which was nice and cool and convenient. "He's weird about chocolate," Suzanne said, giggling. (It took me about seven years to understand the full implications of that remark.) That summer she also fooled around a bit with the gardener's assistant: once in the garage, once behind a sick elm. Our senior year in high school she divided her time between the senior class president and the captain of the basketball team. She swore to them both, of course, that she was a virgin who had once fooled around with a Super Tampax.

"That nose job was marvelous, simply marvelous," Aunt Bea said to my mother, to all the relatives. "Not only does Suzanne look exquisite—frankly, she takes my breath away when she's all dressed up—but her whole attitude seems to have changed." Even her class work improved. She did very well on her college boards and was accepted by Bennington. The school's admission director told Suzanne that the Faculty Committee decided she had a lot of interesting potential.

During her first three months at college she began a stormy affair with her literature professor whose

book on Fitzgerald had won a National Book Award.
He was married and had two small children. They met
in haylofts or under a picturesque covered bridge.

Suzanne had colds and the flu all that autumn.
Aunt Bea thought it was because she was studying so
hard. She insisted that Suzanne go to Miami Beach
during Christmas vacation to recuperate, and I was
invited along. We stayed at the Fontainebleu Hotel.
"Uncle Morris wants to see what it's like. I'm sure it's
much too vulgar for my taste," said Aunt Bea.

And that's how Suzanne met Johnny Poparossa.

Meyer Schoenfeld, a reputed Mafia leader, but
Jewish, was staying in the Presidential Suite at the
hotel. Johnny was one of his three bodyguards.
Schoenfeld—short, wrinkled and balding, his pot belly
drooping over his madras Bermudas—looked exactly
like all the other little old men who stayed at the hotel. He smoked cigars, read the *Wall Street Journal,*
spent most of his waking hours eating bagels hurriedly in the downstairs coffee shop or playing pinochle. But while the garment manufacturers or doctors ("he's the biggest gall bladder man in the East,
he's the biggest prostate man in Cincinnati") played
cards with each other, Schoenfeld played only with
his three young pompadoured associates. Occasionally
his shouts of "shmendrick!" or "shmuck!" aimed at the
inept playing of his companions, could be heard at
adjoining tables. Later Johnny told Suzanne that
Schoenfeld paid them a weekly salary in cash and
then won it back at pinochle.

In the eighth grade we all read *The Amboy Dukes,*
giggling over the dirty parts which one of the boys
had thoughtfully underlined in red pencil. Johnny
was a Duke made flesh. Superhood. With sunglasses,
heavy black greasy-kid hair, a thin olive-skinned Ital-
ianate face. With a radar that I still do not possess,

Suzanne homed in on him the first day by the swimming pool.

Fifteen minutes after we sat down she handed me her sun reflector. "I think I'll get a Coke," she said and sashayed past Johnny and his companions on the way to the poolside bar. She was wearing a leopard-print bikini. Sheena, the Jungle Girl. The three young men looked up admiringly; one whistled. But it was Johnny who stood up as if hypnotized, who left his friends who were practicing their card game and headed after her. Johnny bought her the Coke and they started to talk.

At that moment Aunt Bea came to the pool for her first morning of broiling in the sun. It was fashionable then to return from Florida looking like a well-tanned cowhide. "Where's Suzanne?" I pointed. Aunt Bea tried to see through her sunglasses. "Oh, she's made a friend, has she? That's nice. Maybe he'll have a nice friend for you."

I had my doubts.

Suzanne returned a few minutes later. "That—uh—boy invited me to have lunch with him. I told him okay." She stretched out with her sun reflector.

"What's his name?" Aunt Bea watched Johnny slowly saunter back to his companions, his oil-coated, muscular body gleaming in the sunlight. His friends were laughing and one punched his arm.

"Suzanne, I asked you, what's his name?"

"Oh—uh—Johnny, I think," she mumbled.

"Johnny *what*, Suzanne?

"I dunno."

"What does he do?"

"I dunno."

"Well, what did you talk about?"

"For God's sake, Mother, if I keep moving my mouth, I'm not going to get an even tan." Aunt Bea watched Johnny and his friends with sharp, narrowed eyes.

They had lunch at the Boom Boom Room downstairs. Aunt Bea waited by the door until they came out. "Oh, Suzanne darling, what a co-in-ci-dence!" she overacted. "Your father needs some Alka-Seltzer and I was just on my way to the drugstore. Why don't you introduce me to Johnny—"

The rest of the afternoon was devoted to a screaming, raging fight.

"THAT BOY ISN'T JEWISH."

"How do you know?"

"Because of his name, Popa-roppa-something."

"Because he's Italian, Mother? Is that what you're trying to say? Well, wasn't Christopher Columbus Italian? And you're always saying *he* was Jewish."

"Suzanne, that has nothing to do with—"

"You're always saying anyone who is famous or smart or rich or anything is Jewish. Well, maybe Johnny's Jewish. Should I ask him if he's circumcised—will that do?"

Uncle Morris looked up from his *U.S. News & World Report.* "Did she learn such words at that expensive college? Is that what I'm paying for, Bea?"

"Oh, for God's sake, Father—"

"Don't for God's sake me, Miss—"

"I don't want you to be alone with that boy again, Suzanne. Do you hear me?"

"Mother, you are shouting so goddamn much that everyone in this whole goddamn hotel can hear you—"

"Because he is a *bum.* That's right. The boy you had lunch with happens to be a *gangster bum.* Do I make myself plain?"

"Mother, you can be so stupid—"

"Is that a way to talk to your mother?"

"No, no, let her talk. Let her rage. Let her work out

all her feelings of frustration on me, Morris. I don't care. As long as she stays away from that wop—"

"The gangster bum he works for, Mother, just happens to be *Jewish*—"

"That's right. And he's the smartest one they have, I hear. *The brains*—"

At three the next morning I awoke to find Suzanne coming into our room in her bikini. I was sure we had gone to sleep at the same time, around midnight, after watching the nightclub show. "Suzanne, what's wrong?"

"Go to sleep; you're dreaming."

"I am not dreaming. Where were you?"

"I was so hot I went to take a swim in the ocean."

Our air conditioner was set on "Arctic." Besides, nobody swims in the ocean, even during the day, in Miami Beach.

"Do you like him that much?"

"Who?"

"Suzanne, you don't have to pretend with me. You like him a lot, right?"

"He's okay." She yawned.

"Just okay?"

"I am *so* sleepy." She yawned again.

"Suzanne, sometimes I don't understand you."

"What are you trying to understand?"

"But if you don't like him a whole lot—"

"Aileen, don't worry about it. Okay? I want to go to sleep now. G'night."

"G'night," I echoed, baffled.

Suzanne and Aunt Bea snarled at each other all the rest of the week but Suzanne appeared to be obeying her mother. We sat by the swimming pool; we went out on a motorboat; we went to Hialeah and she won the daily double. Uncle Morris was very impressed. "I just picked the names I liked," she said, smiling sweetly, and gave me half of the $220 she won. At night we ate dinner at different hotels, saw different nightclub shows. A couple of other boys asked Suzanne for dates but she turned them down. "Why didn't you say yes?" Aunt Bea complained. "He looked like a nice boy, a college boy."

"I'd rather just rest."

"All right, Suzanne, if you want to be stubborn, be stubborn. You're the one who'll be missing out on the good times and the fun but you do what you want—"

"I intend to," said Suzanne.

They met every night at 1:30. She was back around four. The last night we were there, she came back with his silver St. Christopher medal and fell asleep holding it. Aunt Bea came into our room early to remind us we had to pack before breakfast. She shook Suzanne awake. "What's *that?*"

"What?"

"*That?*"

"*This?*"

Suzanne looked at the chain intertwined in her fingers as if she had never seen it before. I held my breath. She stretched and yawned. "This? I found it in the corridor when we came in last night. It's some kind of religious medal. I guess one of the Cuban maids must have lost it."

Aunt Bea's mind was hopscotching to other things. "Do you think I should have bought the red straw bag along with the white one yesterday?" The day before we had gone shopping, and Suzanne had been rewarded for her "good behavior" with another bikini and two cashmere sweaters. "It is a smart bag, isn't it, Suzanne? I wonder if we can stop on the way to the airport. I'll go ask your father. . . ."

"I guess he wanted you to have the medal," I said when we were alone.

"Yeah, I think he has his name engraved on it."

"He really must like you a lot, Suzanne," I said. She yawned. In the lobby she gave Aunt Bea the medal to hand in at the office while she bought some magazines for the plane.

"Keep it," Aunt Bea hissed at her. "Keep it, you can put a locket on the chain."

"Well, I don't think that's right, Mother, but if you say so. . . ."

That might have been the end of the Johnny Poparossa episode if Johnny hadn't been sent to Albany on a quick business trip in March of that year. Looking at the road map he noticed that Bennington, Vermont, was near Albany, New York. What a hell of a coincidence! After completing his assignment, delivering a locked briefcase to a state senator and sometime business associate of Schoenfeld's (later indicted for selling stolen Treasury notes), Johnny with a free week-end, drove across the border to see Suzanne.

That weekend Suzanne was in her dormitory room, nursing one of her colds. The hayloft was even damper in early spring than it had been in late fall. Even worse, that weekend she was supposed to be writing a paper on Conrad's *The Secret Sharer* for her professor-lover. Both Conrad and her lover were turning into colossal bores.

"Suzanne, there's a guy asking for you," one of the girls shouted up to her as she sniffed and choked.

She wasn't expecting anyone but, released from Conrad's steely grip, she flew down the stairs, sneezing.

"JOHNNY!"

"BABY!"

They fell into each other's arms. The girls in the living room, entertaining beery Williams boys, looked on enviously. With his pompadour and sideburns, his dark glasses, and shiny bopper's suit, Johnny was super cool.

"Just a minute, Johnny; I'll go get my coat." She dashed up the stairs, her stuffed head miraculously clearing. She signed out for the local pizzeria, an appropriate cover, she decided. They spent the night at the Ethan Allen Motor Lodge.

Johnny was a perfect change of pace from the lit professor who thrashed around in the hay filled with angst after every single time. And the roll in the hay wasn't enough for him. Oh no, he wanted Suzanne to write brilliant papers on the poetry of Wallace Stevens and babysit for his children on Saturday nights. "Darling, it's the way for you to get to know my wife and family, for you to get to know *all of me*. I want us to have more than a *few physical moments* together, enchanting as they may be."

In contrast, Johnny that night whispered *Amboy Dukes* dialogue nonstop in her ear: "Baby, I'm crazy about you . . . Baby, I never met a girl like you before . . . Baby, I couldn't stop thinking about you, dreaming about you. . . ." In the morning he asked seriously: "Hey, baby, you ain't married?"

"No, Johnny."

"Neither am I."

"Gee, Johnny, that's swell."

"So why don't we get married? You think I'm kidding? I'm not kidding. I never asked a girl before."

"You're sweet."

"You don't want to go back to that school, do you? What do you do there? It don't even look like a school. It looks like a Fresh Air Camp they sent me to one summer—"

She laughed. "That's sort of a funny idea."

"What? Getting married?"

"Yes."

"Well?"

"Okay, I guess."

"Today?"

"But we can't get married today, Johnny."

"Oh, yeah? Honey, I know a guy in Albany who can fix *anything*."

The state senator did. Waiving their Wassermans, they were married that afternoon in a judge's study. They drove back to New York on their wedding night. Johnny said he was staying in a friend's apartment on East 57th Street. "It's a girl I know. She— uh—sort of does some work for me."

The apartment didn't have much furniture. One room, one bed, large and round, with pink satin sheets and a mirror overhead. "What else do we need, baby?" Johnny said and Suzanne nodded, trying to smile.

For three days they made love, watched the movies on TV, ate corned beef sandwiches that were sent up from the local deli. They even had long serious talks. They decided they would raise the children as Catholics and send them to parochial schools. "You can't do better than the nuns," Johnny said seriously and Suzanne, still smiling, nodded her agreement. He called up some friends and they arranged a wedding party for the next Saturday night at the Copacabana. Suddenly, at four o'clock on Wednesday afternoon, Suzanne began to get dressed.

"Where are you going, baby?"

"Just to get some eggs, or a steak, or something. I'm sort of tired of sandwiches, Johnny."

"Can you cook?"

"I don't think so."

"Hey, I'll get my mama to teach you how to make spaghetti."

"That's a peachy keen idea."

He gave her $10. They kissed a long deep kiss.

Just as she was about to enter the Gristede's at First and 56th, she turned instead and hailed a cab. She gave her address in Hewlett Bay Park, told the driver she would pay the extra out-of-city fare and then burst into hysterical sobs. She cried all the way home and for two days thereafter, hiding her head under a pillow. It was a week before she would tell her parents what she had done. Uncle Morris pulled every string. At the annulment hearing, dressed in white, she told the judge that Johnny had made her perform acts of sexual perversion. She whispered in the judge's ear exactly what Johnny had made her do. The judge flushed. The annulment was granted.

A couple of years ago Suzanne called me late on a Saturday night. She was in Washington at the Watergate, waiting for her Undersecretary of State to return from an emergency meeting. With nothing better to do she was making a list on stationery engraved "From the Office of the President." No names, just numbers:

~~IIII~~
~~IIII~~
~~IIII~~
~~IIII~~
~~IIII~~
~~IIII~~
etc.

"Aileen, can I tell you something?" she asked me long distance.

"Sure. What?"

(Oh, how many times has she asked and I have answered and she has told. Why do I always want to hear? And why do I have so goddamn little to contribute to this game of do-and-tell? Those are the questions.)

"I've just realized that I have slept with more men than my mother and her mother and her mother and maybe than all my female ancestors added up together."

"Give or take a few pogroms."

"You can include the pogroms."

"So?"

"Guess what that makes me?"

"I can't guess."

"All fucked up."

And she hung up, laughing.

3

*Do you know what I would do if I had
the Venus de Milo in my office? I'd say,
honey, you absolutely must go on a high-
protein diet.*
    —Eileen Beale, Beale Model Agency,
        "Do You Want to Be a Model?"
        Modern Teen Magazine,
        November, 1972

Five days since baby day and still counting, but backwards. Suzanne and I have spent a lot of time poring
over last spring's calendar. But Suzanne can't remember very well. It's all sort of vague and unclear (not
unusual for this lady).

"I don't want to think about it too much, Aileen."

"Then why did you bring it up?"

"Because I think about it all the time."

Suzanne sucked on a piece of her hair.

Her periods were always irregular so how could she
know exactly when she became pregnant? She used
the pill but only when she remembered to take it. No
pill for three days, two gulped on a frantic Saturday
night. She didn't even suspect that she was pregnant
for weeks and weeks. She simply blamed her nausea
on the English food.

"Madame Anapoulis," Paul has assured her several
times these last few days, "it is perfectly normal for
an infant to be two weeks late. The infant does not
know he's late, *n'est-ce pas?*"

"More time to practice, you lucky *gel*," boomed

Hardcastle, whose personality must have been tempered in Coventry during the blitz.

But Suzanne worries that every day which passes proves Nicho is not the father.

"Are there lots of other possibilities? I'm just asking."

We were taking a walk. Suzanne has decided to exercise, hoping it will bring on the baby, the way hot baths and moving furniture around the apartment and drinking half a bottle of Milk of Magnesia would rather explosively bring on one of her sluggish periods. Now she swims with Paul and me twice a day, bobbing like a large pale cork in the turquoise water. And we walk up and down and around her island which is two miles by three miles, hot and rocky and dry.

"If you don't mind my asking—*who?*"

"Oh, just a man I met in London after I met Nicho." Last spring things got a little complicated for Suzanne. She left her groom-to-be in New York waiting under the wedding canopy at the Plaza Hotel and went off to London. She met Nicho in London, left Nicho in London, and met this other man. The mind boggles. And I like to think of Suzanne as languid.

Just then, for instance, she stopped and yawned. We sat down on a rocky edge. I poured some lemonade from the Thermos I carried and drank a cup. It was delicious. Suzanne stuck out her tongue and panted like a dog. Even Hardcastle acknowledges that Suzanne is a supreme panter, able to continue, her tongue hanging out, minute after minute. She likes to do it the way a little girl likes to make funny faces. I refilled the cup and handed it to her.

It was very hot as usual. Here the sun never stops shining, never is covered by a cloud. It will rain soon, Nicho says, but only for a few days. It is a life filled

with unremitting sunshine. I can understand why the
ancient Greeks believed that the sun was the great
god Apollo, driving a fiery chariot endlessly across the
sky. By comparison, in New York, even on the
brightest day, the sun is a concealed lighting effect.

Suzanne wiped her forehead with a silk handkerchief. There was a delicate beading of sweat on her
upper lip. She leaned back, her stomach jutting out,
hard as the rock. She says now she feels stuffed with
baby from chest to thigh, stuffed with bones and
muscles stronger than her own.

"What was he like? This other man?"

No answer. She drank another cup of lemonade.
Even talking, forming words with lip and tongue and
teeth, seemed exhausting in the late afternoon heat. It
was very quiet. Nicho was on the phone, giving com-
mands to his legion of assistants and vice-presidents.
Nothing in that vast organization is done without
Great Caesar's specific approval. Paul, our good
medic, was swimming. We could see his graying head
moving in and out of the water. Hardcastle was in the
kitchen with the chef who adores only her. She eats.
He makes her English trifle, coupe aux marrons,
sacher tortes. We end our meals virtuously with Shim-
mer, out of deference to Suzanne.

"Suzanne—"

She was dozing, her eyes closed. Nowadays she
falls asleep like a cat. I could see a bright blue vein
throbbing on one eyelid. Her breasts are crisscrossed
by a network of pale blue veins and there is a spider
web of veins on the back of her leg. The insides of
her hands are flushed pink. All normal, Paul explained, all the stigmata of this pregnancy.

As I watched, Paul strode out of the water, his slen-
der body handsome in the afternoon sunlight.

*A quickie fantasy. Aileen De Carlo in dia-
phanous veils and doctor-doctor on the beach.
(Rip) "Doctor, doctor, that's not a thermometer...." (Grin)*

Except it always plays better in my mind than in
the flesh.

Paul and I have not managed to continue the conversation we began so promisingly the other day. I
fear he and I have the same kind of problems. My old
classroom discovery, Mr. Eliot, may have summed it
up best: *"Between the idea and the action/Falls the
shadow—"* But Paul now gives me warm friendly
looks at every opportunity. "Aileen (a warm friendly
look)—would you like (a warm friendly look)—the
second section of this *New York Times?"*

Not really. The *Times* tries too hard to remind me
of home. I start thinking about my little rent-controlled West 83rd Street apartment, with the three
Segal locks on my front door. Home sweet home. I
have, all my own, a fireplace that's charming and
doesn't work, a gate at my window, a dozen cock-
roaches who bathe daily in Raid. A sudden flash of
memory: New York in late summer. It stinks, actually.
The dog dirt that lines every street, east or west, the
hot oily popcorn smell of the subways, the stench of
urine throughout Grand Central Station. Who pees all
over Grand Central? I wonder as I race against the
crowd for my shuttle train. You'd expect a better class
of behavior from the Westchester commuters.

When I moved to the Upper West Side Aunt Bea
called and asked in an angry voice: "Aileen, you want
to get yourself *raped?"*

Don't ask.

Suzanne awoke, yawned, and smiled sweetly. "Was
I asleep again?" She looked amazingly pretty even in

the heat. Her face was flushed but rosy, her blonde
hair curled in tendrils around her face. Suddenly she
took a deep cleansing breath. She began to breathe
out slowly, whistling out the air. She massaged her
stomach which appeared noticeably tenser. I could
see a definite secondary bulge within the primary
bulge.

"Suzanne, it's happening," I screamed. I started to
rise, ready to race off for Hardcastle and Paul. But
she shook her head, put her hand on my arm, took
another cleansing breath before she spoke.

"I just felt a twinge, that's all. Ripening contractions, Paul calls them. My lazy uterus is practicing,
too, I guess." She lit a cigarette. "Now what were we
talking about?" she asked vaguely. She unrolled a
length of hair that had been fastened on top of her
head.

"You know. The other man." And only you know.

She made a face. Oh, *him.* "He was English. A journalist. Not terribly special."

A jingle I learned in a journalism class at Columbia
bubbled into my mind:

> Never try to bribe or twist
> the good old British journalist
> For what the man, unbribed, will do
> there is never an occasion to.

"What was he like? I don't mean to pry—" Oh, didn't
I?

"He was handsome. He sort of looked like me."

"That's lucky—"

She gave me a look. "Oh, does it really matter,
Aileen?"

In the past Suzanne liked contrasts. When there
were two at a time, and there have been two at the

same exact time (she told me it happened, giggling, and then told me, huffily, of course, it hadn't.) But when there were two taking turns, it was the good guy versus the bad guy, a nice guy followed immediately by a rat. After Nicho, easy. I said sweetly— "King Rat?"

She considered, chewing her hair. "The Rat Dauphin?"

We giggled together. She rolled her hair back onto the top of her head. "I've been thinking, Aileen. I've been thinking I should tell Nicho all about it? What do you think?"

"What the hell for?"

"Because then he'd know. And whatever he'd feel, he'd feel and whatever he'd do, he'd do. And then I could stop worrying about it."

"Suzanne, that isn't exactly a reason—"

"I didn't care who the father was when I first realized I was pregnant. I didn't think about it that much. I was so goddamned amazed at being pregnant. And when I decided I wanted to have the baby—well, that's all I wanted. I still didn't care who the father was.

"Derek couldn't understand. That's his name. Derek Britten. He kept saying nobody has babies anymore. Babies are out of fashion, aren't they? I left him because he didn't want me to have the baby.

"And Nicho, well, I never expected Nicho to go to all that bloody silly trouble to try and find me. We had a very good time when we were together but, my God, why we were only together for about ten days. I didn't know I was so important to him."

Suzanne, my dear, you see you make this terrific first impression.

Suzanne left Nicho when he was called away to a conference in Geneva. He instructed Suzanne to stay at the hotel in London where they had been together. He would phone her. He had arranged for lavish gifts to be sent. He even provided a duenna, his British secretary, since dismissed. Suzanne has always called her, in retrospect, the lovely Miss Chilblains.

Chilblains, superefficient, taking her job seriously, had drawn up a tight schedule suitable for the likes of Suzanne.

They had one brief encounter.

"Mister Anapoulis thought you might like to shop while he's away."

"I HATE to shop."

"Or have your hair done."

"My hair is done. Been done for years. I just have to wash it occasionally."

"Well, right-o, shall I book for lunch downstairs in the Rib Room in an hour?"

"I'm a bloody vegetarian."

Tempers snapped like rubber bands. Miss Chilblains' pink-tipped nose quivered with sudden fury. Her mid-Atlantic accent reverted to Cockney primitive. "Mistah Anapoulis 'as 'ad other gulls like you," she spat out. "A word to the wise, dearie. Gather ye rosebuds—"

Suzanne picked up the nearest thing at hand, a heavy glass paperweight that filled with snow when shaken. It was Nicho's latest gift, purchased at the Chelsea Antique Market because Suzanne had said she had one just like it as a child. Suzanne took general aim but flung wildly, the paperweight flying across the room, missing its petrified target but shattering the mirror above the bureau.

"Owwwwwwwwwwwww—" Chilblains emitted a horrible Eliza Doolittle scream.

"Get out, get out, get out," Suzanne shouted, as if it were Aunt Bea in her room examining the crotch of

yesterday's underpants. Suzanne's shouts could be heard echoing down the corridor. Doors opened and shut as the terrified Chilblains fled.

In a daze Suzanne packed and split less than two hours after Nicho's cheerful departure. When things get tense Suzanne runs, on little cat's feet.

After Suzanne did her familiar disappearing act (now you have her, now you don't) Nicho hired seven detectives to search London, Paris, the streets of New York with orders—Find Her. A month later one of them found Suzanne Goldfarb begging on the Spanish Steps. Nicho flew to Rome, loaded down with presents, buoyant with expectation. But this Suzanne Goldfarb was a nineteen-year-old N.Y.U. dropout from Forest Hills, freaked out on Moroccan hash.

"But this is not her," Nicho complained, balancing his square bulk precariously on the Spanish Steps. "You fool!"

"It is the name on the passport. You wanna girl with this name, I finda girl with this name," the Italian detective shouted back, gaining the gathering crowd's sympathy. Private detectives are considerably less private in Italy.

Nicho returned to London, feeling like a fool and very depressed. He wanted his Suzanne, he longed for his Suzanne, his fey blonde enchantress. He had cut out a picture from a magazine of a girl advertising eye shadow who looked something like Suzanne (it was). He kept it in the top drawer of his desk, studying it during telephone calls and in the middle of long business meetings. He was suddenly as lovesick as a boy of fifteen. After another month with no success, he hired three more detectives.

"In movies and books private detectives work fast," Nicho explained. "But in real life, on per diem and expenses, they work nice and slow."

She was tracked down finally by a Scotland Yard
man with the right bloodhound instincts. He explained that he had searched for young women of
good families before. Methodically he checked the
records of every maternity clinic in the greater London area. Suzanne had gone to a clinic once for a
checkup, a vitamin supplement, and free milk cou-
pons. He found that she lived in a small bed-sitting
room in Earl's Court and worked behind the counter
in a nearby cafe.

When Nicho was certain that this Suzanne Goldfarb was *the* Suzanne Goldfarb he wanted (the detective brought back Minox photographs), he set out
across London in his Silver Cloud Rolls Royce.

The climactic scene: the Olympia Tea Shoppe on that
fateful day. FRESH SANDWICHES CUT DAILY MORNING
COFFEE AFTERNOON TEAS, reads the creaking sign
above the front door. The windows are smudged and
greasy. The air in the square, dark room is heavy
with the kettle's steam and the smell of day-old hard-
boiled eggs and Wall's pork sausages.

Nicho enters, center stage, a short squat Prince
Charming. (Unfortunately, Nicho was changed from
a frog into a permanent disguise as Rumplestiltzkin.)

He strides purposefully through the crowded
tables, knocking over a couple of chairs. He goes
straight to Suzanne (who is temporarily and memora-
bly disguised as Cinderella). She is at midcounter,
her head bent, washing dishes. Hard at work, humming a rock tune, sucking her hair. She doesn't look
up.

Meanwhile, the proprietress, Mrs. Mulchrone, is
wiping up the tables with a dirty dishrag. She gives
Nicho a hard look. She, for one, doesn't like these
greasy little Pakis.

Nicho (he speaks in a throaty whisper, his eyes damp with surging emotions): "Hello, my darling."

Suzanne: "Ohmigosh (she drops a soapy dish). How did you ever find me?" (Her voice is shrill, her accent lightly tinged with echoes of Earl's Court.)

Nicho: "I lost you, so I found you." (Was he rehearsing that line?) "Come with me, my darling. The car is waiting." (The counter separates them or he would—naturally—sweep her into his short but powerful arms.)

Mrs. Mulchrone (rushing up): "This bloke troubling you, dearie? What's your order, then, mister?"

Nicho (blowing): "Madame, I wish to inform you that Miss Goldfarb is handing in her notice as of this day, this hour, this moment—"

Mrs. Mulchrone: "Sez who?"

(Nicho reaches across the counter and takes Suzanne's arm firmly.)

Suzanne (a whine): "Nicho, please, you're hurting me."

Mrs. Mulchrone: "Have you finished the ham and tomatoes, dearie?"

(It is almost tea time. The cafe is filling with regular customers, slamming the door, taking their cutlery and trays.)

A customer (coming to the counter): "A cheese and chutney, luv, and a cuppa." (Suzanne pulls her hand away and fills a thick chipped tea cup.)

Nicho: "Suzanne, my darling, I know what is best for you, believe me, trust me—"

(Suzanne hesitates, considering.)

Mrs. Mulchrone: "Do I have to get behind there myself, my girl, and give this man his tea?"

(The hot tea splashes over the cup rim, scalding Suzanne's dainty hand. She bursts into tears.)

Suzanne (wailing): "I'm going to have a baby! WAH!"

Customer: "Good luck, luv."

Mrs. Mulchrone: "Shocking goings-on."

Nicho (after a pause and a deep breath): "Congratulate me, my friends, I am going to be a father."

Customer: "Congratulations, mate."

(Nicho kisses Suzanne's damp red hand. Then he tugs her the length of the counter, finally leads her out, her hair covering her face. She is still crying. Transfixed, everyone in the cafe watches as the chauffeur rushes to open the door and as Nicho guides her tenderly into the back seat of the Rolls.

Mrs. Mulchrone: "Well, I never! Bloody foreigners, both of them—"

Customer: "Do I get my cheese and chutney now, luv?"

The Sunday after Suzanne's wedding Mrs. Mulchrone told her story to the *The Sunday People*. "Cinderella Suzanne was like a daughter to me," she wrote with the help of three staff writers. "Everyone liked her salmon mayonnaise but I was personally fondest of her fishpaste and cucumber, her own unique combination on brown bread. I sincerely hope and pray that Nick likes her sandwiches too. I think every woman, no matter how well off, should be able to make a sandwich and a cuppa for the man she loves."

Remembering that comic-opera day, Suzanne said: "My leg hurt. For the first time I couldn't button my skirt. And Mrs. Mulchrone was such a bloody bitch."

"But, Suzanne, surely that's not the reason you went with Nicho?"

"Oh, Aileen, I don't always know how I feel about things until I do something that shows me how I feel. And sometimes even then. . . ." her voice faded.

"Suzanne, you *are* crazy." I laughed.

"I went with him, I think, because I was afraid. Suddenly, I realized the baby was for real. Isn't that a good enough reason?" Her eyes flashed.

"Yes," I said. I had been teasing her, and whenever I do, I always feel ashamed.

After Johnny Poparossa, Suzanne, for the one and only time, had gone to a shrink. Aunt Bea and Uncle Morris insisted—and they had paid. Suzanne and the psychiatrist didn't talk much. "When I walk in he always asks me how I feel and that sort of puts me off—"

The doctor cost $60 an hour, one hour a day, five days a week. She lay on his couch and counted the slubs on his slubbed silk wall covering. Then she multiplied slubs, divided slubs, began to dream about slubs that walked and talked and made perverted slub-like love to her. She fled the nightmarish wall covering. About six months later she met the psychiatrist at a party and let him take her home, spent the night with him. In the morning she told him about her dreams of slubs and he told Suzanne he used to dream about her.

"We should go. The sun's going to set."

"Yes. Another day's over. Damn it."

She yawned, rubbed her back, smoothed her belly. She tried to stand up, tottered; I helped her to her feet. "If this sea monster that's swimming inside me isn't born in a couple of days, I am so going to tell Nicho. I am so." Suddenly, she looked so tired standing there, weighed down by her own body. I helped her over the rocks and she held my hand tightly. I wondered if she was afraid again.

Later that evening on the terrace, Paul looked cool

and handsome in his white linen pants and dark
blazer.

"Madame, how are you feeling?"

"Preggers." She had changed into a long aqua dress
that made her eyes greener and her stomach rounder.

"Tomorrow I think we shall take some extra tests—"

"Why?"

"Just a precaution, I have no concern—"

"Good," said Suzanne, stuffing a handful of forbid-
den almonds in her mouth.

There were roses everywhere. There were no
presents under Suzanne's Porthault pillowcase this
morning. But at lunch Nicho explained that the Good
Fairy had been fogged in over Heathrow. So Nicho
sent the helicopter to Cyprus for red roses, dozens
and dozens, and their scent filled the air. Suzanne
wove a bracelet of roses for me and slipped it on my
wrist. My mother could never manage to teach me,
but she taught Suzanne to knit and sew.

Nicho joined us, wearing his white dinner jacket,
slapping his hands together, filled with his usual ebul-
lience.

"My darling—" He kissed Suzanne's hand. "For us a
treat, a surprise, a diversion—" he has noticed her flag-
ging spirits, her moodiness and it seems to hurt him.
"We shall have a picnic on the temple grounds. Two
thousand years ago, villagers from the mainland
rowed to our island to make offerings to the goddess
and to dine in her sacred grove. So shall we tonight—"

Our little island is called Astarte which was the local regional name for the goddess Aphrodite. There
was a temple on the island though all that is left of it,
a quarter of a mile from the villa, is a few pillars and
a flat stone sunk into the ground where offerings of oil
and perfume were left by the worshippers. Occasion-

ally one of the workmen finds a piece of gray stone with a trace of a carving and gives it to Nicho.

"Would that amuse you, my darling?"

"Sure. Lovely," Suzanne said. "But let's go—I'm hungry, I'm starving—"

The chef and maids, carrying baskets, led the way. Nicho held Suzanne's arm. The path was steep and rocky. The sun, a ball of flame, hung over the horizon, then set suddenly. The maids swooped and lit a dozen scented candles.

The table was laid near the altar stone, covered with a long white cloth.

"Perhaps we shall summon the spirit of the goddess," said Nicho.

"Oh, dear, I hope not," said Hardcastle, sitting down. "I had a friend who went in for seances, that sort of thing. And the stories she told. Made me feel all creepy-crawly."

"If I spill some wine—by accident, of course—she may think it is an offering," Nicho said. He was filling our glasses with champagne. "So—it has happened—" He poured half a bottle of Dom Perignon on the altar stone. It made a puddle in a groove in the rock. Then he opened another bottle.

"Are the old gods still worshipped anywhere in the region?" I asked.

"I doubt it," said Nicho. "The old gods just had a good time. They were happy fellows. Jesus Christ suffered. He is a better god for the modern Greeks. When I have a son, I shall build a church over these stones."

Across the table, Paul looked a trifle uncomfortable, as if he would be held responsible if the baby he delivered wasn't that son.

"What do you want, Suzanne," I asked her once, "a boy or a girl?"

"I hope she's a fool, a pretty little fool—" she replied, straight-faced. Her Bennington professor had made his Daisy read his Fitzgerald.

On the island, along with my paperback of stories from mythology I had been rereading my college copy of *The Golden Bough*. I always bring guide books along when I travel and read them conscientiously in my hotel room. In fact, I have occasionally enjoyed a well-written travel book a lot more than the place I was visiting.

In *The Golden Bough* it explains that Aphrodite (a.k.a. Astarte) was the most important and most popular goddess in this part of the Mediterranean. Small wonder. Her rites included an offering followed by a feast followed by an orgy. The orgy and the feast were sometimes simultaneous. Her priestesses were holy prostitutes who slept with both friends and strangers and used the money they earned for the upkeep of the temple. In some areas young girls, as a religious duty, had to sell their virginity to a stranger and give their payment to the priestesses. They waited at the temple gates. There were few travelers at the time. Some girls—the ugly ones—had to wait years and years.

> "I'm sorry, sir, but she's the only virgin we have on hand. A party of Thracian sailors was through last month and practically cleaned us out."
> "Well, I'll do a lot of things for the Great Goddess, but not that."
> "Think of it as charity, sir—"
> "Sorry, I give at my home temple—"

Poor virgins, they must have been the first teen-

agers—waiting, bored out of their minds, praying for
something, anything, to happen to them.

Around the table our conversation moved in fits
and starts. We ate langoustine, cold chicken, trout in
aspic. Suzanne, thinking she was hidden by the semi-
darkness, stuffed a piece of thickly buttered bread in
her mouth. Paul was watching. He pursed his lips and
shook his head. Suzanne grinned.

There was a sound, a long twang of a note and a
light seemed to glow on the altar stone. Iphigenia,
who was serving Turkish coffee in little gold cups,
gave a high-pitched giggle.

"Oh, dear," said Hardcastle, "you Greeks have
ghosties too—"

The spotlight grew brighter. We were all watching
closely, except Suzanne who kept spooning up her
strawberries and cream. Nicho lit a cigar and put his
arm expansively over the back of Suzanne's chair.

"Very mysterious," he said.

"I wonder if the goddess is going to look like Liz
Taylor?" I whispered to Suzanne.

"Well, she bloody well better not look like
Veruschka or I'm kicking her ass off this island,"
Suzanne whispered back to me.

The effect was very old-fashioned theatrical. When
the altar stone was brightly lit, a man suddenly
stepped from behind one of the broken columns. He
must have been crouched there for hours. He was
dressed in baggy white pants and a white shirt. He
walked to the center of the light and bowed.
Hardcastle applauded. "Very nice," she said. And
then he knelt down. He stretched wide his arms and
began to declaim in a loud voice: "Beautiful lady, I
haf been sent by the Great Goddess Astarte—" he
stopped and crossed himself "—who ees your admirer
and friend. For you, gentle lady, ees so beautiful, so

beautiful—" He talked in a sing-song up and down, but his accent was so thick, it was hard to make out his words.

"—so beautiful, so beautiful—" Obviously, he had learned his recitation by rote, and now he was stuck like a cracked record.

Nicho growled something in Greek.

The man stood up, bowed, then knelt down and began again in a louder voice. "Beautiful Lady, I haf been sent by the Great Goddess Astarte who ees your admirer and wishes to be your friend. For you, gentle lady, ees so beautiful, so kind—" he remembered and gave us a broad happy grin.

Paul and Hardcastle and I were smiling in response but Suzanne had that haughty expression that means she is either annoyed or embarrassed. When her parents took us to night clubs in Miami Beach, singers would often serenade her and comics tell her jokes or flirt with her while the audience laughed and applauded. One night a singer crooned, "Gimme a little kiss, willya huh," while the audience ooohed and ahhed. He kissed her on her cheek and Suzanne whispered in his ear: "Tony, baby, your fly is open."

"The Great Goddess could be jealous but she is not. No, she wishes you good luck, healthy, wealthy, wise—" He pantomimed a belly. "Sons—" He wiped his brow with a handkerchief. "That's all, Boss." He bowed again and we applauded.

Two other men popped out of the darkness. One handed the goddess's messenger a bouzouki and they broke into a lively rendition of the theme from *Never On Sunday*. They were probably tourist entertainers Nicho had had helicoptered in from Mykonos or Rhodes.

"Very lively—" said Hardcastle, humming along. "I think I've heard that folk song before."

"Are you cold, my darling?" Nicho asked. There was a sea breeze and the nights had been growing cooler. Nicho gestured and Iphigenia brought a shawl. He draped it over Suzanne's bare shoulders. "Darling—" Nicho kissed her hand. "Does this amuse you?"

She smiled and shook her head slowly from side to side. "Isn't that the way the Greeks say yes?"

He shook his head. "Yes—" They smiled at each other.

One of the men began to dance, holding a handkerchief stretched out between his hands. It was strong-legged, masculine dancing, with foot-stamps and knee-bends. One of the other men joined him and they danced together slowly with great dignity.

"Aren't they marvelous! Can you dance, Mister Anapoulis?" Hardcastle asked.

"When I was younger—not anymore."

"Da Boss, he is a good dancer," Iphigenia giggled. She was giving me and Hardcastle brightly colored shawls. They were locally made and the wool was scratchy.

"A little gift for you—" Nicho said. Party favors.

"You are too generous, sir. Really—" Hardcastel protested. The shawl made Hardcastle look like a sweet old grandmother.

The dancers stopped and we applauded. The singer began a song that was slower, less melodic; it sounded vaguely Arabic and very sad. I turned to Suzanne. She was breathing slowly and rhythmically. Her head fell against Paul's shoulder. She was fast asleep.

Paul looked concerned. "Madame, she needs her sleep. I think, perhaps, she should go back to the house now. I will be happy to take her back. I am afraid I had a little too much sun today. I have stopped being cautious—which is always a mistake."

"This has been so enjoyable, so picturesque," said Hardcastle. "But I'm getting used to my nine o'clock beddy-byes, too."

"You are all children," Nicho said.

"Madame—Madame—" Paul touched Suzanne's shoulder. Her eyes opened wide like a little girl.

Paul and Hardcastle helped her up. Paul looked at me. I could hardly see him in the darkness but I'm sure he was wearing one of his friendlier expressions: "Aren't you going back, Aileen?"

"I'm not tired."

"*Au revoir,* then, *chérie.* Good night, sir." Together they supported Suzanne between them. Two maids led the way with candles. The singer stopped abruptly. But Nicho clapped his hands together and growled at them. The men exchanged a look and began to play another lively tune.

"So," he said to me, "are you ready for a real drink?"

"Sure," I lied, I who can get silly on two Grasshoppers.

"Metaxa!" he called. Iphigenia scurried to him with the bottle and small glasses. He poured two brimming shot glasses of the amber liquid.

"You should drink it the way vodka is drunk—in one gulp and not with orange juice. The Americans do not understand the Russians because the Americans drink orange juice with their vodka. But now we are talking about Metaxa. So watch. One gulp. Done!"

I watched carefully. I gulped. Firewater mixed with floor wax, equal parts. My esophagus would burn and shine.

"You like it?"

I couldn't talk but I smiled bravely. When I found

my voice it had become a strained whisper. "Delicious."

"Good." He poured me another shot. "*Salud,*" he said. "*L'chaim.*" We gulped together. The second time it burned less but I could taste it more. It was not an improvement.

"That is enough for you," he said firmly. He called, and Iphigenia took away my glass, brought me another cup of thick sweet coffee, a glass of ice water, a dish of dates stuffed with nuts. We had been eating for hours. I chewed on a sticky date.

He held up his glass which he had refilled again. "To you, my dear girl, to you." He drank. "I want you to understand that I appreciate your being here, spending this time with us. I know you are a modern young woman with a life of your own—"

"I was glad to come here if Suzanne wanted me with her. We're family. More than that, we're friends."

"Yes." He took another gulp. "By the way, Aileen, I've been wondering if your aunt has any pictures of Suzanne when she was a child, a little girl—"

Of course we were going to talk about Suzanne.

"Dozens, *hundreds.* There's even a portrait of her painted when she was about eighteen. The hotel artist in Miami Beach did it so you can imagine its aesthetic quality. He made every woman look a little like a movie star. It's Suzanne as a young Grace Kelly, I think." (There was one of Aunt Bea as Barbara Stanwyck, mutual nose dip and all. No, I didn't have my portrait painted.)

Nicho laughed. "I must have that. I will tell the New York office to call Suzanne's mother. And you have given me a good idea, yes, a very good idea. I shall arrange to have a new portrait of Suzanne paint-

ed, perhaps by Annigoni. Yes, she must have her portrait painted. Next year, of course—"

All that love and adoration pouring out of Nicho,
combined with the liquor, made me a little dizzy. Still
I babbled on uncontrollably: "I also came here because I wanted to meet you. I mean it. I was
impressed, sir—you are impressive." I sounded silly
again. But drunkenness is always such a good excuse.

"Me? But I am a dull man," he said "Don't you
think so now?"

"Of course not. But what's most fascinating about
you, I'm sure you won't talk about."

"And what is that?"

"Your past. How it all happened. How you made it
happen."

"There is only half a bottle of Metaxa. To talk I
would need at least two bottles."

"So give me half a bottle's worth." The kid can be
so damn cute.

He laughed. "I would not know where to begin.
What about me would interest a young woman? My
knowledge of shipping rates?"

"Start at the beginning."

He puffed on his cigar. "I have never let myself be
interviewed because how can one explain one's life? A
life happens, that's all. All I can tell you perhaps are
a few little stories. All right. But just between the two
of us. What do they say—not for publication." He relit
his cigar and winked a heavy eyelid. "And stop me,
my dear, whenever I am boring you," he added,
sounding serious.

4

THE MONEY MACHINE,
OR HOW OUR MODERN ODYSSEUS
FOUND THE GOLDEN FLEECE

Notes on a conversation with Nicho Anapoulis:

We talked till the sun rose. The musicians played and played. Iphigenia brought a second bottle and then a third. I shared the third. We all shared the third.

It is now hours later and I am trying very hard to remember everything he said. The clatter of the typewriter keys is giving me a ferocious headache but I want to write up what I remember. Who knows? These are notes worth keeping. I used to do that after an interview with a rock star like Mick or John. ("I was the genius," John once told me. "Just remember, Paul wasn't the genius.")

Nicho: " 'Money' was the first word I ever said, or so I have been told. I suppose it's the truth though it is very surprising because in the village where I was born no one had any money. Once in a while, the people with relatives in America were sent letters filled with stiff green American dollar bills. Very beautiful. A friend of mine who had an uncle with a coffee shop in New Jersey once let me hold and smell an American dollar. From then on I thought American money might be good to eat. To me it smelled delicious, like potatoes fried in oil."

Childhood: "My father owned no land and so he was the town shoemaker, carver, mender. He did a hundred odd jobs. But mostly he sat in front of the door and carved small wooden figures—little animals, figures of men and women, the priest in his robes, a little carving of me running after a ball, my only toy. He was very skillful.

"My mother and her older brother owned a few stony acres on a hillside outside the village that was farmed by the brother and his family. I was clumsy with my hands and could not learn to carve. My father would say to me, 'It is easy, all you must do is find the little figure in the wood.' But I could find nothing. I was afraid that when I grew up I would have no work, and my family, my little children would starve.

"What was our life like? I can still remember everything. Most of the time I thought about food. I was always hungry and my mother always scolded me if I asked for more at a meal. I remember we ate bread dipped in olive oil for our breakfast, maybe a watery vegetable soup for our one main meal and at night bread with olives for supper. At Easter my uncle slaughtered two lambs and we had meat for a week. We pretended to each other we enjoyed it very much. But we were not used to meat and it made us sick.

"I taught myself to count. Because my father made a carved chest for the church, the priest taught me to read. I never went to school because there was no school in our village. The schoolteacher, like everyone else who had some brains, had emigrated to America.

"My mother was a strange woman. She was broad-shouldered, black haired with a face like a hawk.

Fierce." (Last night I thought Nicho looked like a bird, too, a macaw perhaps or a parrot, old and wise and worn.) "When I was about eight she had a baby, a little boy, but the baby was born dead. A year after, she aborted when she was about seven months pregnant. The year after that again the baby died. The embryo was so misshapen that the midwife took it away and buried it and would not let my mother see it. Then my mother became stranger, more distant. She would not talk to us. She would not cook or clean the house or wash our clothes. She prayed in the church all day until the priest chased her home. At night, all night, she cried and would not let my father comfort her.

"My parents slept together in a big bed. I slept in a little bed by the fire. We are talking about over fifty years ago, and yet this one night, I can remember it as if it was yesterday. In the middle of the night, still half asleep, I awoke and heard my mother talking.

"God was punishing her, she said. God was killing the innocent babies in her womb. It was because she was wicked and full of sin and she must confess her sins to her husband. My mother got out of her bed and in her long white nightgown she knelt down before my father. Long ago she said she had gone to the city and worked as a servant girl. One night, only one night, she had been with a man, a sailor off a ship. A month later she came back to our village with a terrible secret. Theirs was a hasty marriage. 'The boy is not your son,' she said that night. 'He is my son. He is not your son,' my mother insisted. The man who until that moment I had thought was my father began to weep. 'I have confessed my sin to you and now we will have sons of our own,' my mother said, climbing

back into the bed and in a little while she went to
sleep. My father, or perhaps I should say my stepfa-
ther, this man I had loved as a father, wept and wept
until he too fell into a restless sleep. I crept from my
bed. Silently I packed a knapsack with a bottle of
water, a loaf of bread, several of my father's best carv-
ings which I thought could be sold. I knew which
road led down the mountains to the city. And before
sunup that morning, I was on the road.

"In a few moments my life had changed totally. My
father was not my father. I had no place. I knew I
had to leave. Everything was lost, everything, and yet
suddenly I felt everything was possible. Can you understand? I was not unhappy. I remember I picked
up a rock and threw it as hard as I could. I remember
it bounced down and down and down. I followed that
rock, singing."

(The relationship of Nicho's childhood trauma and
Suzanne's current problem rather overwhelmed me at
this moment. It still overwhelms me.) "In *Athina* I
starved, begged, sold the figurines for a good price
too—the shopkeeper wanted more but how could I
bring him more? I learned to sleep in doorways, fight
with alley cats for fish heads; I even learned to steal,
fruit from a stall, a handful of dates. If I had been
caught even once, who knows what my life would
have been? Then one day someone—I don't remember
who it was—told me a ship in the harbor of Piraeus
had lost an engine room wiper, the lowliest position
on board. I ran, I begged, I got the job though the
engineer wanted a boy from one of the islands who at
least knew something about the sea. He made me
swear I would not get seasick. If I did, he told me, he
would throw me overboard. He frightened me so

much that I didn't get seasick even though it was a
rough voyage, nearly a thousand miles. We sailed to
Djibouti on the Gulf of Aden. I was twelve years old.
Old enough."

Nicho, the sailor: "I am proud that I was a sailor for
nine years. I could not own ships now if I had not
sailed on ships. I would be ashamed to give orders to
men who knew how to do things I could not do myself. It is an education to be a sailor. I learned languages, geography, history. At night in my bunk, with
a flashlight, I read. First I read the books that every
sailor who bothers to read will read. Cheap novels,
books about the sea. Then a few captains on whose
crew I served took an interest in me, lent me books
on navigation and engineering. I progressed very
slowly but I began to read books on economics, on
trade. Slowly, I realized I had a job only because
someone in my country wanted to buy or sell something to someone else across the ocean. I read about
politics, I read biographies, I read philosophy. I
thought I was a great and original thinker until I began to read the two-thousand-year-old writings of my
countrymen. I read novels, Russian novels, and the
plays of Shakespeare which I read first in French only
because I bought my copy in a secondhand bookstore
in Marseille. During a voyage I used to read maybe
five or six books a week. That was my Oxford University and my Harvard School of Business.

"During those years, I worked exclusively for the Delolandris Shipping Company and by the time I was
twenty-one, I was first mate on their largest freighter,
the *Andromache*. I got along well enough with my
fellow sailors but by that time I knew, and the officers
with whom I worked knew, I was different from most

of the other men who had started as engine room
wipers. I got promotions, raises, I thought I was
treated very well. At that time I was the youngest of-
ficer sailing out of Piraeus. I looked forward to
growing a moustache and becoming a captain in a
few more years. I had some savings which I was in-
vesting. I was even courting a shopkeeper's red-
headed daughter. Her name was Irina. We would
take walks on Sundays and go to the cinema. But I
am ashamed when I think back to what a pompous
fool I was when I was twenty-one. The most dangerous moment in any man's life is when he sits back on
his ass and feels secure and likes the feeling. Excuse
my vulgarity, Aileen, but I am speaking the truth to
you.

"The shipping line's owner was Elias Delolandris,
who was considered the richest man in the city. It
was—what shall I call it?—publicity, of course. The
Jewish money lenders must have been richer but no
one noticed them which is just what they wanted.
Publicity is bad for businessmen. It makes your customers who do not have their names in the papers either jealous or uncomfortable. That's why I don't let
myself be interviewed. I try not to be written about. I
know some of my competitors enjoy publicity. Too
much publicity. So let them have it all.

"Old man Delolandris had no sons and three daughters. The oldest, Elena, was fat and plain. On her upper lip she had a slight but dark moustache. In the
sailors' taverns we called her The Bearded Lady. The
two younger ones were ordinary girls but made
highly attractive by the rumored size of their dowries.
They had suitors falling all over each other, the sons

of rich men who wanted rich wives, double security so that they would not have to work at all. But nobody wanted the oldest, The Bearded Lady, even when sweetened by a small fortune. However, old man Delolandris believed that, like a ship, the first built should be the first put out to sail. The younger daughters could not marry until the oldest married.

"The captain of my ship was an old and trusted friend of Delolandris. The freighter sailed between Buenos Aires and Piraeus. We carried cargoes of Oriental tobacco to the Argentine and returned with our holds filled with wheat. It was the beginning of the Depression. Times were bad. Sometimes half the tobacco was sent on consignment. It was Captain Leander who sold the tobacco to merchants in Buenos Aires. And the Delolandris Shipping Company took a third of the price as payment for shipping charges and commission. Believe me, it could not have been a simpler operation. Only one factor was important, crucial—that the man who acted as sales agent be totally honest.

"Captain Leander did not like me. At first I could not understand why. I wanted to be so helpful to him. I wanted to learn. At twenty-one, believe me, Aileen, I was what you Americans call a little eager beaver. I wanted to go with him when he made his calls on the tobacco merchants. I explained I knew a bit about bookkeeping and that I would be happy to write up the bills, keep the records for him. He grew very angry and told me I was impertinent, interfering, and to mind my own business. I suppose he thought I was already suspicious of him. But it was his strange, hostile attitude that began to make me suspicious.

"One day in the middle of a voyage home I found his cabin door unlocked, half-open, in fact. I knew he was up on deck and would be busy for half an hour or so. Impetuously I went in and began my search for his ledgers. As I was going through the desk Leander and several of the ship's officers came in and caught me. For the rest of the voyage I was confined to my quarters and in Piraeus I was dismissed without pay and threatened with the police. At twenty-one, my career seemed over, my life broken."

At this point Nicho smiled at his memories and lit another cigar. But wasn't he overwhelmed, terrified, devastated? I asked.

"Total failure can be very stimulating," he said. "It gives a man great clarity of vision. My life was in shambles, yes. So what did I do? First of all, I got drunk. I had a woman. A redhead in honor of my fiancée who was no longer my fiancée. Her father had broken our engagement as soon as he heard what had happened. He didn't want a thief for a son-in-law, at least not a thief without a good job. But at the end of a week of drinking and whoring I woke up clear-eyed, clear-headed, with a simple plan in mind. I dressed in my last clean shirt and I walked to Delolandris' house which was in the hills outside of town. I knocked on the door and a maid answered it. 'What do you want?' she asked. 'To see the boss,' I said. She tried to shut the door on my foot so I kicked it open and walked in.

"Delolandris and his family were in the dining room, eating their midday meal. He sat at the head of the table and Elena and her sisters and Madame Delolandris sat on either side. The women were all dressed in black. I remember thinking: one cock and four black

crows. The old man looked at me and kept eating his
soup.

"I told him my name and then I said: 'I've come to do
you a big favor, Mister Delolandris.' The girls started
giggling behind their hands when I said that, and Delolandris laughed too. So I said: 'I'm glad you are
amused but you must have a strange sense of humor
if you laugh when you are being cheated, Mr. Delolandris. Does being cheated really amuse you?'

" 'And who is cheating me?' he asked.

" 'Captain Leander, who is supposed to be your
friend.'

"The old man got angry then. But I said: 'Send a
few telegrams to the Argentine. Say there have been
a few errors. Ask for copies of the original bills, that's
all. Just do not let yourself be cheated because of an
old friendship. I think anyone can be cheated by a
clever thief. But only a fool lets himself be cheated
by another fool." And I turned and left the house.

"For a month I heard nothing. Then one morning I
was summoned to Delolandris' office. He was sitting
behind a big desk. The first thing he said to me was:
'Captain Leander has proved unsatisfactory. I am giving you his command.' I didn't say a thing for a couple of minutes. He looked at me, I looked at him and
at that moment I made an important decision. Finally, I said: 'I love the sea but I am tired of the sea.
I will not earn my living as a sailor again. I want to
work for you in this office.' The old man smiled. Fine,
he said, that would be fine. He could always use a
sharp young man as an assistant. 'But I must have a
captain's salary,' I said. The old man screamed, 'You
are going to be my office boy.' So I said: 'Today, I become a businessman so let us make a deal like

businessmen. For three months pay me nothing. But at the end of the time, if I am worth it to you, pay me a captain's salary as your assistant.' Of course in three months I was Delolandris' private secretary and got the wages I wanted. But he never paid me for the first three months and he never forgot that he once got work out of me for nothing. He never stopped trying to get something out of me for nothing again, the old bastard."

At this point Nicho wanted to stop. "Enough," he said, standing up. "Time for bed."

"No," I said. "More—please."

"You must be bored. Your ears must ache from listening to me ramble on."

"More."

"But there is nothing else but shipping rates."

"I don't believe you."

He smiled. "Do you think Suzanne would be interested in these stories?"

I hesitated, then: "Sure. Why not?"

"I do not think so," but he sat down again. "All right." He poured himself a drink. "I am thinking about things I haven't thought about in years. So what shall I tell you about now?"

"Can I be tactless and ask you about your first wife?"

He didn't seem annoyed. "You would have understood Elena."

"I would have?"

"She was like a reader of that magazine you worked for. At thirteen she was like a girl of sixteen, at forty she was like a girl of sixteen, and I'm sorry to say even at sixty she was like a girl of sixteen."

I would have understood Elena.

Elena Delolandris Anapoulis: "My wife was a very plain young woman and that alone was the tragedy of her life. If only she had been a soupçon prettier her whole life would have been different and my life would have been different and it would have been much better for us both. What shall I tell you about her? My poor Elena. That once she shaved her moustache with her father's straight-edged razor and cut her lip. She stayed in bed for a week with her hand over her mouth until the cut healed.

"My Elena. The Bearded Lady. Her sisters hated her. They tormented her. They pinched her, pulled her hair, made fun of her. To make herself feel better, Elena ate chocolates, pounds of chocolates, and read cheap romantic novels. If she had been a little prettier she might have been a different woman intellectually too. But she was stunted. By the time she was thirty, by the time I knew her, her head and her body were filled with sugar and with nonsense.

"Every Sunday old man Delolandris gave a sort of party. It was the fashion then to have open houses, salons. Wine and tea were served, baklava. I was invited to come. The suitors of the younger girls were there. I enjoyed the parties but for a long time I couldn't figure out why Elena was watching me. When I went out into the garden for a breath of air, she was there. And whenever I was near, she would drop her handkerchief. I was always bending down.

"She began to ask me to take her to the cinema. She liked American movies. Everybody liked American movies then. She carried a photo of Clark Gable in her wallet. She asked me to take her driving. I had bought a small coupe. I felt sorry for her and I took

her out a couple of times. I thought she was dull and
fat and plain. I didn't even wonder why she trembled
when I casually touched her hand.

"I know she fell in love with me because there was
absolutely no one else for her to be in love with. The
sons of rich men in the city had fled from her flirta-
tions ten years before. I was the only possibility, the
bottom of the barrel. She sent me a Valentine which
said: 'I will love you always. I will die without you.' I
thought it was an office joke and tossed it away.

"I did not know it then—I could not know it—but there
was a revolt brewing in the Delolandris household.
The younger sisters thought nothing would come of
Elena's feelings for me and they were tired of waiting
to get married. They wanted their men and they
wanted their dowries. Even Madame Delolandris,
who was an old-style wife, totally obedient to the old
man, was impatient. She wanted grandchildren.

"So one day Delolandris called me into his office. He
asked me to make my intentions toward his daughter
plain. 'What intentions?' I said. 'What daughter?' I
thought. He got very angry. He started to shout at
me: 'You have been taking the girl out for drives, to
the cinema, monopolizing her time. You have made
her fall in love with you and now you say you are not
interested in her. Villain, you will break my poor
girl's heart.'

"I had to think fast. So I said: 'I'm sorry, sir, but I
cannot afford to marry. I will not see your daughter
again.' He bit. 'I will give you a raise. I will buy you
a house as a wedding present. I will give my daughter an appropriate dowry.'

"But I shook my head. 'I swore to myself I would not marry until I was a man of substance, a man with my own business or at the very least a partnership in an established business.' I watched it sink in. 'Get out of here, you little bastard,' he screamed at me. I went back to my desk, whistling under my breath. I thought that would be the end of the great love affair.

"But I had underestimated Elena and her sisters. All of them had hysterics. The sisters threatened to run away with the suitors. The suitors threatened to leave without the sisters. Elena ate herself sick and at the same time threatened suicide three times a day after every meal. Under such pressure, even Delolandris cracked. 'All right,' he said to me, 'what do you want?' I told him and he said, 'Never,' which is always a good beginning for a business discussion. It sets limits.

"We snarled at each other for a couple of weeks, talked sense for a few more. Then I went to a lawyer and had a marriage contract drawn up. The old bastard wanted only to shake hands like gentlemen. I told him I wasn't a gentleman and after working so closely with him I knew he wasn't, so I wanted a contract. I made only one important concession. I said I was five years older than I really was. Elena was ashamed to marry a man eight years younger than herself. So I became five years older. That's why people have so much trouble when they are trying to find out my real age, not that it matters to me.

"So we were married and the day after Elena's sisters were married. Delolandris had had his way: the oldest was married first. The sisters went to Paris on their honeymoons and we went to Canada. Not very romantic. But there were some ships I had heard

about in the Port of Quebec that could be bought
very cheaply and I wanted them. I used Elena's
dowry as part of the payment. No, it was not a romantic honeymoon. Poor Elena. It was not a romantic
marriage.

"A few months later the war in Europe started and
our family left for America. There was nothing else to
do. At that time Elena wanted to have a baby but
nothing happened. She started to go to doctors in
New York. One gave her some kind of hormone shots
that had a good effect on her. They made the hair on
her face disappear. She even lost weight. There was
quite a change in her appearance. She started going
to Lily Daché and Hattie Carnegie and Elizabeth
Arden's. I know because I started getting all sorts of
new bills for her. But I had turned my ships over to
the American government on long-term charters, partly as a patriotic gesture, you understand, partly for
business reasons, and so we were making some
money."

A story Nicho didn't tell me but one that is included
in every article written about him: the dozen old tubs
he bought in Canada and which he turned over to the
United States were heavily insured. Several were lost
during the war. Nicho paid about two hundred thousand dollars for the ships and at the end of the war
realized a profit from them of nearly seven million
dollars in cash. After the war, with the available capi-
tal, he began building freighters. Which became the
basis for his shipping empire.

*During the last half of the last bottle of Metaxa,
Nicho told me two stories, out of context, mystifying,
grotesque. Perhaps he was a little drunk too.*

"Every year my wife went to a clinic in Switzerland for a few months. She had her face lifted, her body remolded. She dieted. At this one clinic, they specialized in what they called the sleep cure. Elena was put to sleep for ten days, given an intravenous feeding every other day, and when she was awakened, she was ten pounds thinner, having never experienced a hunger pang. The perfect diet for the rich who have no will power. She adored it. But on her last visit, when she was turned over (to avoid bed sores) the attendant noticed that Madame was a bit too cold, a bit too pale. Her sleep was deep and permanent. Her heart had failed.

"I was summoned from Paris. One sister came from Palm Springs, another from Rabat. They cried over her coffin. One wailed: 'Elena, Elena, you could wear a size seven. Elena, you would be so happy.' The next day the two of them jetted off in different directions. I had Elena buried in the cemetery of the village near the clinic. I sued the clinic for malpractice, shutting it down. My sisters-in-law were furious. They wanted to go back there for the sleep cure, too.

"I saw my mother dead too. A few days before the family left for America in 1940, I was summoned to my home village because my mother was dying. She had been half-mad for years. I sat in her room and hoped the old witch would just die and never awaken. But she sat up suddenly and spoke in a clear voice, without any surprise. 'So you have come, Nicho, you bastard. I have been waiting for you. I have something to tell you about your father.'

"My heart began to beat very quickly and I leaned forward.

"'I knew your father for one night but for years I have thought about him. He poisoned my life. Now at last I know who he really was.' She beckoned me even closer to her. 'He was the Devil, the Devil himself—' She spat straight at me and then fell back. I began to laugh. I couldn't stop laughing. Of course my mother was dead.

"All my relatives in that village died in the war, killed by either the Nazis or the Communists and I have named a ship for each of the dead except my mother. I am building a yacht in Kobe now which I will name for Suzanne. And I am building a tanker in Dusseldorf—the largest tanker in the world—that I will name for the child and will give to him in his name on his first birthday. This child has become very important to me, Aileen, very, very important—"

I can't remember Nicho saying another word.

5

Where was Suzanne when the lights went out? In the dark. But not for long.

Suzanne met Nicho in London on the day of her New York wedding. It was during one of those power black-outs British labor unions now specialize in. The miners stop shoveling coal, the electrical workers stop putting in the plugs; whatever the cause, the lights go off and for an hour or two everyone scuttles around, holding the candles, keeping their upper lips stiff, muddling through. England's finest hour is when the English cope magnificently with a crisis that any other highly civilized nation would manage to avoid.

Suzanne had just checked into the hotel, gone downstairs for a sandwich and a cup of tea, and was on her way back to her room when the lights went out. In the darkness she stumbled down the corridor, not able to remember the room number, not able to see her key in order to get an important first clue.

In typical Suzanne fashion she was on the wrong floor, having counted floors American-style, one-two-three—instead of British-style, ground, one-two-three—but never mind.

One room at the end of the corridor remained a blaze of light. Nicho's office staff had thoughtfully supplied him with his own auxiliary generator, a model similar to those used in hospital operating rooms. Nicho kept the door of his suite open in order to brighten the gloomy corridor.

Naturally Suzanne looked in. Nicho looked up.

Within ten minutes she was curled up on the couch, drinking champagne and telling him lies.

"Did you know how important Nicho was? Who he was?" I asked Suzanne in London before her Savoy wedding, not to be confused with her Plaza wedding (though quite a few of the same guests attended on the bride's side and gave the same gifts).

"Well, I did ask him if he was one of those rich Greek shipping types and I guess he said yes and that was that."

Curiosity never even endangered this cat, unlike Aunt Bea who kept a Dun & Bradstreet in the bathroom so that she could look up the ratings of Suzanne's dates' fathers while she was on the john.

At roughly the same time Suzanne was brightening Nicho's hotel suite, three hundred wedding guests were at the Plaza in New York, listening to "And This Is My Beloved" and wondering when the hell the ceremony was going to begin. A bit confusing. But then last year was a confusing one for Suzanne. She was successful, unhappy, and thirty pretending she was twenty-six, all at the same time—a dynamite combination. A friend of mine who works for the model agency that represented Suzanne sent me a copy of their last confidential report on her. It sums up lots of things. (I brought it along just in case Herself ever starts getting dewy-eyed about the pleasures of her near-immediate past.)

BEALE MODEL AGENCY

Our motto: "Beauty is only skin deep"

From: BD
To: EB
Subject: Suzanne Felice Goldfarb
Type: WASPish—Masochist *à la Belle de Jour*
Age: 26 *forever*
Height: 5'8"
Weight: 115

Eyes: Blue-green. Unwilling to bleach or shave her eyebrows. Lost two *Vogue* assignments because of this but wouldn't listen to reason. She can be stubborn.

Hair: Blond and long. Does not enjoy using wigs. There has been a report that in a picture in *Harper's Bazaar* she had her shag on backwards. Owes us for three wigs. Must collect.

Hands: Good but not great.

Legs: Great but not fantastic.

Feet: Simply beautiful. Really gorgeous little piggies. No bumps, lumps, nasty calluses. Tapered Grecian toes. When anybody needs feet they think of our Suzanne. It is very gratifying.

Earnings: For the past six-months period: Fair to Good. $18,416.04. For the previous six-months period: Fair to Good. $17,517.87. For the past nine years Suzanne has been just on the verge of realizing her potential.

Job summary: In the past six months Suzanne has had one *Bazaar* cover (the art director said he wanted just another pretty face, so we sent along Suzanne). Also one LHJ hip homemaker cover and one trip to the Panama Canal Zone to shoot

guerrilla-type sportswear for *Vogue.* (The photographer wanted to go to Cambodia—but we
talked him out of that.) The other model on that
assignment in Panama, Marilee, freaked out on
magic mushrooms and was bitten by a baby
tarantula on the first day. Bad luck. The whole
spread was shot around Suzanne.

But SFG's biggest moneymaker was her *Realman
Cologne* TV commercial. It is very popular. Suzanne is at a consciousness-raising session with a
bunch of uglies. A Superstud walks through the
room. Suzanne gets up like she's sleepwalking—
she is very, *very* convincing—and follows him out.
The voiceover (in one commercial it sounds just
like Joe Namath) says what a real woman wants
is a Real Man. The women's libbers have been
going off their nut about it ever since.

General Comments: All in all, Suzanne is a good
model but will never be a great one. She is beautiful, she is narcissistic, she is insecure. But that is
not enough. When she was told that Veruschka
keeps six sets of golden breasts that were modeled from her own around the house and lets
special visitors touch them, Suzanne wrinkled up
her nose and said, "What for?" Even after all
these years, she doesn't understand.

And that is the mentality of model agency execu-
tives. But to be honest the models are worse. I always
loathed picking models for the magazine. Would our
girls identify with this or that sleek-haired snub-nosed
wonder? I loathed going to shootings too. Most of the
models are dolls with perfect faces and heads stuffed
full of sawdust and old rags. I remember at one cover

shooting that went on past lunchtime, our teenage beauty declared: "Oh, I'm so hungry I'm simply ravished." When I couldn't suppress a dry cackle, she laughed gaily too. "I mean I'm simply ravishing," she said and gave a perfect pearly smile.

But back to last year and Suzanne's troubles. Her men were rotten too. Stylish men in New York, the ones who liked to be seen with a girl like Suzanne, seemed to catch modes of behavior from one another like head colds. Last year everyone tacitly agreed that the selection from Column A was kinky sex. The same people who once went to Vera Hruba Ralston Festivals at the Thalia and were into camp, who became the people who went to pot parties and were into universal love, were now into all-night orgies with Afghan hounds.

I myself have never been invited to an orgy. But if I was, I'm sure it would offend my sense of aesthetics even more than my sense of morals. Most people look perfectly horrible without their clothes on. All that wall-to-wall flab. And what if once I got there, I wasn't invited to join in? (It could happen.) I can just imagine myself in charge of changing the Rolling Stone records to Ravel's "Bolero," shaking my head and clucking my tongue, filled with pity and terror in equal parts.

Suzanne called me one Sunday last September. It had been a sweltering weekend. In New York the seasons never take a look at the calendar and depart gracefully; they have to be dragged out, kicking and screaming, making everyone uncomfortable.

"Where have you been?" I had wanted to use her air conditioner.

"Easthampton."

"I thought you hated Easthampton."

"Where would I go if I stopped going places I hated?"

"How was it?"

"Hateful."

"That's nice."

"Marilee got stoned and the Margolins broke up. They must have been married for eight years which is practically a record."

"Gee, that's awful," I said. I didn't give a damn. Sandy Margolin is that vapid sort of girl who believes in clothes the way little old ladies in Italy believe in God. If I ever wonder what I am supposed to be wearing at any exact moment—what shoes or belt buckle or nose ornament—all I have to do is invite Sandy Margolin to lunch.

"And I'm finished with Ralph, the turd." She sounded surprisingly cheerful. Ralph was the current one, a businessman with an elephant-hair bracelet and bottle-green contact lenses. I called him the Ancient Mariner because he liked to tell you the story of his life within ten minutes of your meeting him. He grabbed you by the arm and wouldn't let you go until he had poured it all out. He was a poor boy who had married the daughter of a rich man the day after he graduated from business school. For ten years he had worked hard for his father-in-law and became a partner in the business. Then one day in the mid-1960s, an omnivorous conglomerate out fattening itself gobbled up their small manufacturing plant. They were paid a couple of million plus stock options which they divided equally. A week later Ralphie-boy split. He left the manufacturer's daughter, the three kids, the ranch house in Great Neck. He didn't want to be liked, he wanted to be congratulated. Cinderella becomes independently wealthy.

"Do you know what the son-of-a-bitch did? He

called me into a room and said: 'Hey Suzie, wanna
see some really great pictures?' And the bastard
showed me some real horror shots—disgusting. Oh
God, have I become the sort of girl men show filthy,
filthy pictures to at eleven o'clock in the morning?"

No comment.

"So I told him I'd introduce him to a nice poodle I
knew since he seemed so terribly fond of animals. Oh,
the fucking creep. He drove home alone. Expected
me to take the train. But it didn't matter because I
met David—"

For her, like coconuts, they fall off the trees.

"Who is David?"

"A doctor. A brain surgeon."

BINGO!

"I really ought to marry someone like David," she
said, just like that.

After her parents spent $6,000 getting her first mar-
riage annulled and the records of it destroyed,
Suzanne had said: "Well, at least he wasn't a nice
Jewish doctor named David."

"I better go," she said. "David is coming by to take
me for a hamburger at P.J. Clarke's."

After I hung up I beat to death a water bug that
had lazily crawled out of my drain, and went to bed.
But—no surprise—I didn't sleep. I just lay there
bathed in sweat and self-pity. And okay, I confess,
envy.

Autumn in New York. It was the season of David the
doctor. Son of a doctor, father of potential doctors.
The Nice Jewish Boy Is Alive and Well and associ-
ated with Mount Sinai. David's hair was thinning
slightly and his belly was already a shade too round.
Probably in an elective in Bedside Manner in medical
school, he had learned the secret of perpetual, re-

spectable middle age. When we met he greeted me:
"Aileen—I-hope-I-can-call-you-Aileen-" (No—Doris.)

"I just wanted to tell you how many wonderful
things I've heard about you. I feel we're friends already." A copy of my magazine dangled from his
clean, manicured fingernails. I guess you can't be a
brain surgeon with dirty hands. "I've been reading
this," he said, "And it's very, very interesting."

"Well, it's aimed at a different audience—hahaha."

"Still, it's very well done." His brown eyes oozed
sincerity.

They had a very proper courtship. He took her to
nice resturants and ordered good wine. They waited
in long lines to see the movies Judith Crist liked.
They went to the Central Park Zoo and admired the
seals and the little Puerto Rican children. Suzanne
cooked for him, except that she couldn't cook. She
called up catering services and had beouf Bourgignon
and poulet estragon and quiche Lorraine sent in and
blithely passed them off as her own. He thought she
was a terrific cook—and kept a really neat kitchen as
well.

For weeks and weeks he kissed her good night at
the front door. Once in a while she lured him in for a
nightcap, but that was all. "He respects me. He respects me," she said gloomily. "That's a direct quote:
'Suzanne, I respect you.' Shit!"

Finally he stayed over on a Saturday night.

We met for a victory celebration at Monday
lunchtime. I arrived at Daly's Dandelion first.
Suzanne breezed in twenty minutes later, wearing
blue jeans, a tiny crocheted sweater and fox coat.

"He didn't expect me to be a virgin," she announced loudly as she sat down. Two men at the next
table gave a look. "No, that would be hoping for too
much, he said."

"Thank God," I said. "A realist." We toasted each other with Bloody Marys.

"But afterwards he wanted to know how many lovers I had, if I wanted to tell him. He hoped he wasn't prying."

The two men at the next table had grown silent and were almost visibly leaning in our direction. Their eggs Benedict were turning cold and lumpy on their plates.

"You lied a *leetle* bit," I said.

Suzanne gave me a cool look. "Well, I don't think I've had *that* many lovers. I've never loved any of them. They've never loved me."

Semantics, semantics—and not even true. *Some* had loved her. Johnny Poparossa had loved her. At the annulment hearing, Johnny had cried, the tears streaming down his long pale face, embarrassing his Mafia lawyer.

"So maybe I've been with fifty men, a hundred men." Suzanne shrugged as if the figure was some mad, wild exaggeration put around town by her enemies—"but it's been all rather—well—impersonal, now hasn't it?"

One of the men at the next table fell off his chair.

"Drunk," Suzanne said scornfully.

"So I told him there were three. A beautiful young boy who I knew when I was twenty. He died in Vietnam."

"Naturally."

"An older man. An artist. He was married and his wife was a cripple, paralyzed from the waist down. That was terribly, terribly sad."

"I bet."

"And one silly, mad, casual thing." She finished her Bloody Mary in a gulp.

"He was a little surprised by the mad casual thing.

But he could understand my being despondent about poor Steven's dying in Nam."

"I *am* going to be sick."

She smiled and ordered another drink. I ordered hamburgers for both of us.

"He does it like you would imagine a brain surgeon would—a nice attention to details, precision. He left the patient resting comfortably." She fluttered her eyelashes.

"Suzanne," I almost screamed, "*I don't want to hear about it.*"

She looked offended. The waiter slammed two plates down on the marble table. A sliver of red meat embraced by an enormous squashy bun. I wouldn't eat the bun, I told myself.

"I bet he gives me an engagement ring at Christmas."

What the hell. I bit into the bun.

"Is that what you want?" She didn't answer. "Suzanne?"

She answered slowly. "He's nice enough. He isn't dumb. You know, he does the Sunday *Times* crossword puzzle in ink."

"Wow. Now I understand the great attraction."

"If I ever get a tumor, he'll be there."

"Suzanne, can I say one little thing and forever after hold my peace?"

"Maybe."

"It just seems to me that you have spent the last ten years doing a lot of crazy things mainly to avoid marrying someone exactly like David."

"Oh."

I finished my hamburger. Suzanne pushed hers away untouched. She lit a cigarette. "Well," she said softly, "I really don't care about being consistent."

One of the men at the next table moaned.

＊

For Christmas David gave her a ring. Two carats, blue-white, in a modern gold setting. Bought at Tiffany's. Suzanne was noncommittal but Aunt Bea was beside herself with joy: "He didn't go to Forty-seventh Street, the darling. He is such an idealist."

David's father was dead. His mother lived in Atlanta. Aunt Bea would be running the whole wedding show by herself. Suzanne and David and I drove out for the weekend. I went to visit my mother. My father was at a convention. She was working on her own design, not merely a needlepoint scatter rug but needlepoint wall-to-wall carpeting. "It's easy," she said. "You just keep sewing the squares together." And together. And together.

I went over to Aunt Bea's for Sunday dinner. My mother was too busy to cook. We sat around reading the papers beforehand. "I always think spring weddings are lovely," Aunt Bea said apropos of nothing. "You can use such pretty colors for the bridesmaids' dresses, pale yellow and pale green."

"We're not having any cruddy bridesmaids," Suzanne said. She was wearing her at-home sneer. "I don't know any cruddy bridesmaids."

"Darling, you have lots of lovely friends."

"I do not," which was perfectly true. "Aileen, you can be maid of honor by default."

"Thanks a bunch."

"Just stop making your big plans, mother dear. We don't want one of those big, disgusting, vulgar weddings."

David looked up from the magazine section.

Aunt Bea said: "I think we ought to talk about this right now and get it settled once and for all. Morris, listen—" Uncle Morris was half asleep under the "News of the Week in Review." "What kind of wedding do *you* want, Suzanne?"

"I dunno." She draped herself seductively around David and began tickling the back of his neck. Suzanne was always pawing David suggestively in front of her mother. "How about eloping to Las Vegas, baby?"

David laughed to show he got the joke.

"Personally, I should think you'd want to be married the right way—" Aunt Bea hissed. The *this time* hung in the air unsaid. Mother and daughter exchanged a furious look.

"I really want to elope to Las Vegas, David," Suzanne said. "David, stop working on that goddamn crossword puzzle and listen to me."

"David is a doctor. He wants a proper wedding, of course. Don't you, darling?"

He looked from one to the other, sensing the danger. "Well, I think big weddings can be fun sometimes but certainly it's not necessary. Bea, frankly, Suzanne and I really haven't had a chance to discuss this fully—"

"Okay, okay," Suzanne jumped up. "Let's have a big wedding. Daddy can afford it. Mother wants it. Why should I stand in the way of all this happiness—" She raced up the stairs to her old room.

David looked after her, a frown on his face.

Aunt Bea shrugged and gave a little martyr-like smile as if to underline: *see what I've had to put up with all these years.* "She'll be a beautiful bride. Now, David, darling, you must remember to have your sweet mother send me a list of the people she wants to invite."

"There are a few of the doctors at the hospital I'd like to have—"

"Of course, anyone you want. I'm sure they are all fascinating people."

Uncle Morris stood up abruptly. "When do we eat?" he asked.

"Oh, Morris," Aunt Bea said with tears in her eyes. "I just know it's going to be a beautiful wedding."

The wedding was set for a Saturday in early March, the only Saturday the Plaza had free for months and months. The original bride-to-be for the occasion had been injured in an automobile accident. "Every cloud has a silver lining," said Aunt Bea, trying to be tactful.

"I hate March," Suzanne said. "March is the cruelest month."

"That's April."

"I'm not getting married in April."

It made me a little sad that Suzanne was developing a sense of humor.

Aunt Bea called one morning bright and early. "Suzanne and I are shopping for the wedding dress today, Aileen. I thought you could come along and we could find your maid-of-honor dress. I'm going to buy it for you as a gift, dear. You've been an awfully good friend to your cousin, and, believe me, I do appreciate it. Now, could you meet us at Bendel's around ten-thirty?"

"Aunt Bea, I work, remember?"

"Can't you take the morning off?"

I was going to interview three student revolutionaries. Somehow I knew they wouldn't understand my dashing out to do a little shopping at Bendel's.

"I'll meet you at noon."

"Well, all right," she said reluctantly.

I hate Bendel's. The store is too damn chic, that's all. Everybody in the store, salesgirls and customers alike, is thin and hipless. I hardly ever go in unless I've just been on a diet. And even then I have the feeling that the president of the store is reviewing the customers on closed-circuit TV. She's not watching for shoplifters, just slobs.

That morning, undetected, I found my way to the bridal salon. When I inquired, a salesgirl pointed warily. Clearly a major family battle had just erupted within the confines of the dressing room. Aunt Bea's face was flushed and she was biting her lip. Suzanne was examining herself coolly in the mirror. She was wearing a long ivory-colored sheath that was very straight and clingy. It didn't look like a wedding dress but it did look tremendous on her.

"How do you like it?" Suzanne asked. I nodded. "I'm glad you agree with me. Mother wants me to go to my wedding disguised as a charlotte russe."

"That is not a wedding dress. It's terrible. It's nothing."

"It's four hundred dollars," Suzanne said and looked at herself in the mirror again. "What it really needs is a heavy baroque cross."

"*SUZANNE!*"

"That reminds me," Suzanne said. "I never have bothered to ask which charlatan is marrying us."

"Rabbi Needlebaum is going to perform the ceremony, of course. He wants to see you and David together for a little talk next week. You remember him. He taught you in Sunday School. He's a wonderful man."

Needlebaum was the rabbi of the reform temple in Hewlett. The temple was built in the shape of a Jewish star as seen from the air, a fact which delighted the temple members. Uncle Morris once told me: "Anybody flying in or out of Kennedy can look down and know: Jews live there."

"Needlebaum? That old windbag."

The salesgirl came into the dressing room. "Need anything?"

"We'll take the one I'm wearing," Suzanne said. "But can you send up some necklaces from downstairs? Indian ones, I think; coral and turquoise and gold, something like that. And I don't want a veil but I do want a string of baroque pearls to twist in my hair."

"That sounds cool," the salesgirl said.

Suzanne looked at me. "Now let's find something for you."

"I was thinking of yellow or green—" Aunt Bea said.

"With Aileen's complexion?"

I looked at my reflection in the mirrors.

The salesgirl brought in about five dresses. I had to struggle to get them zipped, which was a little embarrassing. "How about the shirtdress?" Suzanne said, indicating a gown she had tried on.

"It comes in her size but only in white," the salesgirl said.

"Let's see it."

It was comfortable; it even looked all right.

"But only the bride wears white at the wedding," said Aunt Bea.

"Who cares? She needs a heavy gold-and-coral belt and maybe some chains," Suzanne told the salesgirl.

"It's wrong, it's wrong."

"Don't worry, mother. David won't be confused by the color of our dresses. He's pretty quick. He'll marry me."

We picked out the Indian jewelry we wanted, bracelets and necklaces and a toe ring that Suzanne insisted on, then pranced around playing dress-up and admiring each other.

"Sign it, mother," Suzanne said when the salesgirl wrote up the orders. The dresses and jewelry came to almost $1,200. Suzanne stuffed herself into her

sweater and a pair of frayed jeans. "Bye-bye. See
ya—"

"But I thought we could all have a nice lunch at
the Palm Court."

"I'm going to see a hairdresser upstairs. See if he'll
do my hair for the wedding."

"Oh, well—" It was a plausible, even respectable,
excuse. But I knew Suzanne had once spent a night
with this hairdresser. "He did such a great job with
my split ends," she had told me. "I thought it was
nicer than a tip."

"I better go back to work, Aunt Bea." My student
revolutionaries loved to talk. In our afternoon rap
session they were going to tell me why even though
ours was a corrupt fascistic pig society, they had decided it was morally wrong to put LSD in the
Ashokan Reservoir. *Because it's wrong, you rotten
little kids.* (Clearly I was growing more and more im-
mune to the charms of the youth culture.)

"Well, maybe I'll look for a few things for myself,"
Aunt Bea said a little wistfully. "Do you have anything for the mother of the bride? I'm a size twelve."

On Suzanne's wedding day March was at its most
wintry. It was cold, dark, and gray and every half
hour or so the sky would unload and sleet. I stayed in
the apartment with rollers in my hair, practicing putting false eyelashes on. It was my grand gesture for
the occasion. If Suzanne could get married, I could
temporarily blind myself with surgical adhesive.

We hadn't talked much the last few weeks; she was
too busy writing thank-you notes for gifts or going
out to dinner with David's aunts and uncles. I called
her about two that afternoon to be cheerful and encouraging and again about three-thirty but there was
no answer either time. Maybe she had gone home and

was coming into the city with Aunt Bea and Uncle Morris around five. It was hard for me to believe that Suzanne would spend the night before her wedding at her parents' house. But maybe she thought it was an appropriate, symbolic gesture.

About four, Aunt Bea called me. "Hello, darling. Isn't it a miserable day?"

"At least it's not snowing," I said. "I'm sure everyone will make it."

"Can I speak to Suzanne—"

"Suzanne isn't here."

"She isn't?"

"I thought she was with you. I've been trying to get her since about two—"

"I've been trying since about ten-thirty this morning!"

"Oh." Neither of us said anything for a long moment.

"She must be with David."

"But she wouldn't see him before the ceremony."

"Of course she would," I said heartily. "Why don't you call him?"

"But what if she isn't there? I wouldn't want to get him all"—she paused, choosing her words carefully—"concerned."

"Maybe she's gone for a long walk—"

"In this weather, Aileen?"

"Well, they say girls do funny things on their wedding day."

"I know—"

Suddenly my doorbell rang. "Aunt Bea, we're supposed to be at the hotel at five-thirty, right? Suzanne will be there. Just don't get upset." The bell rang again. "I've got to go." I hung up and ran to the door. "Su-zanne, for God's sake—"

A little old man with water dripping off his hat

stood outside. "That's not safe, girlie," he said. "What if I was the Boston Strangler? You should say 'Who's there?' before you open."

"All right," I said, "what do you want?"

"A big girl like you should know better." He shook his head. "No wonder people get killed."

"Thanks for the advice. But what do you want?" I repeated.

"This you?" He pointed at my name scrawled on a manila envelope.

"Yes."

"So sign." He extended a damp sheet and a ball-point pen.

"Who gave this envelope to you?"

"Who was supposed to give it to me?" he asked suspiciously. A paranoid messenger.

"Goddamn, mister, *just tell me*," I almost screamed.

"Okay, lady, take it easy, you'll live longer. I picked it up from a super in one of those little buildings on the East Side. Tenements but they charge an arm and a leg for a one-room apartment in them. I wasn't supposed to deliver the package to you until after four."

I started to close the door.

"On weekends we're allowed to accept tips."

I found my bag and handed him a dollar. "And remember, girlie, the next time you open, ask first. Take a minute. I don't want to see your picture in the *Daily News*."

I slammed the door. In the envelope was a note for me and two other letters. The note was written on blue stationery in Suzanne's characteristically flamboyant scrawl. I sat down before I began to read:

Dear Aileen,

Yes, you're right. As you have probably guessed by now I have taken off, run out. I sup-

pose it is my biggest fuck-up of all time, and I
am giving you the really shitty job of announcing
the news. Please, please forgive me.

But, oh, Aileen, I woke up at four this morning—I have woken up at four every morning for
the past month—and I knew I couldn't go through
with it.

I guess every girl feels she is marrying a
stranger. But I finally realize that David is one
stranger I don't want to get to know any better.

What a scene there is going to be at the Plaza.
Please remember all the details.

I am going away for a while so all I can say is
see you when I see you.

Thanks for putting up with me.

Love ya,
S.

I went to the phone to call Aunt Bea. The number
rang and rang. They had already left for the city.
Then I poured myself a stiff Scotch. It was ten after
five. I had already put on my maid-of-honor dress. I
wondered if I should switch into something simple
and black and funereal. But I buckled on my three-
pound Indian belt, threw on an old raincoat, and
went downstairs hoping I wouldn't find a taxi in the
rain. Just my luck, I found one in half a minute. The
other two envelopes weren't sealed. Suzanne knows
how nosey I am. In the note to her father, Suzanne
had enclosed a ticket from the Ritz Thrift Shop.

Daddy:

I pawned the engagement ring that David
gave me. I needed the cash. Will you please get
it back and give it to him.

Believe it or not, I am terribly sorry that I am
making you unhappy at this moment.

This morning I was thinking we haven't had a conversation since I was twelve and you used to take me out on the speedboat—and even then we didn't really talk.

Good-by.

Your daughter,
Suzanne

The letter to David was the most legible. It looked as if she had copied it over carefully several times.

My dear David,

The only thing I can say is this is better for both of us.

Only a bitch would do what I am doing today. Clearly, I am a bitch. You don't want to be married to such a bitch. Besides it wouldn't be good for your practice.

I'm not the girl you think I am. I'm not the girl for you. But please don't be unhappy about this, David. You're a dream husband. There are hundreds of girls who would love to love you.

S.

The hotel had provided a suite for the bride and her family. Uncle Morris opened the door. He was wearing a dinner jacket with a frilly shirt; his wine-colored cummerbund seemed to fasten directly beneath his armpits. Aunt Bea was sitting at the dressing table, reflected in the mirror. Her strawberry blonde hair had been teased to fantastic new heights. She wore a green dress splashed with glitters. She turned. "Aileen—where is she? What's wrong? There's something wrong. Mor-ris—"

"Just after you called there was a messenger with a

note from Suzanne. I tried to call you at home but I guess you had already left—"

"What kind of note? Mor-ris. I knew it. I knew it. Something had to go wrong—"

"Uncle Morris, she sent you a note too. Here."

He took it, read it, blew out a puff of cigar smoke, clamped the cigar back in between his teeth.

"Morris—*WHAT?*"

He shook his head but didn't speak.

"Aunt Bea—" I began strong—and finished weak, "well, she's not coming."

"NOT COMING? WHAT DO YOU MEAN SHE'S NOT COMING?" She put her hand on her generous breast. "Morris, I think I am having a heart attack," she said in a small terrified voice.

"Sit down, I'll get you some water." I ran into the bathroom. Uncle Morris handed her the note. When I came out, she had begun to cry. "Even Suzanne couldn't do this to me. It's a joke. A terrible joke. Show me the note she sent you, Aileen."

"I left it at home."

"You knew about this. Aileen, how could you?"

"I didn't know anything. I haven't even seen Suzanne for the past couple of weeks. In my letter all she said was that she woke up at four this morning and felt she wasn't doing the right thing."

"And marrying that Italian gunman—that was the right thing to do?"

"Aunt Bea, that was a long time ago so why go into that now? What time is it?" I asked Uncle Morris.

"About six."

"They're all going to be here in twenty minutes. David's mother. His aunts and uncles. They came all the way from Atlanta—"

"Didn't Stanley and Grace come back from Florida early just for this?"

Aunt Bea gave a wail. "Morris, you have got to find her and get her here. Go, go. Go to her apartment and—"

"I'm sure she isn't there. She said she was going away—"

"Some world," said Uncle Morris.

"Morris, what are we going to do? Morris, answer me. Very original—a wedding without a bride." For a flicker of a moment her eyes fastened on me in my long white dress.

There was a knock on the door. We all froze. "Don't tell anybody anything," Aunt Bea said in a hoarse whisper. "Who is it? Just a minute—" she called out gaily.

"Felicitations, felicitations—" It was Rabbi Needlebaum.

"Rabbi, thank God it's you," Uncle Morris said. "We've got this little problem on our hands." Hurriedly Aunt Bea explained.

"Be calm, dear friends, be calm," said Rabbi Needlebaum, taking off his coat. "This isn't so unusual. Girls often get panicky on their wedding day. Marriage is a momentous step. Who wouldn't be nervous? I've talked quite a few young ladies out of their wedding-day jitters." He gave a reassuring half-smile, using only the corners of his mouth. The rabbi never smiled fully as if such an overt expression was beneath his dignity.

"But Suzanne isn't around for you to talk to—" I pointed out, the old killjoy.

"Hmmmm—yes—well, that is a problem. There's no way to get in touch with her? You are absolutely sure, my friends—" He looked at Uncle Morris sternly.

"Morris, go to her apartment, break down the door. Make sure she isn't there. Maybe she left something, a clue—"

"All right, all right." He put on his hat and coat. He looked out the window. It was snowing now. "I'll call you," he said.

The three of us sat quietly, without talking, for a while. There was some liquor and an ice bucket on the bar. I made all of us a drink.

Aunt Bea kept dabbing her eyes. Finally she said: "I wanted a pretty daughter. Every mother does. Maybe it would have been better if she wasn't so pretty."

"She was a very pretty girl," the rabbi said, nodding. I noticed his use of the past tense.

The phone rang and we all jumped. Aunt Bea ran to pick it up. "Oh, it's you, Dora, darling. Ha-ha. Yes, we'll be right down. I was just fixing my eyes. They got a little smudged. That's right. The ceremony is at seven-fifteen sharp. Ha-ha. That's right. See you. G'bye."

"David's mother," she told us. "Lots of people have arrived. Everyone was afraid they'd be late because of the weather so they arrived early."

The phone rang again. "Morris? So? *What?* Where to? Oh my God—all right. Just come back here. Morris, I need you," she said in a low voice. She was clutching her breast again. She turned to us. "Suzanne wrote the number of a flight on her scratch pad. Pan Am 202. He called. It's their round-the-world flight and it left at eleven this morning. She was aboard. Rabbi, tell me, is this what you have children for?"

"Bea, you are being tested, tested like Job—"

I cut in before the sermon started. "Don't you think you ought to tell David right away? The longer we wait, the worse it will be for him. Please, let's give him the letter—"

"I suppose there isn't any reason to wait. Rabbi?" The rabbi nodded. She was crying when she went to the phone and dialed the number of the room where

David and his best man were getting ready. "David, darling—" she used her gay little voice again. "Will you come over to the suite for a minute? No, no, nothing's wrong. Of course, I know it's bad luck for a groom to see the bride. But don't worry about that. No, no, darling, believe me, *NOTHING'S WRONG*." She started to sob again. "Rabbi, just tell me what I did? What did I do different than my friends? All *their* daughters showed up at *their* weddings—"

David knocked.

"Come in," Aunt Bea trilled.

He was bright-eyed but suspicious.

Needlebaum stood up. "Come in, young man, sit down. You remember me, I'm Rabbi Needlebaum."

"Of course, Rabbi."

"Have a drink, darling. Scotch, rye, bourbon? I think we have everything or we can call room service—"

David looked at his watch. "Excuse me, Bea, but aren't we supposed to be doing something kind of important downstairs?"

"There's been a slight change of plans," Aunt Bea said slowly.

"How to cope with rejection—this, my son, is one of the greatest problems of modern life," Needlebaum began as if he had sorted through his files and found the appropriate little number. David looked from one to the other.

"Will you please tell me what the hell is going on?"

"David, here—" I handed him the letter. I felt sick. He read it once, then twice, then a third time. The third time he was moving his lips.

"I don't believe it," he said softly. "I don't believe it."

"Believe it, David. Suzanne's gone away," I said. "There isn't going to be a wedding."

"I wouldn't put it that way," said Aunt Bea.

"Then how would you put it?"

"Well, there's been a temporary misunderstanding—"

"Young man, believe me, you must not take this personally or it will be like a poison in your soul. Young women today are full of great conflicts."

Uncle Morris returned. He looked tired and stooped and there was melting snow on the shoulders of his overcoat. He shook hands with David solemnly. He blew his nose. "Come on, Bea. Let's go downstairs and tell our guests. Let's get it over with. Rabbi, will you help us?"

"Of course, of course." Needlebaum breathed deeply as if he was summoning together his vast resources. He put on his yarmulka and draped a tallith over his shoulders. Aunt Bea, with Uncle Morris and the rabbi holding each arm, left the room. I started to trail out after them but David caught my arm. "I'm sorry, David," I said. "I'm really sorry. But maybe it's better this way."

There were tears welling up in his eyes. "What did I do wrong? I was trying so hard not to do anything wrong—"

"Oh, David—" I squeezed his hand and escaped. I stopped off downstairs in the reception room. Uncle Morris and Aunt Bea were going from group to group whispering and explaining. Everyone patted Aunt Bea's shoulder, kissed her moist cheek. She kept dabbing at her eyes with a blue-green glittery handkerchief that matched her dress. The orchestra played softly, almost mournfully in the background.

"Don't go, stay, have dinner. Listen, it's got to be paid for, so you might as well eat it," Uncle Morris said to a couple who were about to leave.

"Kids today—what is it? The bomb? The pill? The war? Who knows? Maybe it's the pollution."

David's friends were in a small group whispering together. "She thought she was too good for him because she was a model and had her picture in magazines," concluded the best man's wife to a rapt audience. "Well, let me tell you, she isn't worth his little finger."

"I know the most darling girl in the world for him," one of the other women declared enthusiastically. "Has anybody got a dime? I'm going to call her up right this minute."

They all were talking, shaking their heads, devouring dozens of canapes and pouring down the drinks as fast as the waiters could bring them. Suddenly instead of bragging about the son who was a nuclear physicist or the daughter who was married to a vice-president of Jonathan Logan's, everybody was admitting to the son who had dropped out of the University of Miami and the daughter who was a professional hitchhiker.

"Mama, she says to me, mama, you're a dirty bourgeoise pig and you're going to be destroyed. This is what she learned for three thousand a year at Sarah Lawrence."

"At three o'clock in the morning, they call me. 'It's the police,' they say. 'We have your son here, Mr. Goldberg. He has three pounds of marijuana in his car trunk.'"

It was a mass soul-baring and breast-beating. The Wailing Wall with libations and Lester Lanin's second-string orchestra.

I found Aunt Bea to say good night. She was listening to a description of a Hare Krishna marriage ceremony.

"Stay for dinner, darling. We were just sitting

down." She was flushed and growing rosier by the moment. Such an outpouring of love and sympathy and affection.

"No, no, I must go. I have a terrible headache—"

"I can understand, darling, but come with me a minute—"

She pulled me into the room that was decorated as a chapel. It was very cold and dark. The orchids on the wedding canopy were already turning brown.

"Here—" she handed me the bridal bouquet. "She would have thrown it to you; I want you to have it."

"But—"

"Please take it. Somehow it would make me feel better." She sighed. "Everybody has troubles, Aileen. That's life. We all have to learn to live with our troubles."

I kissed her cheek. Her perfume smelled too sweet, like a sugar bun.

"You're a good girl, Aileen."

It was snowing heavily outside. The Plaza doorman couldn't get me a taxi. Walking through the slush I dropped the bouquet in the first trash can I found. Then I walked over to 57th Street and took the Riverside Drive bus home. My shoes and the skirt of my dress were ruined.

I heard the party lasted till after midnight, grew very boisterous, and that Uncle Morris and Aunt Bea cut the wedding cake themselves to roars of approval, cries of "Parent Power!" and the shouts of one drunken uncle who kept repeating: "Kill the umpire! Kill the umpire!"

And at about that moment in London, on the seventh floor of the Carlton Towers, Suzanne was sleeping peacefully and would sleep right through her one o'clock luncheon date at the Savoy with Nicho who, nevertheless, forgave her.

6

FRIENDS FROM ACROSS
THE SEA

Mid-morning on the eighth day after the due date and still nothing but some added weight gain had occurred. Suzanne was now weighing in at 148; her normal weight was 115. She was more or less permanently collapsed on the chaise lounge, her varicose veins spreading like webs spun by a most industrious spider, her stomach curved over her invisible thighs.

"The baby has dropped," Paul announced solemnly that morning, sounding like a Wall Street commentator. "Something will happen any moment, any moment—" He was rubbing his hands together in expectation.

"Promises, promises," Suzanne snarled. Her pouting had become almost demoniac. She fluctuated hourly between fretful sleep and fretful waking.

Only Nicho did not feel the cutting edge of her finely honed whine. Mainly because she hardly spoke to him anymore. I don't think they ever talked that much. Their relationship had not been forged with scintillating conversation. Now he kissed her and she sighed. He patted her hand and she sighed. He had a diamond tiara, formerly owned by one of the Romanovs, sent from Cartier. She looked at it, tried it on, rubbed her forehead and still she sighed. But her spoiled-brat quality didn't seem to disturb Nicho. I think he rather expected his women to be difficult and spoiled. Together, to mollify her, they read *What To Name The Baby?* in English and in Greek.

To me Suzanne confided whenever we were alone, her voice rising hysterically: "I am going to tell him, I am so going to tell him." She bounced around a lot when she spoke. She continually had to relieve a hard-pressed bladder. Returning from the john, she concluded dramatically: "Then I'll have my baby in peace."

"You're being selfish."

"Honest—"

"It can be the same thing."

"Oh, shit, but he thinks I'm so perfect. Sweet, practically an innocent—"

"Suzanne, don't exaggerate—"

"If he only knew what I was really like—" Her eyes reddened again. Suzanne now cried a dozen times a day. Sometimes I think she burst into sobs just because she looked down and couldn't see her feet.

"Oh, shit, what if there's something wrong with the little bastard?"

"Are you really worried about that?"

"All the goddamned time in England they have these horrible pictures in the papers of these little Thalidomide kiddies learning how to broadjump with little flippers for arms or learning how to stand on their hands with little flippers for legs. They're meant to be *inspiring*—"

"Oh, Suzanne—"

"Maybe, I'll be punished," she said dramatically.

"For what?"

"For all the dumb things I've ever done. For being dumb-dumb me. What the hell do you think for?"

"Suzanne, everything's going to be all right." I said it slowly, with lots of emphasis. Nine-and-a-half months needs lots of reassurance.

"No, something's going to happen. I can feel it. Paul says I'm fantastically dilated. He's quite impressed. The Lincoln-bloody-Tunnel. Remember that joke?"

We said it together: "Everything goes in."

"Maybe the baby knows something we don't know and doesn't want to be born. On second thought, all he has to know is what we know," I said.

She dragged herself off the chaise again. She looked like a pregnant cat whose belly is dragging along the ground and who has sacrificed all of her natural grace to her biological destiny.

"Can you believe I've even been wanting my mama?"

"Aunt Bea? She would *run*—"

"Oh, yeah, sure, and she'd rub my back for ten big minutes and then be off looking for bargains in flokati rugs."

I couldn't disagree.

Suzanne went to her room and I drifted down to the beach. Paul was there reading a medical journal. He had stopped wearing his baggy bathing suits and dressed soberly each day in dark slacks and a starched white shirt that was cut like a doctor's jacket. We watched the sea, sitting next to each other, and for a long time didn't talk.

Then suddenly he burst out, stumbling over his words: "Madame does not understand. Inducing the birth—it is more painful that way. Harder for her to control. I do not want this birth to be an unpleasant experience, a terrible experience, for her."

"Suzanne knows that. She isn't unhappy with the way you're treating her. Please, don't think that, Paul. She's just unhappy with herself—" Everyone was feeling the building tension.

"I want to make her as comfortable as possible. As

soon as possible. Yes, this is important. Very important. But childbirth should be a *naturelle* process—always—"

I nodded, half-listening. Childbirth: frankly it scared me silly. So who was I to belittle Suzanne's quite reasonable fears? Once I asked my mother about it. She looked up from her beaded flowers and frowned. Oh, *that*. "It wasn't so bad," she said and went back to her beaded-lilac bush. I thought of all the movies I've seen with women writhing and screaming, hands pulling on the bedstead, eyes bulging. Even a stick of an actress turns into a full-fledged tragedienne enacting a birth scene.

And what about that hot-water-and-plenty-of-it routine, which always made my skin crawl? The drunken doctor sobers up in time to deliver the hysterical schoolmarm, wife of the sheriff, while the rustlers and/or Indians attack the wagon train. "Hot water and *plenty of it*." Even that sounds terrifying. How much is there to wash on mother, doctor, or baby?

I was about to ask Paul, mainly to lighten his mood, when he said in a small choked voice: "My wife—our baby—was induced. Yes, it was a long time ago. And yes, there are different drugs, there are different methods, of course. But I shall never forget what a terrible experience it was, a tragic experience."

He wanted to talk. He was brimming over. I wasn't sure I wanted to hear. Whenever a friend is about to lay a long sad tale on my brother, he says in a plummy baritone: "There are a million stories in the Naked City." It usually has the desired effect: prolonged silence. But I couldn't do that. Not to Paul.

He was looking at me expectantly from behind his glasses.

"Tell me about it," I said sympathetically. "I mean if you want to—"

He wanted to. He took a quick eager breath. "It was a long time ago. My wife was very young. We were married when we were students at the university." He hesitated and then glanced at me. "She was pregnant."

"Oh."

"Are you shocked, Aileen? I did not think you would be." He looked concerned.

"Of course I'm not shocked," sounding shocked that he could think that of me.

He nodded, reassured, and then continued. What he was saying was so important to him. It was supposed to be important to me, too, if I cared about him, even a little.

"She was pregnant and we were both Catholic. Both very serious and very young at the university. But we were children still. And the first thing we did, foolishly, stupidly, was to tell our parents. And so after that, there was nothing for us to do, no other choice but to marry.

"When she was about eight months pregnant we went to visit her family. They had a chalet in a small village in the mountains. About an hour after we arrived at the chalet, she fell down the old stairs."

"How terrible. How really terrible." I didn't like this story at all.

"I don't know how it happened. I still think about it after all these years. She had become clumsy, gained too much weight perhaps. She was not happy. She was eighteen years old and she wanted to be a schoolgirl, not a mother.

"There was an old doctor in the village. He thought that the baby had probably died in the fall. But he was not certain and believed inducing the birth would be the right thing to do. I disagreed. I felt we should let nature take its course, that we should wait. But I was still a young student and my wife's parents would not listen to what I had to say. And she said, my wife: 'At least it will be all over.'

"The birth was induced that night in the chalet. I assisted. My wife she was in terrible agony. Hour after hour. The baby was born alive. A boy. But we could not keep him breathing. I realized afterwards that the baby died because of the doctor's ineptitude and clumsiness. My wife went into shock, began to hemorrhage. We had no drugs, no facilities, no equipment. Nothing. She died early the next morning from loss of blood."

"Paul, oh, Paul, how terrible—"

"Yes, it was terrible." He paused and looked at me. "Of course I knew I had to become a gynecologist because of this experience. Before that I had thought I was going to be a surgeon. But now I am happy each time I put a healthy baby into the arms of a woman who wants that baby. I am happy every time a baby is born easily and without much pain."

"Oh, Paul," I said softly and took his hand.

"Thank you," he said, "for understanding."

The simple cause and effect of Paul's life amazed me, dazzled me. Most people I know never know why they do anything and rather pride themselves on the lack of simple rational motivation, including Suzanne, expecially Suzanne, who, when in doubt, runs. While one kernel of experience was an explanation for Paul's whole life. No matter what the tragic cause, it must be sort of a comfort to know why you're doing what you're doing. Perhaps what the whole modern mixed-up world is suffering from is a lack of deathbed promises.

"I do not usually tell people about my life, Aileen.

But I find you a most sympathetic and interesting person."

"Thank you," I said.

"I have opened my heart to you. May I continue to speak frankly and openly? May I continue to unburden my heart?" He gave his little shy smile.

"Well—" But then I nodded.

"Can you understand that during the past years it has become increasingly difficult for me to establish— hmmm—personal relationships with women. Because of my occupation. Do you understand? I have so many professional relationships—"

I had let go of his hand. We were both staring tactfully out at the water to avoid eye contact.

De Maupassant once said all cats were black in the dark. But what if all cats were black daily between nine and five? If women were one long pap smear after another, I could understand wanting to wash one's hands of females at the end of a busy day.

"But Aileen, I must admit, I find you most attractive, most attractive. Am I being too plainspoken?"

"NO!—"

"Yes, most attractive—"

A couple of other times men have told me that, while other ladies left them unmoved, I, and I alone, had that certain something. I realized they were probably handing me a line but even if they weren't, their lavish compliments didn't flatter me. Rather, their single-minded enthusiasm made me feel a little peculiar, as if they were men with decidedly off-beat tastes. I want to be loved, sure, but I don't want to be used as someone's exotic aphrodisiac. Or maybe it's simpler than that. Maybe I never want the ones that want me the most. As the great American philosopher Groucho Marx once said, "I'd never join any club that would have me as a member."

"Doctor! Mademoiselle!" Iphigenia was running down the path.

Paul bolted. "Perhaps Madame—at last—" We rushed to the bottom of the path.

"You come—"

"Yes," Paul said, "of course."

"Da Boss, he wants you."

"But is Madame all right?" I asked.

Iphigenia pantomimed tears. "She cry again—boo-hoo—boo-hoo." She gave a happy smile, pleased with her interpretation. We all raced up the path.

Nicho was on the terrace, smoking a big cigar and drinking his vodka neat. It was about eleven and he was still wrapped in his gold-colored terrycloth robe. Usually he was dressed before seven. He looked worried and tired. "I am sorry to disturb you, my friends," he said quietly. "But something has come up. These things happen. I must fly to London this morning."

"London?"

The phone rang on the table. Nicho picked it up, listened, then growled a few words into it and hung up. "Yes, it is most unfortunate," he said, "but one of our tankers has gone aground in the English Channel. It has already released ten thousand tons of oil. The loss of oil is, of course, very worrisome at this time of shortages. And there is also the danger that the oil may wash up on British beaches and pollute them."

LOSS OF MUCH NEEDED OIL. THREAT TO THE ENVIRONMENT: A double whammy of screaming black headlines.

"My dear wife—our dear Suzanne—is, of course, very disturbed that I will not be here for the next few days. I am disturbed myself." He was pacing up and down.

"Can you send someone else?" I asked.

"There is no one else, my dear. I must be available to the British press, the British government. I must find the cause of this unfortunate little mishap. And I must supervise the clean-up operation myself. How can I stay on my own beach if the beaches that thousands use are in danger? Besides, it would be damned bad publicity."

The phone rang again. Nicho listened for a few moments, then began to spit out some rapid-fire French. Overhead his white-and-red helicopter approached. He hung up the phone angrily and stubbed out his cigar. "I will fly from Cyprus. A plane is waiting for me there. I will be in London by early afternoon. The British papers are already full of accusations. They are convinced my friends in the desert and I are trying to drive up the price of their petrol. When it comes to business the English are quite polite to each other. But how they love to smear anyone who is not an Anglo or a Saxon." He looked at Paul and me. "I do not want to miss the baby's birth. But such things happen. I have been told that my father did not attend my own birth. So maybe it is in the family tradition—" He gave a gruff laugh. "Monsieur, we will keep in constant touch."

"Everything will be all right, sir. Please, do not worry—"

Nicho left us abruptly.

Paul said: "Perhaps you ought to go and see Madame now." We both remembered Iphigenia's tearful pantomime.

Suzanne was lying across the bed, red-faced, tear-stained.

She looked at me. "Do you know what that fucking tanker is called? The Elena-fucking-Anapoulis. Isn't that bloody ironic?" Her stomach jumped indignantly.

The baby had moved or turned or poked out a little bony elbow.

"Terrible things happen when Nicho leaves me," she whispered dramatically. "Terrible things." Her stomach shifted gears again. It was absolutely riveting. Suddenly for the first time I wished she would have the baby right away. It seemed more important than anything.

She cried softly, the tears running down to the corners of her mouth.

"He isn't leaving you. He's just going away for a little while."

Nicho knocked and came into the room, dressed for battle: beautiful tailored blue suit, white starched shirt, red, paisley silk tie. His shoes gleamed like mirrors. A pair of darker-than-usual sunglasses hid his heavy eyes.

Nicho seems to have no vanity, I think because he has honestly assessed his physical appearance and knows there is not much value in his being vain. He seems most comfortable in Mexican sandals, a pair of dark slacks and a soft, loose sport shirt. But when necessary, in order to achieve the appropriate effect, he will subtly bedeck himself. For his trip to London he wore two wide watchbands of beaten gold and carried a vicuna overcoat.

"Darling—"

Suzanne tried to get up but couldn't make it. She groaned softly and wiped her smudged face with the back of her hand. When Nicho bent to kiss her I left the room though I heard her sigh. Outside suddenly there were several more helicopters zooming up and down, a great clatter of helicopters.

"What the hell is going on?" I shouted over the din.

"Journalists," Paul said, extending an arm upward. "Oil spill in the Channel during the time of oil shor-

tages. It is—what do they say?—a big, big story? They
are British and French journalists, I would imagine."

I watched the hovering helicopters, feeling as if I
were in a combat zone.

After a few minutes Nicho came out, with Suzanne
clinging to his arm. He looked at the helicopters. "Do
you know what they want?" he said. "The bastards
want me on a beach reading the *Wall Street Journal*
with a bottle of champagne and a woman who is not
my wife. That is what they want. They don't want me
to go to London and get something done. These un-
imaginative sons-of-bitches." Suddenly he roared out a
string of Greek expletives. I had read once that Nicho, when angry, could curse like a Piraeus stevedore.
Iphigenia and the other maids who clustered around
broke into embarrassed giggles, their hands over their
ears.

"When I go, these bastards will go too. There is
nothing for them here without me. You will not be
disturbed."

Nicho solemnly shook hands with Paul and
Hardcastle, kissed me on the cheek. "Call me at any
time. Or use the Telex in my study. It connects
directly with the London office. I'll probably be in the
office most of the time. I'll sleep there. So we can be
in touch at any time."

Then Suzanne walked with him to the helicopter
and kissed him good-by. Her belly kept them apart;
they just managed a lip-to-lip kiss. While they kissed,
the airborne helicopters bounced up and down excitedly, like a swarm of wasps sighting a particularly
succulent prey.

Nicho climbed aboard, waved to us once more, and
began to read a report even before the helicopter took
off.

"I'm going to pee in my pants," Suzanne said and

raced inside. If he bothered to look, Nicho might have thought she was overcome with emotion. The other helicopters followed Nicho's. They turned east toward Cyprus.

The rest of the day dragged. Suzanne moaned, groaned, pulled her quilt out on the terrace, and did her psychoprophylactic exercises for the two-thousandth time. "Good *gel*," said Hardcastle. "Game *gel*."

During lunch and the long afternoon, Paul kept giving me warmer, friendlier looks which took the form of speculative, melancholy looks. I'd glance up from the *New York Times* to find him staring at me. I'd smile. He'd smile. We'd both look down at the papers we were reading. What with Suzanne's delivery and sexy old me, he sure had a lot to look forward to.

That night there was a message on the Telex from Nicho. He had arrived safely and the situation was approximately what he had expected. The tanker was being towed to port, still discharging oil. New equipment was being sent from West Germany to help speed the clean-up operation. He would be back as soon as possible. Suzanne read the message and cried some more.

I put her to bed and sat with her. She reached out to grab my hand. "You're my best friend."

"I know."

"You're my *only* friend. The only friend I ever really had."

I nodded.

"I wonder why." Then she fell asleep, chewing a great clump of her golden hair.

The next morning during breakfast a helicopter returned to the island. It hovered menacingly above our heads while we ate.

"Didn't he get the word?" I asked.

"I wish he'd go away," said Suzanne. "He's giving me a bloody headache."

Another day, another dolour.

"Madame, what if it lands—what shall we do then?" Paul asked.

"Don't be silly. Why would it land?" Suzanne asked.

"Why is it here?" Paul replied.

"I suppose we can tell whoever it is that this is private property, so kindly bug off," I suggested. "If we're forceful enough, he'll understand."

"Hmmm—" Paul said. "Hmmm. Perhaps, *chérie*. It all depends on what language our visitors speak, *n'est-ce pas?*"

On the island was our brave little group with Hardcastle in the kitchen as usual. The chef was teaching her puff pastry in exchange for tourniquets.

And there were also a dozen fluttery maids and two sturdy handymen. We talked French and they talked English. Iphigenia, I concluded, was our only translator.

"Look—" Paul said suddenly, standing up. "Madame, look." Near the temple was a flat field that Nicho's pilot occasionally used for a landing site, though there was a smaller but more treacherous clearing near the house. This pilot, less familiar with the terrain, had chosen the larger site. The helicopter was coming down slowly but deliberately, like a fat lady trying to sit down on a small stool.

"Oh, shit—well, do something." Suzanne hissed at Paul.

He gave a very Gallic shrug. "*Chére* Madame, what shall I do?" I decided I liked Paul's Gallic side.

Three maids had drifted onto the terrace to watch. Iphigenia, her head to one side, looked perplexed. "Not De Boss—"

"No. Not De Boss," Suzanne said. "Iphigenia, go and get Stephanos and Christian. Tell them to come here. Iphigenia—" She repeated what she had said in a kind of baby-talk-badly-pronounced Greek. She had studied the language for a few months. A tutor who must have thought his fortune was being made, came to the island three times a week to give her lessons. But she couldn't remember what she had learned from Monday to Wednesday, and Nicho teased her gently. Irritated, Suzanne stopped the lessons and probably broke the tutor's heart.

The workmen were on the other side of the house, laying mosaics on the bottom of the pool. The filter system had already been finished. Nicho had planned that the pool's bottom would be a giant mosaic of Venus on the half-shell, the Venus looking suspiciously like you-know-who. But Suzanne had vetoed that idea. The mosaics were now abstracts based on Cretan motifs symbolizing prosperity and fertility.

In the field we could see two men climbing stiffly out of the helicopter.

Stephanos and Christian came around the corner. They took off their caps, bowed respectfully to Suzanne. "Paul," she said coolly, "take these men with you and go over to the field and tell whoever it is that we don't want any today. Try to be pleasant, but get rid of them."

Paul gestured to the workmen and the three of them started down the path. The helicopter's rotors began turning once more. The two men, one tall and one short, who had disembarked from the chopper were walking slowly toward the beach while the helicopter rose again immediately, straight up.

"Suzanne—SUZANNE!"

She nodded; she was watching, too.

"Suzanne, you know, I have this funny feeling that

whoever they are, our visitors are going to be around
for a while."

"I see—oh shit—I see." Suddenly she began to
giggle. "What a bloody mess. What's Nicho going to
say?"

Paul had reached the beach. So had the other men.
They met in the middle of the sand. From a distance
it looked like a tableau: *Dr. Livingstone, I
presume?*—At least they were talking to each other.
The helicopter was now heading back to the mainland.

We watched anxiously, trying to figure out what
was being said. "They must talk English or French.
Paul isn't having any trouble communicating with
them, at least—"

Suzanne bounced up and down excitedly. "What
are we going to do? How are we going to get them
out of here? Damnit, will you think of something."

"Well, we can get the helicopter from Cyprus. Or
get that helicopter"—which was fast disappearing—"to
come back, I guess. And there's always the boat."

"A speedboat," said Suzanne disdainfully.

"It works." Nicho had a snappy Chriscraft tied up
on the beach. Occasionally he went zipping through
the water as a way of relieving tensions after an
hour-long conference call.

"Remember when my father had a speedboat and
he wanted my mother to call him captain?"

"Captain Goldfarb," I laughed.

"And he would get seasick just crossing Hewlett
Bay."

"And didn't your mother book on a round-the-world
cruise?"

"That's the way she paid him back. Poor Daddy.
Seventy-two straight days, hanging over the rail."

Suzanne touched her hard stomach and turned back
to the beach.

"Don't worry. Paul and I will get them out of here
somehow," I said. She kept rubbing her stomach, not
answering. "But who do you think they are? What do
you think they want? Suzanne?"

She pushed her bulk away from the table. "I don't
even want to know. If they ask for me, just say I'm
indisposed. I *feel* indisposed." She went into the
house.

Paul and the two men were climbing the path. Stephanos and Christian remained on the beach. I
poured myself a cup of coffee, nervously ate a croissant without Suzanne's hungry eyes on me.

Paul was breathing heavily as he led the way. The
day had become as bright and hot as usual and perspiration beaded his forehead. He spoke to me sotto
voce: "*They say* they are journalists. *They say* the pilot was supposed to wait." He shrugged.

One was tall and thin; the other, weighed down
with cameras, was small, bent over, monkey-like with
a hairline an inch above his eyebrows and his eyebrows one straight fuzzy line.

"That's right," said the tall one affably. "There's
been a frightful mixup somehow. I am sorry. You see,
we were just setting down to ask if we could stay a
bit and have a nice little chat and that pilot up and
leaves us stranded. Probably didn't understand one
word we were saying, of course. Did he, eh Mick?"

The other one grunted.

"Wasn't even a Greek. He was one of those Turko-
Nazi-God-knows-what, Levantine mixtures spawned
in the alleyways of Istanbul types that are so
charming in mystery thrillers but are considerably
less charming when they have your life in their
hands. Personally, I think his instrument panel was

made of hashish and that's why he didn't understand
what we were trying to tell him which was to wait—"

Another grunt of agreement from Mick.

The tall one glanced down at me again. "Oh, dear,
I know you're wondering what you're going to do
with us. Well, don't worry, my dear. We'll find a way
to get back. Where there's a will, there's a way. And
there is a will—" Then he smiled suddenly as if he
had just let me in on a marvelous joke. He had the
most dazzling smile. Superdazzling. I smiled back. So
did Paul, I noticed. It was almost involuntary. Our
eyes held. I pulled my gaze away. He was incredibly
handsome. Fair straight hair, bright blue eyes, a long-
ish but elegant nose. A beautiful Englishman.

Somehow I shut my open mouth, found my voice,
and managed a question: "Excuse me for asking, but
what are you doing here? What do you want? Mr.
Anapoulis isn't here. He left for London yesterday."

"I know. How well I know that, my dear. The
bastards—excuse me, but that is the only word possible for the fools at my office—informed me of the
salient fact about an hour ago in Nicosia Airport. So
what the hell am I doing here? I asked them. Those
were my words precisely. 'Oh, sorry, old man, but
there's been a bit of a mistake. Somebody was supposed to send a message for you to disregard the first
message. Didn't you get that message?' Would I be in
bloody Cyprus if I got the message, I asked the fellow. Of course not."

"Of course not," I repeated.

He smiled.

I smiled. Our verbal interaction was rather like a
snake charmer and his snake.

"Look, my dear, do you think me and my young
friend here could have a beer? I'm sorry to be so
boorish as to ask but I'd so appreciate it if you could

manage that for us. We're awfully, awfully dry. He's
come all the way from Paris, old Mick has. Haven't
you, old thing? And d'y'know—" He glanced at his
watch. "About five and a half hours ago I was fast
asleep in the Hotel Angleterre in Rome. *Arrivederci,
Roma*—" He gave a little wave and a big luscious
smile.

"Iphigenia, two beers, please," I called. He sat
down casually and looked toward the beach. "This is
very nice though. I have to be honest and tell you
I've found myself stranded in worse places. Remember Biafra, eh, Mick?"

Eh-Mick gave a short knowing lauúgh.

"Do you enjoy being here, Doctor? Doctor Lavelle,
isn't it? I recognize you. I've read some stuff about
you, sir. Damned interesting, too.

"I trust it isn't too hard being here. Not the worse
place for a short-term practice?"

"Hmmm—yes—it's beautiful," Paul said uneasily.
There was the click of a camera suddenly. The little
photographer began taking pictures of Paul and me
and of the view. It was annoying.

"Aren't you supposed to ask first?" I said to him but
he made no understandable reply. He just kept clicking away. Suddenly I understood why celebrities
smash cameras.

Iphigenia brought out the beers and the steins that
were kept specially chilled just the way Nicho liked
them.

"After you've had your drinks I really think we'd
better find some way of your getting out of here, Mister—"

"Oh, but I'm being dreadfully rude, aren't I?" he
said with a tantalizing hint of that awesome smile.
"Forgive me again, my dear. The uninvited guest
hasn't even managed to introduce himself properly

now, have I?" He stood up and extended a long hard
hand. "Derek-Britten-London-Daily-Express." He said
it like it was one long complete name.

Just in time I caught my mouth dropping open
again and shut it with a hard snap. Derek was
watching me very carefully with those glorious long-
lashed blue-green eyes. I was surprised but only because I wasn't thinking. If I had been thinking it
would have been easy to guess. What I mean is, coin-
cidences happen all the time, don't they? Small world.
Bloody infinitesimal.

"And who are you, then, my dear young lady. Fair's
fair—"

"I—uh—well, I'm Mrs. Anapoulis' cousin."

"Yes, you look a bit like her. I mean, I've seen pictures of her and you look quite a bit like her. Yes,
there's a strong family resemblance."

He was lying, of course, through his long white English teeth.

"Thank you," I said, "that's quite a compliment,
because, you see Mrs. Anapoulis is considered to be
quite—well—pretty."

"So I've heard. Where is the lady? Is she around?"

"Unfortunately Mrs. Anapoulis is not feeling very
well today."

"Nothing serious, I hope." He looked concerned.

No, but it's going to be. I shook my head. We
traded reassuring smiles. Suzanne had said they
looked alike and they did. Tall and blonde and elegant. He was wearing a beige safari jacket, a pair of
chinos, and Gucci loafers without socks. Derek-Britten-London-Daily-Express was a movie foreign corre-
spondent.

That summer long ago when Suzanne discovered
teenage sex, while she was out, I stayed home and
watched the Grade B movies of the late forties on

TV. That summer I fell in love with movie foreign
correspondents in dirty trench coats. Derek was the
updated version.

He lit a Gauloise. The right cigarette. It had been
then. It still was. I sucked my tongue. We were both
waiting. He looked down at the beach and then back
at me.

"Ah—the wine-dark sea," he said solemnly. He
turned his head quickly and his smile flashed like
lightning across the hot summer sky. I knew, I knew
Suzanne was in the doorway behind me.

"Hello, Derek—" her voice was husky and honey-
toned.

She had changed into a gold-colored caftan and her
hair was up in a cluster of curls. She looked like a
very bulky, very festive Christmas package.

Derek jumped and raced to her, his arms wide. He
had to stretch them a little wider. "Hello, Suzie, my
lovely, lovely girl. Oh, but you are looking bloody
marvelous—"

The photographer crouched on the floor, grunted,
and took a picture as Derek tried to pick her up,
couldn't manage, then kissed her instead, first on the
cheek and then lingeringly on the lips. When they finally pulled apart there was a hint of tears in
Suzanne's blue-green eyes, and a look of triumph in
Derek's blue-green eyes. The only sounds were Paul's
shocked intake of breath and the click of the small
simian photographer's automatic Leica.

7

ANAPOULIS FLIES IN

*"I have come to help, of course, why else?
What do you want me to say? I have come
to pour oil on troubled waters?"*

London Daily Express

Over lunch: "I am not going to be interviewed,
Derek. I haven't got anything to say."

"I guessed as much, luvie. Don't worry about a
thing. Don't worry. It was the office's stupid idea. Not
that I didn't want to come and see you." He smiled at
her and sipped a glass of retsina. "Cinderella
Suzanne, that's what they called her."

A toss of golden curls which were drooping. A delicate beading of droplets which dampened her upper
lip. "It was so stupid—"

"But you were news, luvie. News. And I'm afraid
your husband is news right now. We don't like Nick
the Greek mucking up our Channel or helping to
drive up the price of our petrol. This incident is quite
unfortunate, quite unfortunate—"

Mick, who sat hunched over, one arm protectively
around his plate of salade Nicoise, grunted an agreement.

"The poor little birdies. I've read they can't fly
when their feathers get coated with oil. Oh, how hor-
rid for them. I do hope Mr. Anapoulis can do something," said Hardcastle.

"I'm sure he's trying," Derek said and then looked

at Suzanne. "You know when I saw that picture of
you, the picture of your wedding, I bloody well
couldn't believe my eyes. I'd just gotten home. I'd
been in Bangladesh. Bangla-bloody-desh, armpit of
the subcontinent. The next morning I'm having a cup
of tea, I open the papers, and there's a picture of you,
the blushing bride on page one."

"Page three," said Suzanne, making ringlets with a
nervous finger.

"Quelle surprise," said Derek. "I had picked up a
touch of fever out there. I looked at that paper and
by the afternoon I was flat on my back in the London
Clinic, practically delirious. They said it was the same
bug. A relapse. They were wrong, of course. I know
what made me sick."

"Oh, Derek," Suzanne said softly.

"Hate to change the subject," I interrupted, "but
about that helicopter to pick you up?"

Derek looked at me and flashed a small but potent
smile. "We'll work something out, my dear. Leave it
to me."

"Yes," Suzanne said, sounding vague, "Derek, you
really must figure out a way to get yourself out of
here. You shouldn't even be here." She gave a snort of
a giggle and put her hand over her mouth. "Excuse
me," she said.

"Today," I said. "Ha ha, I don't want to sound un-
gracious, but shouldn't you go today?"

He looked at me again and this time he didn't
smile.

"Yes, today," Suzanne said, softly.

"When are you going to have the wee bairn?"

"Last week."

"It's late, then?"

She nodded, pushing away a scarcely touched plate
of salad.

"Probably lazy like its old da—"

"Oh, no, Mister Anapoulis is a whirlwind of activity," said Hardcastle, all school*gel* loyalty.

"Excuse me," Suzanne said, trying to get up gracefully but rattling all the dishes as she pushed against the table, "but I try to take a nap every day after lunch."

"I could use a bit of shuteye myself, y'know. I'm a bit short. Just got into bed last night in Rome—was it only last night?—when the office called. Haven't really had more than a few hours in days and days."

"Poor Derek. I'll have Iphigenia show you to a guest room."

"But what about the helicopter?" I was sounding a little shrill.

"Don't worry about a thing. I'll call the airport as soon as I've had a sleep. How's that? You'll let a man have the rest he needs, won't you? Mick-o needs a bit of rest too, don't you, m'boy?"

The photographer had exchanged plates and was now polishing off Suzanne's lunch.

Paul stood up. "Madame, with all the excitement, I would like to take a blood pressure reading now."

"What excitement?" Suzanne sounded a little irritable. "What excitement? Really!"

"That's right, doc. The excitement's in the Channel, I'd say. Unfortunately for all concerned, ten thousand tons of filthy oil is floating toward Southend free of charge while the price on land is rising practically every hour. That's the big story. There's nothing much happening around here. Anybody can see that. Except my office." And Derek smiled.

A knock on my door. "Come on in, Suzanne."

She was wrapped in a robe. She had removed her

makeup, applied a mask, and even set her hair, for the first time in weeks.

"Well?" she said. "*Well?*"

"*Well* what?"

"Well, what do you think of him, of course?" She sat in the white lacquer bentwood rocker and rocked nervously, anticipating my reply.

"I don't know him. And I don't want to know him."

"But you must have a reaction, a first impression. Something. You don't like him? But you couldn't like me so much, if you didn't like him at least a little." So there.

"Suzanne—don't you think—now try to be sensible. Don't you think it would be better and simpler if he'd just get the hell out of here—and fast?"

She leaned back against the rocker and closed her eyes for a moment. Finally, halfheartedly, a murmur: "I guess." She began to peel her face mask off in long onionskin strips. Underneath, her cheeks were pink. "It was just that I really was a little crazy about him in London."

"But you're not in London now—"

"All right, all right! But he's handsome, don't you think?"

I nodded. "Yes, he's handsome."

"And we do look alike. And he's like me. He is. I guess that's why I feel so comfortable with him. We worry about the same things."

"What things?"

"Oh that when you're so pretty-pretty on the surface there's nothing much inside."

"Suzanne, just look down. There's *plenty* inside."

"That's not what I mean. But being pregnant helps take away that emptyheaded dummy feeling that I always used to have—"

"Suzanne!"

"And Derek's rather a super lover. A lover-ly lover. Probably the best I've ever had."

"*Quelle* testimonial."

She stuck her tongue out at me, then laughed and lit a cigarette. "You do want to hear about it—about us?"

I didn't reply. No, for once—funny—but I didn't want to hear. The dawning of Confidante's Lib.

"Throw me a pillow," she said. "I've got to get comfortable." I knew it was going to be a long session.

"When I left Nicho's hotel I stayed with a model I knew for a couple of days. And one night we went to a discothéque together. It was a terrible, terrible place. Very chic and very in. Everybody raved about the mah-ve-lous food, dahling. As a matter of fact the food was bloody awful. And because I was the new girl in town, a dozen men were looking me over, sort of slobbering over me.

"And it got to me, Aileen. Like everything, I mean. The horrible dark little discothéque, the nauseating goopy food, the dozen chinless wonders trying to flirt with me. It gave me this horrible smothery feeling which is a feeling I often get. I guess I've never even told you about it, have I? I hate it so. The smothers. It isn't easy to explain. But I got it at the hotel when Nicho's old bitch of a secretary started ordering me around and making me feel cheap and stupid. I got it the morning of my wedding day with David. It's sort of like a plastic bag is being put over my head while everybody is smiling encouragingly at me. Do you understand? Nobody notices the bag but ME! Everybody else thinks I look perfectly lovely as usual, while inside I am fighting for breath, choking, practically disappearing and there's no one to tell. Nobody notices what's happening but me. I'm choking and everybody thinks I've never looked better.

"But while I was sitting there quietly suffocating, Derek breezed by and smiled at me, his wonderful smile—have you noticed his smile?—and in a moment—I know it sounds corny but it's exactly the way I felt—like I was breathing fresh air again.

"Well, we danced that night, Derek and I. He held me tight even during the fast numbers when you are supposed to shake. He wouldn't let me go. And he kept murmuring in my ear. He called me an American import, the best American import he'd seen in quite a while, even better than hot foamy shaving lather.

"About midnight Derek said: 'Got anything to say bye-bye to, luvie?' and I said, 'No one, nothing.' And we went outside and got into his car.

"Derek's flat was so dirty and dingy that I could write my name in the dust on the mantelpiece. He said his charlady had been in the hospital and he never remembered to get himself another. But I liked the place. I did. The chairs were just chairs, the table was just a table. No big deal. There wasn't one goddamn thing in the whole place that was chic or clever or artistic. Nothing was worth anything so nothing was even a big bargain.

"Later I found out you had to put a shilling in the gas meter to get the fire started and it even cost sixpence to take a bath which can be a real drag when you're undressed and forgot you haven't any change. And Derek's sheets were gray. Not Bill Blass pearl gray either. But after we made love on his old gray sheets, I thought—well, I thought Derek's dingy flat was the most romantic place I'd ever seen.

"In the morning he made tea and toast for me. With bitter orange marmalade smeared on the toast.

He said he couldn't live in America because they gave you grape jelly in little plastic packets with your toast in the morning. And he said it wasn't the violence in Americans that surprised him but their docility. No other people would accept little plastic packets with grape jelly in them except Americans.

"Afterwards when we had gone back to bed, after that, he said: 'Well, luvie, I think you better stay around for a while,' and I said, 'Well, okay.' Then he said: 'Where are your things then?' and I said vaguely, 'Oh, I'll go and get them sometime,' and he laughed and said no, he'd get them.

"All I wanted then was to fit into Derek's life. And his life was like a pattern. We got up late, had break-fast—and after that first morning, I made the tea and toast. He made a few phone calls. He went to his office around noon and the first thing he did when he got there, I found out, was go and have a quick drink. Then he had a long lunch with his chums. He did his work late in the afternoon. But on a lot of days, he didn't have anything much to do so he just hung around a Fleet Street pub.

"At first I didn't mind the sitting around and drink-ing. I'd eat a sausage roll and listen to the chat which I didn't understand. It was sort of like background music. When I started to feel tired and sickish, I didn't like it too much. And when Derek came home too sloshed to do anything but fall asleep muttering in my neck what a smashing girl I was, I didn't like it at all. But even when I was annoyed or depressed I still had the feeling, this tender feeling toward him. I just felt so tender and dozy and sexy and nice just being around him." She smiled, remembering.

Love, Suzanne, love—maybe you were in love for the very first time.

She lit another cigarette, looking thoughtful, blew

out a puff of smoke, continued: "During this time I wasn't doing anything. I didn't want to work. I felt lethargic, hardly able to move around. So I spent a lot of the day in the flat just cleaning it up. You know how I always hated even picking up a pair of pantyhose I'd thrown on the floor? Well, suddenly I was washing and scrubbing Derek's flat like crazy.

"Well, one night after we made love and I was just lying there listening to Derek sleep, I felt so tender toward him that I hurt, my throat, my breasts, all over. And then I sort of touched myself and I realized I really did hurt. My breasts felt sort of heavy and peculiar. I got out of my bed and went into the bathroom and turned on the light. I looked at myself carefully. And at that moment, I knew. That's all. I looked at myself in the mirror. I thought I was going to get that smothery feeling again but I didn't. So I just went back to bed, pushing Derek over to his side, and fell asleep.

"I didn't do anything for a couple of days. I didn't want to tell Derek. I thought I should go and see a doctor and make sure even though I was sure. The doctor I finally went to was horrible. He was an old man with a yellow face and yellow fingernails which I couldn't stand to look at. He gave me a quickie examination, hurting me, and said of course I was pregnant and that he was getting tired of these stupid, careless sluts who couldn't be bothered to take precautions. He said he had an hour free on Thursday and that an abortion was a hundred pounds, cash on the barrel. That was his fee for one and all. He wouldn't charge his sainted mother a penny less.

"I asked how pregnant I was and he said good and pregnant. But I said I wanted to know exactly. I guess he had heard the question before because he caught on right away. He said: 'Oh, you girls are so very naughty these days.' He said he couldn't tell exactly if I couldn't tell exactly but he thought it was about six or seven weeks. So it might have been Derek but it could have been Nicho. There's been no way for me to tell ever, right from the start. Which is really weird, isn't it—about the weirdest thing in the world."

I nodded my head, agreeing. About the weirdest thing.

"I was just in a daze the rest of the week. I didn't go on Thursday. I was just too busy being nauseous and sleepy, but I wasn't unhappy. I just kept feeling this tenderness flowing out of me, aimed mostly at Derek but sort of covering everything. And I began to wonder: had I felt so warm toward Derek because I was already pregnant when I met him and being pregnant had changed my body and my head? Or had I become pregnant by Derek because I felt different toward him because I was sort of in love with him for the first time? For the first time ever, maybe I was in love—"

I didn't have to tell her. Hell, she knew.

"Aileen, remember, I had been crazy and careless before, lots of times, hundreds of times, and nothing had ever happened. So which came first?"

Like the chicken or the egg or the rooster.

"When I finally told Derek, at first he got mad and told me I was a brainless bird. And then he said, oh, buck up, luvie, an abortion's really nothing. It's like having a tooth out. And then he began to wonder where he'd borrow the hundred pounds. He asked me the name of the doctor I'd seen, got on the phone, made another appointment for me to have the abortion.

"But I had already decided I wasn't going through with it. I hadn't reasoned it out or thought about the future. I never once thought about the baby as a baby. But I just knew I wasn't going to have the love, the tenderness, the new way I was feeling scraped out of me. Oh, sure, it could have been Derek. But there had been so many men before, other men, and it had been pretty good in bed with them, too. But I never felt the way I was feeling. I wasn't going to take any chances on Derek. I couldn't do that. I had to take my chances on the baby.

"So when I got back to the doctor I said to him: 'Do you have a back door? Please, just keep the money. I want to go out the back way without my boyfriend knowing.' And he said: 'Well, now I've heard everything.' But after a moment he said, 'It's some kind of con, is it? Whoever is waiting for you outside is going to come back and say I've done something to you, make me pay him back the money.' I said I'd leave a note. I wrote Derek: 'Thanks for the air fare. I'm going home. Good-by' and gave it to the doctor."

"But after that," I said, unable to contain myself, "did you keep on feeling the same way *without* Derek?" *Warm, loving, tender, sexy, cozy.* Suzanne's emotions sounded like the names for seven pervert dwarfs.

"Well, until my leg started hurting."

"Then you didn't miss Derek?"

"I guess I did, but then I didn't." She added after a moment: "But I'm glad he's here now."

"Suzanne!"

There was a knock on the door. "Suzanne, are you in there?" Derek called.

"Yes," she answered in a breathy little-girl voice.

"Hey, you were supposed to be taking a nap, bad girl. Listen, luvie, I thought I'd walk over and inspect your temple. Suzie, you're the only girl I know who owns a ruin. Most girls I know just live with them. Come and give me the guided tour. Please."

She was rapidly unwinding the curlers from her hair. "All right but we have to walk slowly."

"Yes, nice and slow," he said. "I'll just go downstairs and get us some light refreshment. I'll be profoundly disappointed if your lord and master drinks anything less impressive than Rothschild Lafitte. Don't be long, luvie."

"Give me some perfume," Suzanne whispered to me.

"Ask him about the helicopter," I whispered back. "Suzanne, you have to be sensible. Suzanne!"

She picked up my brush and began to beat her mane into shape. "I'll just be a minute, Derek," she called. She sniffed at the bottle I offered. "That's perfectly terrible."

I had to agree. It was a sample generously given me as a farewell present by the beauty department of the magazine.

"Where's your eye shadow?"

I gave her a puny, tarnished tube.

"Aileen, why don't you get yourself some decent makeup?" she wailed.

I shrugged. "When I grow up," I said, which is really the way I feel. I trailed her back into her room. Suzanne had a special makeup table. Her entire triple dresser was covered with bottles and tubes and little jars. It was like Bloomingdale's cosmetic counters. Everything was there except the other customers.

It took her twenty minutes to apply moisturizer, base, cheek gel, shadow cream, powder, brow beautiful, eye shadow, false lashes, mascara, underliner, overliner. She even plucked her eyebrows. I enjoyed watching. There was a sort of ritual to the performance. Suzanne enjoyed herself a lot too. Snow

White whistled while she worked. She was frighteningly cheerful and had more energy than she had shown in weeks.

"How do I look?" she asked after applying a finished coating of coral lip gloss.

"Pregnant."

She laughed and looked in the mirror, pleased as punch with what she saw. Mirror, mirror on the wall, etc. She wiped an invisible speck off her gleaming cheek. "I guess I have been feeling a bit like the back of a bloody bus," she said.

"I'm sure Nicho finds you perfect this way."

"Yes, I guess, he finds me perfect. But I am not perfect. I am far from bloody perfect."

She looked at her mirror again. "Oh, I know, I shouldn't care about looking attractive now but—" And all the time she kept looking at herself in the mirror, giving herself these encouraging little smiles, a purse of the lips, even a raffish grin. "Aileen, nothing's going to happen. I mean there's nothing that can happen. I mean—you know—well, I really can't. Not really.

"And even if I could, I wouldn't. I mean, I can't even bend over." She bent over. "Gee, I didn't think I could bend over."

"Suzanne, I don't want to rush you, luvie, but, for God's sake, woman, the champagne is getting warm. We can't let that happen, now can we?" Derek shouted up the stairs.

She bent over one more time, smiled, then blew me and her mirror a little kiss. Sure enough, she was still the fairest. For the first time in weeks she raced quickly and almost lightly down the stairs.

The room was heavy with her flowery perfume. Her dressing table was stained with dabs of blue eye makeup and spills of powder. I stared into the mirror.

All the elements were here for another of Suzanne's little escapades. A full-scale escapade. Unconsciously, I drew a heart pierced with an arrow in the powder. Hurriedly, very hurriedly, I blew it away, getting the sweetish powder in my mouth, up my nose.

While Derek and Suzanne explored the temple ruins, which meant sitting next to each other, knee-to-knee, and talking intently, the rest of us tried to keep ourselves otherwise occupied. Hardcastle, game old thing, tried to draw out the little chimp of the photographer. "Where are you from, dear boy?" she asked.

His reply was a sound, not a word, totally unintelligible to me.

"I knew you were from Glasgow," she cried delightedly.

She also managed to find out that his name was Mick Finn. Mickey Finn. No wonder he didn't talk much: he didn't want to introduce himself.

Paul read the *Journal of the American Medical Association* and clicked his tongue with disapproval at most of the articles. He stopped me as I walked past going nowhere. I kept sneaking glances at Derek and Suzanne's silhouette. They were now holding hands.

"Pardon, Aileen, but a question—"

"Yes, Paul?"

"This man, this journalist, he is an old friend of Madame's?"

"Ye-es."

"A strange coincidence his coming here."

"Ye-es."

Paul spoke slowly, "In a way—perhaps I am wrong— but I feel Mister Anapoulis left me in charge. I feel I should be doing something about getting both these men to leave. It is very awkward for me—"

I murmured a noncommittal murmur and left Paul

looking nervous and upset. I went into Nicho's study.
Through the window I could see Derek and Suzanne.
He now had his arm resting lightly on her shoulder.

On the Telex machine there was a message: SITUA-
TION IMPROVING RAPIDLY. HOMEWARDS WITHIN THIRTY-
SIX HOURS. TRUST ALL IS WELL. REGARDS NICHO. I ripped
it off and put the message on Suzanne's dinner plate.
An hour later she read it, yawning. Her afternoon at
the temple seemed to have exhausted her. Her
makeup faded, she looked pale, drawn, and tense
again.

Afterwards I learned about their sacred-grove conversation. Derek had dwelled on one point.

"I love you, Suzie. Goddamn it, I love you. Had I
known the baby meant so much to you, I would have
wanted the baby, too."

"Derek, what's the difference now?" Suzanne had
said softly. "We're not in London now. There's nothing we can say or do now, is there? Our relationship
is finished."

"Do you know, luvie, I nearly killed that doctor?
Nearly knocked out all his front teeth. I was almost
up on charges. I thought he'd hurt you. I couldn't believe you'd just take off like that. I didn't believe you
wrote that silly note. If I had only known— If I had
only known how you felt about the baby—"

"Oh, Derek," Suzanne said softly. "What difference
would that have made? I was just another bird to
you. Now wasn't I just another bird?"

"No, no! I loved you. Suzie, I loved you then and I
love you now—"

"Derek, please don't keep saying that."

"I LOVE YOU."

"Derek, I am getting very nervous—"

"I LOVE—"

"Please, let's talk about something else."

"What else is there for us to talk about, you gorgeous little fool? Will you let me kiss you?"

"No, of course not!"

"Woman, that's my child inside of you."

"As a matter of simple fact, I don't know that it is."

"Stop telling silly little lies. That doesn't make it better, it makes it worse."

"I'm telling you the truth. I really don't know."

"I'll be damned if I'll let another man claim my baby even if he is some kind of bloody zillionaire. Goddamn it, you can't still buy babies that are wanted even if you can buy practically anything else in this bloody world."

"The baby could be yours or it could be Nicho's. That's the truth. The only thing I'm abso-bloody-lutely sure of is that the baby's mine."

"And mine. Your husband is an old man."

"He isn't that old and he's an extraordinary man. A wonderful man."

"He's a rich son of a bitch so he's extraordinary. If he was a poor son of a bitch, my dear, he wouldn't be so extraordinary. But the hell with him, I'm talking about us, Suzie girl. Remember us, Suzie, the way it was with us."

"Yes, I remember."

"So do I. I can't forget it."

"Derek, please, what good does it do?"

"Maybe he wants you and the baby. I can understand that. But I can't let it happen. Suzie, I need you and the baby. Honestly, I do. I want to change my life. You know that. I want something to be important to me. And you, you with a baby—that would be important. Do you know, I think you're more beautiful now than ever. Please let me kiss you, Suzie—"

"Derek—"

"One kiss—"

"Oh, Derek."

They kissed. A long kiss.

"I went to Bangladesh to try to stop thinking, to try to stop worrying about you. To try and just forget you. But even there I couldn't. No, Suzie, you are not just another 'bird' to me. Suzie, we were right for each other. Just plain right for each other. And we can be right for each other again, can't we?"

"Derek, I want to go home. Please, my leg hurts."

"Home? This isn't a home, Suzie. It's a goddamned shrine."

Dinner was silent and awkward. Hardcastle was looking around a bit quizzically, as if something weren't quite right but she couldn't figure out what it was. Mick, too, was off his feed. He had only three portions of everything he could reach.

"You should eat more," Derek, who was on his second bottle of champagne, said thickly, watching Suzanne pick at her roast lamb. "Woman, you're eating for two."

"That's an interesting dieting theory," Suzanne said.

"And where's your milk? You're supposed to drink milk. Isn't she, Doctor?"

"Madame takes calcium tablets and drinks skimmed milk."

"Derek, stop taking care of me. It simply isn't your style." She laughed nervously.

"Well, I'm going to start taking care of you. You'll see; you'll be surprised what a bloody good job I do of it, too."

Watching Suzanne's tense face, Paul asked: "Are you feeling all right, Madame?"

"Yes, I guess—" she said with a faint smile.

"Well, I'm taking her up to bed now, Doctor. I'm sure you'll agree that's what she needs," Derek said firmly, though he was a little wobbly when he stood up.

"I can manage by myself ... oh, all right." The Telex message from Nicho fell off her lap. She didn't notice, and stepped on it.

"Just a minute—stay there," Derek said and disappeared into the house. Suzanne made a sulky face but she stayed. He came back a few minutes later, carrying a glass of milk. "For you, luvie, it's warm to make you sleep."

"I hate warm milk. I hate it."

"I want to see you drink it all up. Now that's a good girl."

"Madame does not need that milk," Paul said coldly.

"Oh, well, it can't hurt me, can it?" Suzanne said with a little laugh and let Derek take her arm.

"He certainly is a bit nervy, isn't he?" Hardcastle said as they went inside together. "Well, these Fleet Street boys have to be, I suppose."

"I would like to see him out of here. I feel he is disturbing Madame. Wasn't he supposed to call for a helicopter? Hasn't he done anything about that? Perhaps I should call myself. It is so awkward—my position—" He looked imploringly at Hardcastle and then at me.

"I'm sure they'll be off in the morning, sir," Hardcastle said crisply, reassuringly.

"Well, yes, I suppose."

"I think I'll go up and see Suzanne," I said.

Derek was coming out of her room. "Tucked her in. Even though the baby is awfully bloody late, everything's all right, isn't it?"

"Yes. But Suzanne isn't supposed to get upset or excited or—"

"Of course not, of course not. After you've said

good night—and don't be long, you're quite right she needs lots of rest—pop down and have a brandy with me. I want to get to know you better. And I want you to get to know me. Frankly, I think I'm going to need a few friends around here." He gave me a flashing smile. "I'll be waiting for you."

Suzanne was curled up in her bed, her eyes shut tight.

"Are you okay?"

"Hmmmmmmmalmost asleep," she said in a little voice. "That hot milk works wonders—"

"I'm glad. And tomorrow we'll get Derek out of here. Right? And the next day Nicho will be home. Right?"

"Hmmmmmmmmso sleepy." She made a delicate but convincing snoring sound.

"Good night." I went out shutting the door.

Halfway down the hall I remembered that the shutter opposite her bed was open; I didn't want the morning light to awaken her too early. I went back to her room and opened the door very quietly. Suzanne was sitting up in bed, holding a magnifying glass and applying another coating of false eyelashes, one by one. She was humming contentedly, much too happily engrossed to notice me. Quietly I shut the door again.

By the pricking of my thumbs, by the sinking feeling in my stomach, by the pounding in my head, I knew we were now deep into a Suzanne escapade. And there was nothing I could do about it. Nothing I *should* do about it. Except watch. Observe. Pick up the scattered pieces. Maybe hold the hands of those she hurt. Damn her! For a minute I wanted to go back into her room and shake her hard. No. Then I wanted to go back into my room and start to pack. Instead, I just went slowly, fatalistically down the stairs. I was, after all, just an onlooker.

"So there you are," Derek said. Paul, Hardcastle, and he were sitting on the terrace. "I was just wondering where you were—and how she is?"

"About the same as usual."

"Good. Would you like a drink? Brandy, my dear?"

"Why not?"

He poured me a stiff one. I wanted a stiff one.

"So our lady is all nice and cozy for the night."

"She's trying to get that way."

"Perhaps I should check on Madame too. That leg—"

"Don't. She's all right."

"Physician, heal thyself and have another drink."

"Perhaps—" Paul relinquished his glass and gave me a little friendly smile.

"Mr. Britten was just telling us such an amusing story," Hardcastle said.

"Not really," Derek said diffidently, his eyes bright.

"Oh, yes," Hardcastle insisted.

"Just been talking about one of my many disastrous encounters with our lovely royal family or how I was bitten in the arse by one of the Queen Mother's corgis."

Hardcastle giggled.

"At least it evoked some sympathy from Princess Anne. And it takes a lot, unless you're four-footed, to get some sympathy from that filly, I can tell you. When I saw her later in the day, she called me over and asked me how I was. And I said: 'Honored, ma'am, honored.'"

Hardcastle and Derek laughed together. He *did* have charm, lots of easy charm, and he could use it. Wisely he was starting with Hardcastle, the softest touch in the place.

"But those days, I'm glad to say, are over for me. No more writing gossip columns. No more royal tours, thank you. Chasing after celebrities, being sneered at by Prince Philip, are a young man's game. Champagne and caviar, I've decided, are bad for the liver—bad for the soul—"

"And what do you want to write about now?" I asked.

"Things that are a bit more important to me, a bit more important to the world, than whether one aging movie star loves another aging movie star. So it's revolutions and riots for starters. I flew into wartorn Belfast and wartorn Biafra and wartorn Bangladesh. It's a bit phoney in some ways, too. I don't deny it. But I'm seeing a bit more of life."

"Then what are you doing here?"

"Touché, my dear. Just happens, I was in Rome, closest at hand. Not that I minded. But to the editors we're all interchangeable bodies. Little pegs they move around the board in the foreign room." He went to the bar. "Now this is damned good brandy. I can still appreciate that. The trouble is, when you try to make yourself a more serious person, you're stuck with all your old frivolous tastes."

Nobody said anything for a few moments. Derek, acting the host, quietly refilled our glasses.

"Really, Mister Britten, you do lead an exciting life," said Hardcastle finally.

Derek smiled sweetly. "Not bad."

"You see so many interesting places, so many important things."

"Sometimes, Sister, sometimes. But do you know what I mostly see are hotel rooms, cable offices, and, oh, yes, airports. And nowadays cable offices, hotel rooms, and airports, especially airports, all look pretty much the same.

"For instance, last year I went to a conference about oil in Iran. It was held in a marvelous old city

called Isfahan, glorious old city. Well, I worked hard
during the conference because it was a big story.
When I got back to Teheran the desk clerk in my hotel asked me where I'd been. 'Isfahan,' I said.

"'Oh, marvelous,' he said. 'How did you like the
great square?' 'The great square! Mmm—I'm afraid I
didn't see it,' I said. 'Well, then, how did you like the
great carpet factory? It's the largest in the world.'
'Sorry, old man,' I said, 'I didn't get to see that either.'
'Well, then, what about the Great Mosque; surely you
saw the Great Mosque?' 'No, I didn't see it.' 'Then
what *did* you see?' 'Well,' I said, 'I saw the airport,
the hotel, the cable office—' "

Hardcastle laughed. Derek had made one sure con-
quest.

Paul stood up. "Mr. Britten, this has been most interesting and now I do not mean to be rude. But tomorrow—the helicopter—"

"I will take care of everything, Doctor. I promise
you that tomorrow I will take care of everything that
needs to be taken care of. Now don't worry about it.
Don't be concerned. Your only concern is your patient. Isn't that so?"

"Well—yes—yes—" Paul agreed and said good night.

Hardcastle stood up too, a bit reluctantly.

"Well, good night," I said, joining them.

"But, Aileen, my dear girl, you can't go yet. We
haven't talked." Derek took my hand. His hand was
cool but slightly damp. "It's been real interesting—"

He wouldn't let go.

"Good night, *chérie*," Paul said to me, looking back
as he left the room.

In the corridor I heard Hardcastle say: "Well, he is
rather charming, now, isn't he? Admit it, sir, he is." I
didn't hear Paul's reply.

"I really wanted to talk to you," Derek whispered in my ear. "It's important, sweetie. Please."

He made me sit down next to him. "Aileen, dear girl, have another drink."

I shook my head.

"Well, I'm going to have another one. You're sure you won't?"

"Oh, all right. Maybe a little one."

"Good. Good." He went to the bar. "At least El Greco doesn't stint on his liquor."

"He doesn't stint on anything."

"Well, why should he? I noticed the taps in the bathroom. Are they really gold?"

"Probably."

"How marvelously, uncaringly vulgar."

"I like Nicho."

"I'm sure you do, sweetie. Power and money are damned beguiling."

He poured our drinks and sat down again. "Look, Aileen, my dear, I have something I want to share with you. Something important I want to tell you—"

Am I beginning to look like the perfect all-weather confidante? Suzanne always, Paul the other day, now Derek—pouring out their hearts, laying their little secrets on me. Does anybody notice anything about me but my ears, for God's sake? I swallowed the brandy in one burning gulp.

"Aileen, your sweet cousin, Suzanne—"

"Mrs. Anapoulis—" I murmured.

"Suzanne, our dear Suzanne, means a great deal to me. Did you know that?"

"Well—"

"Yes, you know that. You know something about it. About us. Don't you?"

I gave a cautious half-nod.

"Well, our dear Suzanne means a great deal to me. A great deal more to me than I ever realized. She truly does. Matter of fact, it's been quite an important revelation to me." His voice was fuzzy with emotion.

Beauty and the lack of availability can be damned beguiling.

"And the baby. Even the baby now means a helluva lot to me too, you know." Those bright turquoise eyes were reddening slightly. Derek looked at me closely, watching for my reaction. But there was no reaction.

"You don't believe me, do you? You think I'm acting or something? Is that it? You know, my dear, you are hurting me very much because you don't believe me."

"What do you want me to say?" I asked him tonelessly.

He got up and walked across the room and poured himself another drink. After a moment he said: "How can I convince you that I am not talking rot? How can I convince you that I really feel the way I say I feel?"

"You don't have to convince me. Derek, you don't have to convince me of anything." Why does everyone always want the reassurance of someone else murmuring in sympathy and nodding in agreement. Do we all have so many doubts about the depth or sincerity of our emotions that they can only seem real to us if they seem real to an impartial observer?

"Will you do me a favor, Aileen? Just stay here for a moment. I want to show you something, my dear."

"I'm very tired, Derek."

"I think you can wait just a few more minutes before going to bed. I don't think that's asking too bloody much, is it? And this is rather important to me. Ra-ther important." I realized that Derek was finally ra-ther drunk.

"Okay, okay—"

He went up to his room. I wanted to sneak away quietly to get upstairs to my sanctuary of green-and-white and wicker. But he was back again, in a moment, blocking the doorway.

"Here—" he said dramatically. "Here it is." He held out a dirty, stained cloth.

"What the hell is that?"

"A rag. A bandage. I don't know quite what to call it. A memento, perhaps, yes, a memento mori. I used it to bind up a man's wounds in Bangladesh. Didn't help much. He died."

"Oh, God." I sat down.

"A nice man. My taxi driver when I was there. Got to know him rather well. One day he didn't show up at the hotel. I was worried so I went to look for him. I found him in the hovel where he lived. He had been beaten in the night. He had been trying to protect his wife and daughter from a band of soldiers. And he succeeded, I think, although he was just about dead for his efforts. But as I was binding up his wounds and trying to figure out how the hell I'd find a doctor, he said to me. 'It's all right, it's all right. I did what I had to do. A man is just a man. But what is important is that he cares about someone, he protects someone.' He didn't say it, maybe he never used the word, but I think he meant what is important is that a man loves someone. I wrote a story about that man. Damned good story. Best story I've ever written."

I didn't say anything.

"Now do you understand why she is so important to me?"

"Well—"

"All right, all right; never mind. Forget it. Forget

what I've told you. It doesn't matter. But at least you strike me as a fair and honest girl, Aileen, and this isn't your business. What happens between Suzanne and me happens between us. It only concerns us. It's only important to us. So just stand clear, will you, my dear?"

"Good night, Derek," I said. "Good night, good night."

For half an hour, which turned into an hour, I thrashed around in my bed. I couldn't sleep, and since I thought I wouldn't sleep all night, I decided to get a book from Nicho's study.

Going down the stairs, I heard Derek talking softly. It took me a minute to realize that he was on the phone.

"Of course it's going to be a bloody good story. Would I still be here if it wasn't a good story? All right, all right, but if you can't trust my judgment for another twenty-four hours—

"Well, yes, that's simply marvelous that he's turning into a goddamn hero, sinking the fucking oil. Going to replace the shipment, is he? Maybe even double it? And he's going to establish a wildlife sanctuary on the south coast? Tears are coming to my eyes, mate.

"Listen, I told you I was getting some fairly good stuff. If I say it you can believe it or—all right, all right. Yes, I'll talk to you tomorrow at the same time. All right." He slammed down the phone.

"Oh, the little bastard," he said softly.

I moved back, pressed myself against the wall as he came out but he still saw me.

"Hello there." He was carrying a drink, swaying slightly.

"I couldn't sleep and—"

"And you were looking for me? I'm flattered,

sweetie. Thanks, but you see, I'm afraid, I already have a date. Rather an important date."

He climbed halfway up the stairs. He turned and looked back at me. "I know you won't believe me—but I do care about her, I do. And I'm not going to lose her. So come on, come on, have a good look since you're so bloody nosey." He turned and finished climbing the stairs.

From below, I heard him knock on Suzanne's door. I heard her soft murmur, his answering whisper. The door opened, shut, was locked from the inside. I even heard him drop his shoes on the floor by the side of the bed.

8

DEUS EX MACHINA

—This is a Watchbird watching a Watchbird who is beginning to hate being a Watchbird. In such a circumstance there are only two alternatives: Close your eyes. Or learn to fly. Yourself.

When I am depressed, confused, uncertain, I sleep and I eat. I awoke the next morning around noon and roared for Iphigenia and my breakfast. I wanted to get it down before it was time for lunch.

She carried in my tray and opened the shutters. The sunlight filled my room.

"Madame—" she began and made a shrugging gesture.

"What? Where is Madame?"

"She take a walk. Wit dat man." Even in pidgin English, Iphigenia's allegiance was clear.

I put on a robe and went out to the balcony. They were walking slowly down the beach. She was wearing her lacy white maternity dress which gave the impression of a tent covered with mosquito netting. There were flowers tucked in her hair. Derek reached for her hand. She hesitated. He took it. She pulled it away but slowly, slowly. I slammed a shutter, nearly decapitating my thumb.

Finally I made myself get dressed and go downstairs. Paul, Hardcastle, and even Mick were sitting on the terrace but everyone seemed deeply absorbed for once, in not looking down at the beach.

"Aileen, are you all right? I was concerned you were not quite well."

"Oh, no, I'm fine."

Mick made an unintelligible sound which Hardcastle seemed to understand perfectly and to which she responded. They wandered off together.

Paul came up to me. "Madame, her blood pressure has risen perceptibly."

I wasn't surprised.

"She should be in bed." She's been in bed. "Resting—I tried to tell her, but—"

I didn't reply. Am I my cousin's keeper? I went into the study. Paul followed me.

"Aileen, I have been thinking. Is there not some way we can get this man off the island? Aileen, he is a pleasant enough fellow, I suppose, but his influence on Madame—"

Another cable had come from Nicho during the night. SLIGHT DELAY. STILL HOPE TO RETURN BY TOMORROW MORNING. TRUST ALL IS WELL. I ripped it off to give to Suzanne.

"Aileen, couldn't we just call for the helicopter? Tell the pilot that these men must be removed. One phone call to the airport in Nicosia. That would not be so difficult to accomplish."

"The helicopter would just appear," I said, thinking about Paul's suggestion. "A *fait accompli.*"

"Yes," Paul said, "*exactement.*"

"And we'd tell the pilot that these men must go."

"And I shall also tell the workmen," Paul said. "Explain to them that our uninvited guests must be made to say *adieu.* I will make them understand."

"Alert them. Have them ready."

Paul snapped his fingers. "Done."

"It's a good idea, Paul. A good idea."

"Yes, a good idea."

We grinned conspiratorially at each other. Outside I heard Derek and Suzanne. "Aileen, are you in there?" she called.

I didn't answer.

"How about a little drink, Suzie?" Derek was saying. "I'd say champagne was in order."

"Why would you say that?"

"You know why, luvie."

"Derek, I've told you. Nothing's decided. I can't decide anything now. Oh, Derek, don't—"

"I couldn't help it. You look so blooming, Suzie. Now, I'll just go and see about a nice cold bottle."

Paul and I looked at each other. "A good idea, Aileen," he said again.

I snapped my fingers. "Done."

I quietly picked up the phone and dialed the code necessary to get the operator. There was no sound on the line. I tried again. And then again. "That's funny," I whispered. "I suppose there's something gone wrong with this receiver. I'm going to try the extension on the terrace, just to see if I can get an operator." But a nasty little shiver of suspicion was crawling up my neck.

Suzanne was lying on the chaise lounge, her eyes half-closed. She looked up at me. "Oh, hi—" She looked away.

"How are you?"

"All right, I guess," she said gloomily.

"Where have you been?"

"Nowhere. I mean, where the hell can I go? Amagansett?"

"Temper, temper—"

"Oh, can it, will you," she snarled. Mother Earth had turned moody again.

"Here's a message from Nicho—just in case you're interested—"

She snatched it from me. "He'll be back in the morning?" She leaned back and shut her eyes. The vein in her eyelid was throbbing.

I picked up the phone.

"Who are you calling?"

"Nobody—" because that receiver was dead too. Derek couldn't be that low, or could he? Besides he'd want to be able to phone his little exclusives to London.

Back in the study, I pressed the Telex starter button. No cheering "go ahead" light. It was dead, too. We were cut off from the mainland. We were cut off from everything and everyone.

"You can forget about calling the airport," I told Paul.

"What's the matter, Aileen? What's wrong?"

"I'm going to try and find out."

We sauntered back onto the terrace, looking casual. "Oh, hello—" Derek said cheerfully. "Want to join us in an aperitif? Champers. The perfect before, during, and after drink. If you can afford it."

"No, thanks," I said and Paul shook his head. He poured a glass for Suzanne and handed it to her. She took it with a sigh.

"We must have a toast."

"No, Derek, please—no!"

"What shall it be? To the baby, to the future, to—"

"Will you please shut up, Derek," Suzanne snapped. Her mood was deteriorating rapidly, from merely Suzanne-lousy to downright Suzanne-filthy.

"Oh, Derek, by the way, did you use the phone this morning?" I asked pleasantly.

He colored slightly. "No."

"Well, something's happened to it since you used it last night to call London."

Suzanne looked up. "You called London last night, Derek? Why did you do that?"

"Oh, the phone. Oh, yes, yes, I was going to tell you about that. Yes, come to think of it, I'm sure there's something very wrong with the phone. You can thank those two eager workmen of yours. They've been finishing the swimming pool, eh? Well, I guess Anapoulis must have once tried to explain to them that electricity and water don't mix. Poor bugger, he did too good a job of it. I guess he was planning a phone extension near the pool, was he? Has to be near the blower at all times, eh? Well the two of them noticed the cable this morning so they hacked it out and buried the ends of the bloody thing. They told me what they'd done when I was taking a walk early this morning. They were so damn proud of themselves, too. Isn't that a laugh?"

"No, Monsieur," said Paul.

"I don't believe it," I said. But remembering a workman putting in a washer in my sink and somehow ruining the plumbing in the kitchen for a week, I sort of believed him.

"The primitive mind," said Derek. "Fascinating but irrational. Suzie, did I ever tell you about that week I spent in Madagascar?"

"Who were you calling in London, Derek? You didn't answer me." Suzanne was trying to sit up straight, which was now impossible. Arranged on the chaise lounge, she looked like the cat who had swallowed not only the canary but the cage.

"It isn't important, luvie. Did I ever tell you about Madagascar?"

"But who were you calling, Derek? Derek? Aileen, if you know, then you tell me—" she said.

The moment was tense. Everyone looking at each other. Paul reached for my hand.

"All right, all right," Derek said. "I was talking to my office. I had to check in with them. But I was just putting them off."

"You rat," she said. "You snake—"

"Suzie, can't you trust me?"

She didn't answer. She was clutching at her stomach, that great enormous stomach. "Ooooooooh," she moaned. Paul and I leapt up and were hovering over her. "It is all right, Madame, it is all right."

Derek was pale and perspiring. "Are you all right, luvie? Is she all right? Suzie, luvie, talk to me," he implored.

"I'll take you upstairs and examine you there, Madame. Relax now, easy, easy."

"Lean on us, Suzanne—"

Together we led her to her bedroom. She kept her eyes closed tight. Derek hovered while we helped Suzanne up onto her bed.

"Do you think your labor has begun, Madame?" Paul was touching her stomach gently.

"Noooo, it isn't that." Tears were squeezing from under her closed eyelids. "I can't feel the baby anymore. Not since early this morning. Oh, God, have I done something to the baby?" she cried out.

"Now, now, Madame, calm yourself. I will examine you." He looked at us. "Please, we must be alone."

"Just call me if you want me, luvie," Derek said and grabbed me as we went out the door. "Does this doctor know what the bloody hell he's supposed to be doing? I know he fixed up some Parisian scrubber but so what? She shouldn't be stuck away in this place. She should be in a proper hospital. In the London Clinic."

"It's what Suzanne wanted."

"What she wanted? What the bloody hell does that have to do with it? You mean Nick the Greek actually does what she wants!? *Quelle* miracle! I wish to hell there was time to get her out of here."

After about ten minutes Paul came out of the bedroom, looking worried. "As I feared, Madame's legs are swollen. One leg is extremely swollen. Also, her blood pressure is much too high. In the last twenty-four hours Madame has managed to exhaust herself both mentally and physically—"

"Can I see her now?" Derek said.

"I, as her physician, want her to rest this afternoon, to rest completely. No visitors."

"I'm just going to make sure she's all right."

"If you were truly concerned about Madame you would leave her alone now."

"No," Derek said, "I'm sorry; maybe you don't understand but I can't do that." He went into the room.

Paul and I drifted downstairs together. The day had become faintly overcast as if to accentuate the emotional atmosphere. Everyone was tense and uneasy. The maids gathered in little twittering groups to whisper and giggle. I was sure they were talking about Derek and Suzanne.

Perhaps to cheer himself up, the chef laid out a marvelous, festive lunch. Fresh langoustine followed by delicate buttery lamb cutlets, culminating in a luscious chocolate mousse. The chef was pleased, I think, because he'd made a new friend in our simian photographer. It seems Mick, who was based in Paris, spoke French well. Perhaps he could learn English as a second language.

Paul ate quickly. "I have decided to induce the baby," he told Hardcastle and me. "She is very tired. The baby's heart beat does seem to be a little erratic. I do not like the sound. And the baby is quite large, really quite large." He stood up abruptly. "So, we have waited long enough for nature. Now we must do nature's work ourselves."

He and Hardcastle went to double-check the equipment in the infirmary unit. I went upstairs. Derek was in Suzanne's room. When I knocked, he opened the door a crack. "She's sleeping," he whispered. "Go away. Go away!" But when he went downstairs for some ice and soda water, I finally managed to slip in. "Suzanne? Suzanne?" I whispered.

Her eyes flickered opened. "I'm not sleeping. I'm just pretending. I can't sleep," she said. That vein was still throbbing on her eyelid.

"Suzanne, are you okay?"

"Give me that pack of cigarettes and the matches." She lit one of Derek's Gauloises and inhaled deeply "Shitty cigarettes." She kept looking up at the ceiling as if she did not want to meet my eyes. "Remember when I told you I sometimes feel there's a plastic bag over my head?"

"I remember. The smothers."

"Yeah, well, guess what, cousin, I've learned something important at last. I used to think other people put it there. Other people who were so stupid or so crude or so unfeeling, who were trying to force me to do something I didn't want to do. Now I know I let them put it there. Shit, I put it there myself." She sat up and looked at me. "Why can't I ever hold anything in my head? Why can't I ever say, this is it, this is the most important thing. This is what I care about. Why do I change my mind every goddamn minute? Why can't I ever really know what I really want?"

"Nobody knows what they really want anymore. Do I know what I want? You've got everybody's disease."

"He keeps saying he loves me. He keeps saying he wants me and the baby. And I should tell Nicho I want to go with him. He says we belong together—"

"You don't have to do what *he says*."

"He says, if I don't tell Nicho, he'll tell Nicho about us. And that Nicho will never want me if there are any doubts about the baby."

She began to cry again.

"But you were going to tell Nicho yourself."

"It's different now. And I didn't tell him, did I? I didn't know what to do then. I don't know what to do now—"

Great plastic tears were rolling down her cheeks.

"Suzanne, don't—oh, don't—"

Derek came back into the room. "I thought you were asleep. You know you shouldn't be disturbing her. She needs her rest."

"Neither should you."

"Please go. Look at what you've done. You've upset her. Don't cry, Suzie. Come on, I've brought you some lovely soup and I want you to have it now."

"Suzanne—"

She ground out her cigarette and put her head under the covers. The smothers. "Oh, Suzanne, don't do that!"

"I'll take care of her now. I can manage her. So will you please get out."

"Oh, Derek, for God's sake, you, you—" But I left without a row. When push comes to shove, somehow I can't. Suzanne was a large, unmoving mound under the covers.

Toward evening it was Paul who finally cleared Derek out of the room. "I wish to examine my patient one more time. Then she will have a sleeping pill. Only her maid will sit with her tonight. Personally I think you should leave as early as possible—tomorrow morning, Mr. Britten."

"I am certainly not going to do that, Dr. Lavelle.

But even if I wanted—which I don't—how would I manage my departure? Saint that I am, walking on water has never been my forte."

"There's always the speedboat," I said.

Derek snorted. "Bloody dangerous. I hate boats, hate water. Once in Africa I had to swim a crocodile-infested river to get a story. If you've ever had an old croc snapping at your arse, I can tell you, it gives you a permament allergy to oceans, rivers, and streams."

Quite drunk, Derek kissed Suzanne tenderly on her forehead, her cheeks, the bright-pink palms of her hands. She chewed on the silken edge of the quilt, no longer talking.

We all went to our rooms early that night. Of course, I couldn't sleep again; I couldn't even read. It worried me that Suzanne seemed so desperate and depressed. I, too, in my way wanted Suzanne always golden, even silly, never anguished like this.

At midnight there was a knock on my door. "Suzanne, you should be asleep," I said, getting up.

"No—*c'est moi*"—a whisper. "I am rather tense, Aileen. I could not sleep. But I did not think it would be wise to take a sleeping pill this night. May I come in for a few moments? I need to be with you."

"Of course," I said in a stage whisper. I opened the door.

He was wearing striped silk pajamas and a neat wool robe. He smiled tentatively. I smiled back. "Come in, sit down, please. I'm glad you came to talk." I gestured toward the rocker. The only other place was the bed.

Suddenly with one quick movement, he grabbed me, kissed me, threw me down. He was surprisingly powerful.

"PAUL!" I screeched and pushed hard. He bounced back up like a toy man with springs.

"Pardon, pardon, Aileen, but I thought you knew my feelings for you."

"I didn't know your feelings were *rape*."

"I truly regret if I have offended you, Mademoiselle. I will not disturb you again." He gave a stiff little bow. *"Bon soir."*

"Paul, oh, Paul—for God's sake—you don't have to go like that, I mean—well, you surprised me, that's all."

He hesitated.

"Paul, I do like you, I do. It's just—"

He sat down on the edge of the bed. "But we are adults, yes? And adults should not behave like children."

"I suppose."

He blew me a little kiss. It wasn't quite his style. I sat opposite him on the other side of the bed and took a breath. He reached for my hand. I gave it to him. We both stretched out warily. He wants me. He likes me. Why not at least try? I told myself. I took another of those deep cleansing breaths.

Now I suppose is the time to make an important personal disclosure. No, I am not frigid. So *there*. Rather, I am tepid, very, very tepid.

By the way, this little confession has never been drawn out of me before, not even by my closest and nosiest friends, not even at the one women's lib consciousness-raising session I attended.

Once Masters and Johnson came to the magazine to be interviewed about "What Every Teenager Should Know About Sex." As it turned out, they thought teens should know a helluva lot more about sex than our advertising director did. Still Masters and Johnson, serious, humorless, pudding-plain, impressed me. The vaudeville team of copulation.

"Presenting for your edi-fi-ca-tion and en-ter-tainment Masters and Johnson, their team of acrobats—all

double-jointed—and their famous Magic Lantern show."

I interviewed them for the magazine but never asked a single personal question. I couldn't. But since then, in my head, Mrs. J. and I sometimes have long searching dialogues, trying to find the solution to My Problem and How I Failed To Solve It.

J.: Miss Walker, I have been wondering if perhaps your orgasmic response occurs whenever you close your eyes and concentrate on some fantasy figure of yourself, Aileen-Yvonne, shall we call her, and her treatment at the hands of various salacious Arab gentlemen.

A.: Good try, Virginia, but I don't think that's it. Because almost all the time I concentrate on my own specially tailored versions of A Thousand and One Lurid Nights.

J.: Then perhaps it is some special quality of your male partner. Is it some special skill on his part, or perhaps the size and shape of his whazzit?

A.: His *whazzit*? Is this the way a sex expert talks?

J.: Just answer the questions, dear.

A.: Well, no. Because no matter what his size or his shape or his skill, the second time around is usually a great big nothing. In fact, it doesn't seem to have anything to do with him or me or the mood I'm in or the record playing on the phonograph or what he whispers in my ear. There is one thing though—

J.: Yes—YES.

A.: Most of the great moments in my sex life have followed Chinese dinners.

J.: Interesting.

A.: But, then, most of my adult sex life has followed Chinese dinners.

J.: We could still try some research on MSG.

Paul and I, our hips pressing. The bed was fairly
narrow. He snuggled down and I snuggled up. We
kissed but gently, tooth to tooth. I was glad I had just
brushed.

"I tell you the truth, Aileen, usually I am—how do
you call it—one big flop." Terrific.

But I said, "Don't worry, Paul. You don't have to
impress me. It's going to be all right." I touched him.
"Take your robe off."

"You wish me to, *ma chérie*? You are sure now?"

I nodded yes and smiled encouragingly though
honestly maybe it would have been a lot simpler to
have gone to sleep. Still, why not try? Suzanne had
said that sometimes bodies understood each other
without words. And she, too, was an expert.

His pajamas were monogrammed. He folded his
robe neatly at the foot of the bed. Then he got under
the covers and turned off the bedside lamp. He lay
back, his hands at his sides. "I knew you were a
warm, giving woman."

"Thanks."

For a while I felt I was working with modeling
clay.

He moved a little. "Ahhhhhah—" He reached for
me. "Aileen, you are lovely, so lovely—but let me,
chérie. Ah, how does that feel?"

"Mmmmm."

"I am not hurting you?"

"No."

"Nor there?"

"No."

"Nor there?"

"Paul!" Goddamn it, he sounded like he was giving me an internal.

"Forgive me, I did not mean. It is—what is the word?—a habit, yes, a habit—"

He kissed my hand. *"Ma chérie, ma chérie,* just one more little question."

"What?"

"Do you take the birth control pill?"

"Not any more."

"Hmmm. Interesting. The pill has such a bad reputation these days in England and in America. Are you wearing a diaphragm?"

"No, Doctor."

"When did you have your last period?"

I told him.

He sat up. "But this is not an absolutely safe day. Are you irregular?"

"Occasionally," I said from between clenched teeth.

"Then there are no absolutely safe days for you. You understand that?"

It was one sexy conversation.

"Then I shall have to protect you," he said. The optimist.

"Don't bother," I said, getting out of bed. "I'll put on my diaphragm."

"You had it fitted within the year? It is the correct size?" he called out to me as I went to the bathroom.

I wonder why he hadn't managed to give me a Wasserman the day before.

When I came out of the bathroom, he had taken off his pajamas and folded them neatly on the back of the chair.

"Aileen, Aileen, I kiss you there and there and there." Suddenly he was a whirlwind of activity.

"Paul—" I was quite amazed.

"Yes, I am just like other men—why not?" He gave

me that coy little smile again. I really didn't like it.
"So, my darling, are you ready?"

*Are you kidding? Can one fool one of the foremost
gynecologists in western Europe?* I closed my eyes.
Two minutes, two and a half. He moaned softly in my
hair and clung to me. "Aileen, Aileen, you are a wonderful girl." He kissed my forehead in gratitude.

Then he got up briskly and put on his pajamas. He
went to the bathroom. Naturally, he was washing his
hands, and I was sure he was using lots of soap.

"I should go back to the room. I should not stay
here. It would not look right." He sat down on the
bed and took my hand. "But I want to be close to
you, *chérie.* I will stay for a moment." He stretched
out his head on my shoulder and fell almost immediately into a light sleep, breathing noisily with an open
mouth. I was strongly tempted to give him a hard
shove but didn't. At least he didn't think we were
strangers anymore. And I suppose it wasn't unpleasant having him close, sleeping contentedly. I
took off his glasses and put them on the night table.

"Good night, Paul," I said. "Good night, darling."
Just to say the words.

I must have slept, too, because I woke in the morning to the sound of running feet and a high-pitched
cry. Paul rolled over and fell on the floor. "*Mon
Dieu,*" he groaned, "*Mon Dieu.*"

Someone was shouting loudly in the hall. I started
for the door. "Wait, wait—" Paul said. He got up and
put on his glasses. He tied his robe rather primly. "It
will look a bit odd our being together. Perhaps you
should say you had an ache in your stomach this
morning and came up to my room. Yes, and I came
back to examine you. Aileen, I am only thinking
about you, about your reputation—"

The shouts in the hall grew louder. Outside there

was a vague distant sputtering noise that struck me somehow as familiar. I opened the window shutters halfway and looked out. For once, it was gray and misty and the waves were high. There was a boat moving away from the shoreline. I studied it a moment before I realized it was Nicho's speedboat. Then with a terrible foreboding I knew what was happening: Suzanne was gone; Derek had taken her away. "Paul, Paul—" I cried out and he rushed to me. "Do you see that boat? I know it sounds insane but I think Suzanne is in it." I felt sick.

"No, no, it is not possible."

"That son of a bitch," I said. A romantic elopement. But it was Suzanne's fault too. "It is possible, Paul. You know it is very, very possible."

He looked uneasy. "Please understand, I can no longer be held responsible for the care of this patient" he said quickly, then sat down in the rocking chair. He shook his head while gnawing at a neat fingernail.

Outside in the hall the screams grew louder. What the hell was going on out there? I opened the door just a crack. Derek was standing over Iphigenia as she wailed and wailed.

"Derek? But I thought—"

"I'm sure you did," he said grimly. He turned toward me but kept his hand on Iphigenia's shoulder. He was red-eyed, unshaven, looking like he, too, had just woken up.

"No, no, I no do nothin'—" Iphigenia wailed.

"That's a bloody lie."

"I sleep, dat all."

Derek turned back to me. "She's gone off in the boat."

"Alone? That isn't possible."

"Quite right. Suzanne could not have got into that

boat herself, could not have got it started. She had some help. Didn't she? Didn't she?"

Iphigenia wailed. "I no do nothin'—"

"Why did you help her? Are you too stupid to realize the danger she's in now?"

Iphigenia sobbed, her face in her hands.

"All right, all right. Control yourself, for God's sake, Derek." I went to Iphigenia and bent over her. "Nobody is going to hurt you. We just want to know what happened, that's all." She kept sobbing. "You must tell us. Iphigenia, please. It's important." Out of the corner of my eye I saw Paul sidle out of my room and tiptoe down the hall.

Iphigenia looked up at me through her stubby fingers. "I no want her to do this, Lady."

"I understand. Now just try and tell us what happened. Please."

She wiped the corner of her eyes with her apron, then her nose. She spoke in a rush of words. "She no sleep much. She wake very early. She say she wanna go outside. She say she wanna sit in the boat. think about De Boss. She very upset. Okay. So I help her in da boat. It is good luck, I know, for a sailor's wife to be in boat when she about to haf a baby. I tell her dat—"

"Bloody hell," Derek sputtered.

"Go on, Iphigenia."

"Dat's all."

"Iphigenia, go on. It's important."

"Stupid cow," Derek said.

She glared at him. "Well, she ask me how to start the boat. She ask me. She tell me to show her. She yell a lot. I must do what she say. She my boss, too, right? Dat's all. I swear." She crossed herself.

"But that can't be quite all—"

"Oh, yes, Lady, I forgot. She cold. She say she very

cold. So I gif her my cloak. Go to the house for a
shawl. I come back and—" Iphigenia burst into tears
again. She covered her face. I noticed one of Suzanne's
Minoan bracelets pushed up high on her arm. Suzanne
had done more than yell; she had bribed Iphigenia.

Paul came down the hall, now dressed in slacks and
a shirt. "What has happened?" He sounded irritat-
ingly casual.

"Nothing much," said Derek just as casually.
"Suzanne's gone crackers, that's all. Your patient is
out on the speedboat right now. You know none of
this would have happened, Dr. Lavelle, if I had been
with her last night."

"None of this would have happened if you had
never come here, Mr. Britten," Paul said.

"All right, all right. Shall we try to forget our differences at least for the moment and concentrate on
what we're going to do? I assume there isn't another
boat on the island—"

"No."

"Bloody marvelous for a great shipowner. Has he
got any binoculars at least? I'd like to get a better
view of what the bloody hell is happening out there."

"Yes, I think so." I remembered there was a pair in
Nicho's desk drawer.

Iphigenia followed me to the study. "I sorry, Lady.
I sorry. I know she crazy but not that crazy—"

Ten minutes later we were all spread out on the
beach—Paul, Hardcastle, Derek, and me—wringing
our hands and passing the binoculars back and forth.
Mick screwed a telephoto lens that looked like the
barrel of a gun on his camera. He took picture after
picture. "Stop that!" I yelled at him. How could he be
so unfeeling? He looked at me blankly. "Fewkin'
dramatic," I think he said.

The speedboat did an occasional mad dash in one

direction, then drifted for a while in another and then again did a mad skittish dash, as if Suzanne were turning the wheel back and forth abruptly. The boat was too far away to see her clearly. Wrapped in Iphigenia's cloak, she was a dark formless lump. I grabbed the binoculars from Derek and focused them. Suzanne was slumped over the steering wheel. She seemed to have lost all interest in trying to maneuver the boat.

"Give me those glasses," Derek demanded and took them back. "How could she do something so bloody stupid?"

Easy. When things get uncomfortable, Suzanne runs. When Suzanne has to make a decision, Suzanne runs. When Suzanne feels guilty, afraid, unsure, like a little girl who has made a mess on the floor, Suzanne runs. And through pure instinct she makes the running away so spectacular that one forgets why she's running. Suzanne tossing in the waves: her most spectacular escape yet. Suzanne splits, splits apart. I shivered in the raw wind. I was becoming very afraid.

"This is dreadful, simply dreadful," said Hardcastle. "Poor *gel*." Poor *gel*, indeed. The boat was bouncing up and down in the foaming gray waves; and the gray sky was growing even darker.

"Gentlemen, we must do something," Hardcastle said. "Gentlemen, we simply must. It's our duty, our responsibility—"

"May I have the binoculars, please," Paul said quietly. We watched him as he took a long careful look. He lowered the glasses slowly. "Do you think one could swim out to the boat?"

"Not me, mate," Derek said quickly. "I told you, I'm not much when it comes to the briny deep."

"But, sir, how could you? It looks like miles," Hardcastle said. The boat was about half a mile out and drifting farther away.

"Of course you couldn't swim," I said. The sea had been transformed overnight from our gentle Med into a strange northern ocean, cold and dangerous. "Can you see her now?" I asked, feeling more frightened when the waves obscured the boat. I began to realize that with one fierce roll she could be tossed into those high dark waves.

Derek grabbed the glasses from Paul. "It's all right," he reported. "She's crouched down on the seat. Good thinking, luvie. Hey, what do we do if she starts to have the baby out there, Lavelle?"

Paul did not reply. He was looking out to sea, his head to one side and a pained expression on his long thin face. "But I am a fairly strong swimmer," he said finally.

"I hope you're satisfied, because this is all your bloody fault, Lavelle. I hope you realize that. This couldn't have happened if I had been with her. I ought to punch you in the mouth, you—" Derek turned toward Paul and raised a clenched fist.

"I will do it. I can do it." He said it mildly, with just a little quaver in his voice.

"No heroics, doc," Derek said.

"I will do it," Paul said again, more strongly.

"Here, here," said Hardcastle.

"Damn it, I'll swim for her too, then," said Derek. "If you can do it, I suppose I can do it."

"I am going to the house to change," Paul said.

Derek was unbuttoning his shirt. "I think I need a little drink." They went to the house together.

I looked through the binoculars again. There was a doughnut of black on the seat, which was Suzanne. Seeing her more clearly wasn't reassuring.

"Oh, dear," said Hardcastle. "All this tension is making me giddy." She sat down abruptly on the damp beach.

"Are you all right?" She was a bit flushed.

She nodded, her head back. She was panting. "Just need a minute to relax my old muscles, dear *gel.*"

Derek returned, carrying a bottle of Scotch and wearing one of Paul's bathing suits. Paul had on tight black elastic trunks, goggles and flippers. He handed me his glasses.

"Have a drink, doc," Derek said mournfully. "Warm us up." They both took long slugs from the bottle.

"Will you be all right?" I asked.

Paul shrugged, very French again.

"Maybe," Derek said, "if I have another drink."

The waves were fiercer, the wind whipping them more furious. Suzanne's cloak seemed to billow around her like a black cloud. Derek and Paul were both shivering.

"*Au revoir,*" said Paul.

"*Bonne chance,*" Mick said beautifully.

"For queen and country. Bloody hell," said Derek. They both walked to the edge where the pebbles became the sea. Together, they plunged in. Paul did a smooth Australian crawl, Derek, more of an English dog paddle. But both of them seemed to be moving in slow motion, while the boat was rocking back and forth to a staccato beat.

"They'll never make it," I said. I had a vision of Hardcastle and me plunging in to save them. But who was around to save us?

"Wait—" Hardcastle said. "Just a minute now." She was holding the binoculars up at a peculiar angle. "Oh, dear, it's not easy to see with these things. I'm not quite sure how to focus. But look, can you see— way over there—"

"What?"

"There." I searched the heavy skies. "Oh, yes—" she said.

"Let me look."

"Can you see it? It's not my old eyes playing tricks, is it?"

"There!" Mick was pointing too, looking through his telephoto lens. "There!"

It was a black speck far to the south. A few moments later the speck had taken shape, and a minute or so later, we could hear its metallic clatter above the sound of the waves. A helicopter, a beautiful gleaming white-and-red helicopter. Nicho was coming home.

"What a picture," Mick chuckled madly. "What a bleedin' picture. *Stern*, for sure. And fewkin' *Paris Match*."

"Where's Dr. Lavelle and Mr. Britten?" Hardcastle asked.

"Drownin'" Mick chirped. They had both disappeared for the moment. Hardcastle began to shout and wave her handkerchief. Paul was fifty yards from us now, still doing his determined Australian crawl. Derek kept going under the waves.

"I suppose they'll look up. Eventually."

The helicopter, intent on the island at first, didn't seem to notice the boat beneath it, nor the swimmers. On the beach Hardcastle and I, twin madwomen, waved and shouted and jumped about to attract its attention or Paul's or Derek's. *Somebody!* It was like a nightmare in which everyone is moving slowly and nobody is where they are supposed to be.

The helicopter began to circle as if it were going to land. "Oh, no," I wailed. Even Mick loudly echoed my anguished cry. But then the helicopter paused as if it finally understood, and circled back toward the boat. It hovered, then dropped down for a closer look, then dropped down once again until it was about fifteen feet above the boat. The noise of the rotors made

Derek look up. Then Paul. They stopped swimming and started treading water. Hardcastle and I clung to each other. "It's just like the telly," she said breathlessly. "Oh, dear, oh, dear, I better sit down again," she said and began fanning herself with her handkerchief. Mick gave a child-like laugh of pure glee. A life-and-death and new-life-to-come situation. He just kept clicking that fewkin' shutter.

I grabbed the binoculars. Suzanne had pulled herself back into a sitting position, the hood of the black cloak falling off, revealing her long blonde hair which gleamed even in the dull gray light. Her hair was whipped around by the down draft of the rotors. She looked up for a moment, then collapsed again, curling herself over the steering wheel.

"I wonder if she's in any pain."

"She's in labor, I think, poor *gel*," said Hardcastle crisply. She took the binoculars. Derek and Paul were swimming toward the shore. Out of the side door of the helicopter a rope ladder was dropped. Fluttering in the brisk wind, it hung about three feet above Suzanne's bent head. But she would never be able to hoist herself up; someone would have to go down to the boat.

A moment later, a figure swung carefully out onto the ladder. It was Nicho. He had taken off his jacket, tie, and shoes; his sleeves were rolled up. He looked paunchy and squat but his square shoulders and short arms were powerful. The ladder swung erratically back and forth as he began his steep, frightening descent.

"*Quelle* picture! *Quelle* picture!" Mick roared. "A bleedin' hundred million blowing in the wind," I think he said.

I kept watching the figure of Nicho moving slowly down the ladder. Halfway down, he seemed to slip. I screamed, Hardcastle screamed and we buried our heads in each other's shoulders.

I looked up first. Nicho was clinging with one hand to the ladder, pressing his body against it for support as he found his footing. He hung there for a moment. "Oh, dear," Hardcastle said, "oh dear."

"That was too close," I said. We were both shaking.

Derek surfaced suddenly close to shore. He staggered out of the water and up the stony beach. He was gray and cold and shivering. "Are you all right?" Hardcastle asked, reaching for his hand and feeling for his pulse.

"A drink—" he gurgled.

"A stimulant *would* be in order."

He gulped from the bottle, then turned and retched. His face was a pale green. He took another, smaller drink and kept it down. Then he lay back on the beach, still shivering.

I looked at the boat again. Nicho began descending again, more slowly this time, stopping at each rung of the ladder, resting for a moment, then stepping down again. From the last step Nicho jumped down hard. The speedboat rocked in the water as he landed. The foam rose, obscuring them completely for a long moment. I raised the binoculars. Nicho, I could see, went straight to the wheel and eased Suzanne out of the way. They didn't embrace. She hardly even seemed to acknowledge his presence. She was probably in shock.

Derek sat up and grabbed the binoculars away from me. "Let me have a look."

Paul came out of the water. He was cold and shaking, too. "A cramp," he said and slumped down next to Derek. "In my shoulder. It will be all right in a moment, I think." He tried to grit his teeth against the pain.

"Is the cramp here, sir?" asked Hardcastle, massaging his shoulder with her broad hands.

"Yes, it is a little better. May I see, please?" he asked Derek, indicating the binoculars.

"Certainly." Derek handed them over. A certain comradeship had blossomed during their swim. "Have a drink, old man."

"No, *merci.*" Paul groaned softly, standing up. "I must go to the infirmary. Get a stretcher for Madame."

"What about us?" Derek asked, and belched.

Paul moved his shoulder up and down. "It is loosening up." I handed him his glasses. He hooked them over his ears.

"I'll come with you," Derek said.

"No, it is not necessary. The servants can help. Rest. You swallowed a lot of water."

"You're telling me. More than I swallow most years."

The boat, with Nicho at the wheel, was headed straight toward the island, cutting through the water at or near full throttle. He steered the boat toward the pebbly beach, smashing it up on the shoreline about fifty yards from where we were standing, cutting the motor at the same time. Hardcastle and I ran along the beach to them. "Do you think she'll be all right?" I asked. "Do you think so?" For once, Hardcastle did not reply.

Suzanne was sitting up, staring straight ahead, unmoving. Oh, God. Hardcastle said softly, "Madame? Madame?"

"Suzanne, are you all right?" I couldn't help shouting. "Suzanne!"

"Puh-lease, don't break my concentration," she declared, continuing to stare as she took a deep breath. "There! Goody! I didn't forget my cleansing breath—"

"Ver-r-ry nice," Hardcastle said.

"I think I should change from first-stage breathing to second-stage breathing now. What do you think, Sister?"

"Well—" Even Hardcastle was ruffled by Suzanne's composure.

"The contractions are coming very fast. Oh-but-I-am-having-another-contraction-shit—"

"Cleansing breath, Madame."

"I remember," Suzanne said. And then she began to pant.

A sweet beatific expression crossed her face.

"Game *gel*," said Hardcastle. "Game *gel*."

Paul came down the path, followed by the workmen carrying the stretcher. He had changed into a crisp white jacket and white trousers. He stood on the beach and called out: "Madame, how are you?"

She glared. Puh-lease, mustn't break her concentration. She took a cleansing breath. "It hurts a bit but I'm doing my exercises. I'm definitely second stage but I can't time my contractions. My watch got wet—" She extended her soggy Piaget. "And I think my water broke but, well. it was kind of hard to tell."

"I think we should try and get you on the stretcher now—"

"Oh, but I can walk. I want to walk. Could you just help me get out of here?"

Nicho had been watching silently, without expression. He stood up and moved to Suzanne. "Lean on me," he said. I waded into the water; so did Paul. Nicho pushed, we pulled. Suzanne panted. We finally managed to get her out of the boat. She rested her head on Paul's strained shoulder. He winced slightly. She batted her eyelashes up at him. "You see, I just needed a little shaking up—"

"That is not exactly what I had in mind, Madame—"

"But it did the job." She began to giggle but her face changed. "Oh, it hurts, it hurts, Paul."

"Cleansing breath—Pant!"

"They're coming"—pant, pant—"too damn fast."

"Next time do the third-stage breathing."

"Is it"—pant, pant—"almost over?"

"Perhaps. It cannot be very long."

"I want to see my baby. I want to see my baby. I kept thinking out there, dummy, I'll never see the baby—"

"Madame, you will see your baby. Just try to concentrate. Now pant. Blow."

Her face was getting red. They walked slowly, Paul and Hardcastle almost holding her up. She seemed enormous, stately. After a long contraction, she turned and called in a soft voice: "Nicho, Nicho, I want you to be with me."

He didn't answer her. He was still standing knee-deep in the water, looking angry. A thunderbolt of rage might burst forth if he spoke.

Paul said hastily. "After I examine you, Madame, then Monsieur Anapoulis can be with you. But we must examine you now—and quickly."

"Nicho—" she called out sweetly, not moving. "Nicho, I need you, I really need you—"

"I am coming," he said finally and waded ashore. He was limping badly.

"Your leg—" I said.

"I think I twisted my ankle jumping during my great heroics. It can be looked at later. It is probably nothing." Suzanne, now blowing, now panting, seemed in better condition than anyone else. "Aileen, who are these men?" He frowned.

Derek and Mick were hanging back, still part of the way up the beach.

"They're British. A reporter and a photographer.

We tried to get rid of them. But something happened to the phone line. A lot of things have—uh—sort of happened."

"I see," Nicho said grimly.

Derek approached, trying to look casual but dressed in goose pimples and a too-small tank suit. He couldn't quite carry it off.

He extended his hand, flashed his glorious gleaming smile. "Mr. Anapoulis, sir, this might be an odd way of meeting but I must say it's still a great pleasure, a very great pleasure indeed. Derek-Britten-London-Daily-Express—" He sneezed suddenly and then again.

Nicho limped past without acknowledging Derek's outstretched hand. He went to Mick instead and pulled the Leica out of his grasp and flung it backwards behind him into the sea.

"Owwwww—" Mick wailed as if he had been struck. He doubled over in pain.

"You really shouldn't have done that," Derek said. "Mr. Anapoulis, that wasn't a very sporting thing to do."

Nicho cursed softly.

"Mr. Anapoulis, I have a few things to say to you, so I suggest we have ourselves a nice little chat as soon as possible."

"And I have something to say to you, Mr. London Daily Express. Get dressed and then get the hell out of here." And Nicho limped slowly up the path.

In a pregnancy the last wait is the longest. For half an hour I paced the terrace. After he got dressed Derek came out to sit and drink and wait, too. Nicho was in the infirmary with Suzanne. Oh, how I hated the waiting. Next time, I promised myself, I'd be the one having the baby. It couldn't be worse than the waiting.

Iphigenia came out to the terrace and whispered to me timidly: "She okay? Oh, please—"

"We hope so. We think so."

"I sorry, Lady. But I do what she tell me. Maybe she crazy. But I do what *she* wants—she tells De Boss?" She was no longer wearing the Minoan bracelet.

"Tell that stupid cow to bring me another bottle of Scotch," Derek shouted and sneezed. Iphigenia scampered off, happy to be serving us again.

The helicopter had landed crisply in the clearing near the house. Nicho's pilot was tall, blond and German. Once Nicho had told me: "I use Germans for technicians, Swiss for accountants, Frenchmen for public relations, and Englishmen for butlers."

"And Americans?"

"Pah! Americans are only good when working for themselves."

"Mr. Britten?" The pilot approached, the workmen standing behind him. "Mr. Britten?" he repeated.

Derek looked up, squinting. The sky was slowly clearing and brightening, though the day was still cool.

"Who the hell are you and what the hell do you want?" Derek asked, sneezing again.

"The helicopter is ready to take you to Nicosia Airport, sir. A reservation has been made on a TWA flight, leaving Cyprus"—he glanced at his watch—"in precisely one hour and seventeen minutes."

Mick was sitting at the edge of the terrace on the flagstones, sulking over the loss of his camera. He had hung all his other cameras around his neck and was holding them close, hugging them as if to protect them. The pilot looked down at him. "There is a reservation for you, too, uh, sir—"

Derek put down his glass and yawned. "And how

did you manage to make these reservations, old man? I know the phones are kaput—"

"The helicopter radio is working. Mr. Britten, may I suggest that you pack and prepare for your departure."

"Get stuffed."

"Mr. Britten, I have been told to take you to the airport in Nicosia. I cannot tell you how distressing it will be for me to employ any kind of physical force in doing so." The pilot frowned as if aggressiveness were totally out of character for him.

"For God's sake, man, a woman is having a child in there and you're yammering away about arrivals and departures like it mattered, you insensitive clod." Derek blew his nose.

The pilot hesitated and then said: "I'm sorry, but there was nothing in my instructions, sir, about waiting until a baby is born. The TWA flight is leaving Nicosia Airport in one hour and fourteen minutes, and you, sir, will be on it."

Deliberately Derek poured himself another drink.

There was a chorus from the infirmary.

"Push! Now!"

"Again!"

"Voila!"

"Push! Push! Push!"

"Ohohohoh—" Suzanne's ecstatic high-pitched croon.

Then, at last, there was the cry but not a baby's familiar shriek. The sound was deeper, more experimental, more joyful.

I ran to the infirmary door.

Derek was grinning. He raised his glass high, then lowered it to take a long drink.

A few moments later, Nicho stepped out the door, tearing off his surgical mask.

"A boy! A perfect boy!" He was grinning. He kissed

me and then wiped his eyes. "I have been waiting a long time for a son," he said hoarsely.

I hugged him. "Can I see Suzanne? Can I see the baby?"

Nicho was looking at Derek over my shoulder. Derek was looking at him

"I want that son-of-a-bitch out of here," Nicho said coldly.

"I think the pilot is just getting his bag. How much does the baby weigh? Nicho? Nicho?"

"The child is quite small." Nicho moved away from me. "No—maybe it is better if I talk to our Mister Britten now," he said thoughtfully.

I clung to his arm. "I want to see the baby."

"Go and see them. Go. She was magnificent at the end. Very calm. Very brave. I am proud of her."

I hesitated at the infirmary door. Nicho limped toward Derek. Derek stood up and walked toward him. They met halfway but Derek didn't take the chance of extending his hand again.

"Mister Britten, the child is male and appears to be healthy and alert."

"I'm glad. That's good to know. That's bloody good to know, sir," Derek said softly.

"We must wet the baby's head. Champagne, I think, would be the drink for this occasion—"

"I'd say so, indeed—" Derek tried a tentative smile.

"And a cigar. Have a cigar. In America, I believe, when a baby is born, they give out cigars. I don't know why. But it is not a bad idea—if it is a good cigar."

"Not bad at all. Jolly good." Derek lit up, seemingly content but his eyes were watchful. Iphigenia brought out a bottle of champagne in an ice bucket. Nicho opened it and the cork flew across the terrace.

Nicho poured.

"To the child—"

"To the lad—"

"To my son—"

Derek hesitated for a second but they drank together. Nicho threw his glass down and crushed it with his heel. He gave a wince of pain. "A custom," he explained, "an old Greek custom."

Derek threw down his glass. "Right-oh," he said. "When in Rome—" He had to stamp a couple of times before he broke his glass. Nicho called to Iphigenia to bring more champagne, champagne for everyone, the maids, the workmen, even Mick leaning against a potted palm was given his tulip glass.

Derek sat down. "I'm very glad we are having this opportunity to talk," he began, shifting around in his seat. "Because, well, I have something very important to talk to you about. And I think we can talk, talk openly. We are both men of the world—"

"Oh, yes, yes, most certainly," Nicho said. "In fact, Mister Britten, on this great, this auspicious day, I have decided to grant you an interview. I hope you are pleased, Mister Britten. As you know, I rarely give such interviews. But because of all that has happened today, I have decided to share some thoughts with you." And Nicho smiled, showing his dark little teeth.

"I didn't think we were going to talk, well, professionally," Derek began. "Is that really what we have to talk about, sir?"

"I am rather surprised, Mister Britten." Nicho's eyes were cold. "Usually reporters want to interview me. But the oil has been dealt with successfully. I am no longer the despoiler, the foreign devil, the villain. Perhaps I am yesterday's news, and you, young man, are in a hurry to catch a plane."

"All right, all right, I want the interview," Derek said slowly.

Nicho refilled their glasses. He laughed suddenly. "You know, I am suffering from jet lag, exhaustion, a sprained ankle, yet I'm beginning to feel much better, almost good, damned good."

"I feel rotten," Derek said.

"My son was born today," said Nicho.

"Mister Anapoulis—"

"Don't interrupt," Nicho said sharply. "Listen! Don't talk and don't interrupt. I don't like it."

Derek ground out his cigar and lit a cigarette.

"Do you know the most important difference between being rich and being poor, Mister Britten? I was thinking about that this morning, flying home. It is not in what a rich man possesses that the difference lies. Oh, it may be very pleasant to drink a good wine, smoke a good cigar, buy one's dear wife a diamond necklace. But that is not what matters very much. True luxury is being able to ignore what one wishes to ignore. And that is exactly what a rich and powerful man can do."

"All right," Derek said, a bit thickly, "Let's just discuss what needs to be discussed, Mister Anapoulis—"

Nicho held up his hand. His face was bland, expressionless. The sun had suddenly come out from behind a cloud. Nicho put on his dark glasses. "Are you sure you will remember what I'm saying? I am sure your readers will be very interested."

"Mister Anapoulis—"

"Mister Britten, shall I give you a good quote? Here's a damn good quote. Do you know that I think my greatest asset in business is the ability to make decisions," Nicho continued smoothly, conversationally. "Remember, young man, and be sure to tell your readers that. A lot of men in business can't make decisions. But if I have a talent, that is my talent. And I believe. I make the right decisions because I *believe* they are the right decisions."

"I refuse to sit here and let you play games with me—" Derek said, a hysterical note suddenly rising in his voice. "Suzanne, the child—"

"Sit down," Nicho roared. "I am not playing games with you, Mister Britten. No games. But perhaps you simply cannot understand what I am telling you. Must I put it so bluntly, must I say to you that, yes, I can ignore the truth if I choose and make a new truth? And believe in that truth and so, for me, it is the truth—"

"Nonsense! Balls!"

Nicho laughed.

"Look me straight in the eye, Anapoulis, look me straight in the eye and I'll tell you a truth, the real truth—" Derek said and lunged across the table, knocking over the glasses and the bottle. The champagne poured out, a steady stream down the table.

Nicho sat back, smoking his cigar, turning his glass in his hand, a puddle of champagne forming at his feet.

"So you want me to speak plainly, Mister Britten. You want that, too. I know that British journalists are allergic to subtlety, to irony. Well, perhaps I am, too. All right, then. Let me tell you this. I know everything there is to know about her. How could you be so stupid to think I wouldn't? What do you have to tell me now? She's my wife and I have a son. And the past, the truth of the past—whatever that truth—does not exist because it does not matter a good goddamn to me—"

Hardcastle was in the infirmary doorway, her surgical mask covering her face.

"Mister Anapoulis, you must come quick, sir. It's a

bit of a shock, sir." Nicho clutched at the table. "Well, it seems there's another baby, another boy, sir. She said she felt something and she gave a push and out it popped. She's quite a *gel*, sir. Super pelvis. So believe it or not, it's twins, identical twins and she wants you—"

Nicho gave a great loud roar of laughter and ran, stopping only to pick up a glass and another bottle of champagne before he went into the infirmary.

Derek looked at me. "Another boy, another son. Well, well—" he said slowly. "It isn't fair. More than anything else in this whole rotten world, we have to have a bit of the truth."

The pilot was carrying Derek's suitcase and portable typewriter. "We must leave right now. TWA will be holding the plane for us—"

"No," said Derek. "I'm not going. Not until I see her, not until I see the infants—"

"I am sorry, Mister Britten, truly sorry I have to do this. But I have to follow my orders, sir." He nodded to the workmen who grabbed Derek and began pulling him toward the helicopter.

"Get your hands off me!"

"Mister Britten, that was not very nice," the pilot said mildly. "Please do not try to kick me in that place again."

"Get your hands off—" Derek looked at me as they pulled him along. "Tell her if she wants me, tell her if she needs me"—Suddenly he stopped struggling and went slack. "Oh, the bloody hell with it!"

While Derek was being strapped into his seat, the pilot remembered Mick. He found him skulking around the infirmary with another telephoto lens on another camera.

"I just wanted to tell the Sister good-by," he said

very clearly and cheerfully surrendered his film. He had hidden another roll in the top of a sock.

As the helicopter took off I knocked on the infirmary door. Nicho opened it, grinning. "Good. Good. She wants to see you now. There's something I want to get for her—"

The door to her room was open. She was sitting up in bed. I went and kissed her cheek. Her hair and face were still damp from perspiration. She was grinning, too.

"How are you?"

"My bottom hurts like bloody hell. The first little darling's head, I think. To tell you the truth, Aileen, it's more like giving birth to a basketball than to a little baby."

"I heard you were terrific."

"Not bad, not bad at all. Have you seen them yet?"

"Not yet."

"So what are you waiting for? Go and see them. They just happen to be beautiful, wonderful, and perfect. But you tell me what you think. Be honest."

They were next door. Baby One in an elaborate bassinet draped with white and yellow tulle. Baby Two in a dresser drawer lined with blankets, the drawer balanced on an unmade cot. Another bassinet would be sent from Nicosia in the morning.

They were reddish-brown with heads of thick, dark hair. One opened milky eyes and looked at the light and made a strained crying face but no sound came. Exhausted by his efforts, he fell asleep again. Their features were flattened and swollen, miniature Golden Glovers who had won a long hard fight. They looked very much alike.

Paul came in, wearing a surgical mask. His eyes were crinkled, so I knew he was smiling. "Never heard a second heartbeat clearly," he said. "For a while I suspected twins but then I thought I was wrong. I did not want to risk taking an X-ray. One was exactly behind the other, hiding. Very cunning fellows. Birth is always a mystery." He pulled his mask down and kissed me suddenly. I couldn't respond. I pulled away.

"Aileen—"

I went back to Suzanne.

Her eyes were half-closed. She was delicate again, the husk of her pregnant self. She opened her eyes. "Wonderful?"

"Wonderful!"

"Beautiful?"

"Beautiful!"

"Intelligent?"

"Brilliant. I can tell from their bulging foreheads."

"Shit. Their noble brows, you mean. One more little question—"

"What?"

"Derek?" she whispered.

"Gone."

"Oh." A pause. "Did he want to go?"

"Well—he left," I answered lamely.

"Okay, okay—"

"My darling." Nicho was standing by the door. "A little something for you." He gave her a blue-velvet Cartier box.

"Happy birthday," I said.

A diamond necklace gleamed against the velvet. "Pretty," Suzanne said.

He clasped it around her neck and then kissed her ear. Twenty-four perfect diamonds. "I am having a little something made up for you, Aileen—"

"Nicho, please, it isn't necessary."

"But I want you to have something, something nice."

"Nicho, really it isn't—"

"My babies," Suzanne said. "I want to hold my babies. I don't even know why I'm crying." She looked at me. "Really I don't."

"Post-partum hysteria."

"I want my babies," she cried. "From now on they are my real jewels," she said dramatically.

"A sweet thought, little mother," said Nicho, kissing her forehead. "Such a sweet thought."

The next day a picture of Nicho kissing Suzanne on the forehead, holding a glass of champagne while she looked at her two infant sons made the front page of the *London Daily Express* and *Asahi Shimbun* and a week later the covers of *Stern*, *L'Europeo*, and (fewkin') *Paris Match*. It was accompanied by a brief story: "Twins for 'Cinderella Suzanne' by Derek Britten":

"My husband is the most attractive man I've ever met," beautiful, blonde Suzanne Anapoulis told me breathlessly just hours before giving birth to her silver-spoon sons. "He is vigorous, energetic, lives every day to the fullest. His greatest ability? In both business and in his private life, he knows how to make decisions and live with them."

A couple of weeks later, while Suzanne was nursing, Iphigenia brought in that day's mail. She handed Suzanne a postcard. Shifting the baby from one breast to another, Suzanne read aloud: "'Your husband got me fired. Thanks, bitch.' Did you, Nicho?" she asked softly.

"I think I wrote the owner of the paper. This island is our property, our home. I do not want my home invaded by the press," he said smoothly. "It is a matter of principle to me, my darling. Why? Does it matter to you?"

She kissed the top of the baby's downy head. "He's asleep, the silly. He'll be hungry again in an hour, of course." She passed the baby to me. I laid him in his carriage. I handed her the other twin.

"Does it matter, my darling?" Nicho asked again.

"Does what matter? Oh, no, no. Not really." She tenderly put the next baby to her breast.

"He was a rather ordinary young man. Not bad-looking. I suppose I could get him another job."

"But would he want that?" I asked, unable to control myself. "I mean—"

"He would not know it was me," Nicho said mildly. "And if he ever found out—the job would be so good that he would not care, he would not let himself care." Nicho laughed at the expression on my face.

"Look at him eat, the little piggy, the little precious—"

Nicho tore up the postcard and put the bits in an ashtray. Then he took off his sunglasses to watch Suzanne nurse—with pleasure, with wonder.

9

AND SO GOOD-BY

This I know now: inside every Jewish princess is a Jewish mother waiting to give birth.

Suzanne, la mama. She wanted to do it all, and she wanted to do it herself. From the start, she was determined to nurse both babies at every feeding.

"Well, Madame, I hope you'll have enough milk," said Hardcastle, sounding very doubtful.

"I'll have enough milk."

"Sister Hardcastle will give the 2:00 A.M. feeding, of course, and perhaps one bottle in the afternoon," said Paul.

"No, I'll do it—"

"Madame mustn't exhaust herself."

"You need your sleep. It is not necessary. They should learn to take a bottle, too."

"I want to do it all," Suzanne said with a new determined look in her eyes.

The babies slept, ate, cried, plumper each day. Suzanne, when she wasn't nursing, would hang over their bassinets.

"He smiled—"

"Gas," said Hardcastle. "A bubble—"

"He smiled at me."

"He's sleeping, Madame."

"Goddamn it, I think I ought to know if my own

son smiled at me." She no longer liked Hardcastle who "interfered," she said. She ran off to find Nicho who almost appreciated the babies' genius enough.

"And Ilg and Gesell say most babies don't smile for at least a couple of months—"

She called Creative Playthings in New York, ordering mobiles, Crawl-A-Gators, Busy Boxes, picture books.

"Madame," Hardcastle laughed, "don't rush things—"

There were already half a dozen books on childraising on Suzanne's night table. I even caught her reading *Teach Your Three Year Old To Read.* "Time flies," she said.

I liked to watch the babies going through their instinctive paces. They rooted for Suzanne's breast—a turn of the head, a snap of the jaws—like small animals smelling the milk.

When I held a twin, he would bury his soft head into the hollow of my neck for warmth and safety. Feeling secure, he would then dare to lift his wobbly head, venturing a little look around. After a moment, he would collapse back against my shoulder, no longer focussing but staring intently with the mad monkey-like gaze of the newborn.

Totally absorbed, Suzanne dressed them and undressed them. She even examined their dirty diapers. Only a mother reads diapers like an oracle. Suzanne was never bored.

Nicho still worked most of the time—talking on the phone, reading reports, meeting with his aides who were flown to the island by helicopter and then whisked away again. Every evening he came into the nursery to watch benignly as Suzanne bathed the babies, fed them, or simply fussed over them if they were asleep.

Often, in her new Mommy-voice, she'd snap at him: "Dar-ling, puh-lease, put out that stinky cigar. I just know that smoke can't be good for their little lungs." Obediently, even meekly, Nicho sacrificed his Havanas. But he resisted any of Suzanne's efforts to turn him into a suburban bottle-wielding daddy. He wouldn't feed or even hold them, saying: "For the first seven years all children belong to their mothers. And mothers belong to their children. At seven a boy, by instinct, should then turn to his father. And that is when he begins to become a man. I will wait for my time."

Suzanne also fussed at Nicho because the babies had not yet been named. In the Greek Orthodox church babies do not have proper names until after their christening, and they are usually christened months after their birth. As he vowed, Nicho is having a small whitewashed church built over and engulfing the temple ruins. An architect from Cyprus has already drawn up the plans. The christening will be held in the new church. Nicho has planned a great party, inviting hundreds of guests. I will be the godmother for both twins. "Who else?" said Suzanne. In the meantime, Nicho called his sons "Hector" and "Achilles."

"I hate those names," said Suzanne. "Hate those names." Somehow I think the babies have been named.

Paul and Hardcastle left us when the babies were three weeks old. The night before he returned to Switzerland, Paul came to my room. During the weeks after the babies were born, he came calling once or twice after midnight. But our lovemaking remained awkward and strained.

That last night Paul held me tenderly, seemed more considerate. He even left the bedside light on at first but then switched it off because we kept looking straight into and then away from each other's eyes.

"I have not made you happy this way," Paul said. "I know that, Aileen."

I started to protest but stopped when he put his finger to my lips to shush me. It was the most genuinely sensuous gesture he had made toward me. I was touched by it.

"Wait—wait, ma chérie, and listen to me. I know I am no great Don Juan, no great lover for you. But I think that, between us, things could get better—truly."

I didn't answer because I felt so uncertain about Paul, myself, the future. I told myself I had to start thinking about ME, ME, ME—to stop avoiding so assiduously thinking about myself.

"You are a kindhearted girl and have been kind to me. I want to please you, too, very much—" And he tried—oh, how he tried—working over my body with a doctor's lifesaving effort. I was only moved by the seriousness and ingenuity of the attempt.

He kissed me good-by with a sigh. "Will you come and see me in Geneva? Come and see me soon. Aileen, we can be good friends and perhaps more than that. This is important to me. It is important to you?"

I gave him another cool kiss for an answer because I had no answer. I think we both knew I was kissing him good-by.

"Au revoir, Aileen."

"Good-by, Paul." I couldn't say 'adieu' like they do in the movies. Too corny. Too true. "Au revoir," I tried. Paul winced ever so slightly at my pronunciation.

On the day after the babies were born I dutifully cabled Aunt Bea: TWINS STOP EIGHT POUNDS SEVEN OUNCES STOP EVERYONE PERFECT STOP SEND EXTRA LAYETTE AILEEN.

The layettes, in their brown Saks boxes, arrived two days later carried by one of Nicho's planes to Cyprus and taken by helicopter to the island. Aunt Bea's tear-stained letter accompanied the packages.

> My darling daughter,
> Today my heart is overflowing with tidings of joy. Though there can be pain in being a mother—and how well I've known that pain—and I think you know what I mean—it is still the greatest joy a woman can have. (No matter what they say about other things these days.) So enjoy your babies when they are babies, enjoy your children when they are children. It's never easy, and it gets harder but there is nothing else like it—

Aunt Bea called every other day from Nicho's New York office to ask about the babies. She kept telling Suzanne she wanted to visit us.

"Puh-lease, Mother," Suzanne whined in reply. "It wouldn't be safe. You'd bring all those dreadful New York City germs."

A couple of days after Paul and Hardcastle had departed, Suzanne got another phone call from Aunt Bea.

"Hello, Mama." Suzanne had become casual and relaxed about the phone calls. She liked to talk about the babies. She talked while she nursed. (She did practically everything while she nursed.)

"Hello, darling. How are you and darling Nicho and the little darlings?"

"Just fine, Mama. This is such a clear connection. The best we've had. Our new phone line from the island is such an improvement—"

"You think so? Hahaha. Guess where I am, darling."

"Guess where you are?"

"Cyprus—"

Suzanne jumped so that the baby popped off her breast and gave a fierce angry wail.

"And what an awful place it is. There isn't even a decent airport shop. The humidity has collapsed my set like a pancake—"

"Mama—"

"I felt I should be with you. Why not? Is that so terrible? I wanted to see the babies. How many grandchildren do I *have*? Besides all my friends were a little surprised that I hadn't come before. Suzanne, you're not angry with me—Suzanne, answer me—"

Suzanne spoke slowly: "It's all right Mama. If you're here, you're here. I mean, it will be nice to see you. Nicho has to call the pilot. He'll bring you here to the island. I'll see you in about an hour. Good-by, Mama."

She hung up the phone. "Shit, shit, shit. Guess who's coming to dinner?"

"I think I've guessed."

She looked at the twin in her arm; she looked at the twin in my arm. "Poor kids, you're going to meet your dear old granny."

As if on cue, they both began to wail. "Well, I told you they were smart. Oh, shit, I better tell Nicho. Poor Nicho."

"Don't worry. He's too big to cry."

Exactly an hour later, Aunt Bea descended gingerly from the helicopter. Strawberry blond frizz whipped by the wind. She was dressed jauntily in a beige safari suit and antique gold bangles.

"My dear Madame Goldfarb," Nicho went to her, bowed, took her arm. "It is a pleasure to welcome you to our home."

"Nicho, darling, call me Bea, please. Madame Goldfarb—I don't know, it sounds like I should be packaging cosmetics. *Su-zanne*," a half-sob broke in her voice. "Su-zanne, you don't even have a little kiss for your mother?" Wordlessly, Suzanne accepted her mother's kisses.

Aunt Bea looked at me through her aviator sunglasses. "Aileen, darling, you look wonderful. See what a suntan can do?"

Suzanne was silent and expressionless. She was wearing a stretched-out maternity dress stained with her own milk, no shoes, her hair long and streaming, tied back with a piece of wool.

"Well, the first six months are terrible, right, darling?"

Aunt Bea continued, ignoring Suzanne's silence. "I remember. Do you think I don't remember? And you had colic. Always crying, always trouble right from the start. But you were beautiful. She was always beautiful," Aunt Bea said, and looked at Nicho. "A little rosebud. So where are they? Do you think I flew six thousand miles only to see my beautiful daughter look like a slob? I remember how you looked when you wanted to look like a slob. Didn't I live through the slob stage too? I came to see my grandsons."

Suzanne stared at her mother, her mouth open. I held my breath, certain of a minor tantrum. Instead

Suzanne laughed suddenly. "Oh, Mama, Mama, will you ever change?"

"Why should I? The babies! I want to see those wonderful babies."

At first the twins screamed more lustily than usual when Aunt Bea picked them up. Suzanne had to comfort and calm them. Finally she put a baby in her mother's arms. "Mama, hold their heads—don't let them wobble—"

"That's right. I remember now," Aunt Bea said softly, following Suzanne's instructions. She sat in the rocking chair and hugged one baby into submissive content silence. "A-ha, baby," she hummed a tuneless, wordless lullaby. For once, the nursery was quiet.

Dozens of presents poured out of Aunt Bea's luggage. Snuggies and sweaters and robes and stuffed animals. Cowboy suits and embroidered bibs and blankets and a dozen shiny silver spoons. From the Hadassah ladies and the Temple Sisterhood. From the Great Books discussion group. Even from Aunt Bea's new tennis instructor. "Aileen, your mama knit carriage covers with Greek key designs in pink and baby blue angora. Adorable. Adorable!"

That night she helped Suzanne give the babies their cereal. The twins loved their nighttime meal of pasty glue. When they saw the bowls of cereal, their hands shook with impatience. Their mouths kept opening, dribbling with anticipation. They reminded me of little old men at the Horn&Hardart whose only remaining pleasure is Cream of Wheat.

Aunt Bea took one twin and one bowl; Suzanne, the other. "I'm sure they sleep much better with a full stomach," Aunt Bea said ladling in a mouthful.

"But I only give them as much as they want, Mama," said Suzanne. The liar. She stuffed.

"Of course, of course." Aunt Bea pushed down another mouthful. "He loves it—loves it—"

"I know—" Suzanne gave her twin a heaping baby spoonful.

"Suzanne, let me tell you. Darling, you really are surprising me. You really are doing an A-number-one job with these children."

"Mama," Suzanne said in a soft voice. "Mama, I'm glad you're here."

For the next few days Aunt Bea helped Suzanne with the babies, made fawning and polite conversation with Nicho, and occasionally gave me critical, searching looks. Nicho showered her with a variety of gifts—a flokati rug, an elaborate gold necklace, a small old krater. "About 4 B.C., the dealer said," Nicho explained. "How interesting," said Aunt Bea. "Nobody else I know will have a planter like this." She was happy and Suzanne remained tolerant and pleasant. But I had even less to do than usual.

"She certainly likes being a mother," I said to Nicho one night when we were having coffee. We still had trouble, cold sober, making conversation. Aunt Bea and Suzanne had gone to the nursery after dessert to watch the babies breathe.

"Yes, she's content now. It is best that she stays so content," he said. Then he got up, puffing on his cigar, and went to his study.

I was alone again. At last, I began to think about going home.

The next afternoon I went to the nursery to help bathe the twins. Aunt Bea and Suzanne, with shirtsleeves rolled up, had already finished. They both looked at me a shade guiltily. "Aileen, sweetheart, sit down, sit down." Aunt Bea's greeting was effusive, too effusive. She was toweling vigorously, ignoring Achilles' wails.

"I've been thinking about you, darling," Aunt Bea said when she finally had her twin down. "I'd love to stay here longer but Uncle Morris is beginning to complain. And Uncle Morris needs me, too. So I'll be leaving the day after tomorrow. I wondered if you wanted to fly home with me."

"Well, that's funny, Aunt Bea, because I've been thinking about going home, too."

"I'd hate for you to go; I'd really hate it," Suzanne said, a bit dutifully. She was glancing over at the twins who were both fussing. "But it isn't fair my keeping you here—"

"What are you going to do when you get home?" Aunt Bea asked as she rubbed Hector's back.

"Open my door. See what's been stolen."

"Seriously."

"I am being serious."

"All right, all right, Aileen—but after that—"

"Call my mother."

"Your mother is now working with Plexiglas. Very interesting. She's already built a cocktail table and a shower stall."

"Oh God."

"And then?"

I almost said catch up with an old boyfriend but didn't. "I suppose I'll have to get a job."

"What kind of job would you get?" Suzanne asked.

"Some kind of dumb magazine job."

"No, you're not. Surprise, surprise. You're going to work for Nicho and me, for us. Name a salary. Go ahead, name one—" Suzanne was smiling. Suzanne was learning to be the happy giver of gifts, too.

"Just a minute—what kind of job?"

"I don't know. Whatever you want. Just doing things for us." She gestured vaguely.

"Personally, I think Suzanne and Nicho should have an apartment in New York, something nice," Aunt Bea prompted.

"Yes, yes, that's right. You could look for an apartment, Aileen. And decorate it. And send me things I want. I've asked Nicho's office in New York a dozen times for some books and they still haven't sent them. They are so dumb."

"It would be nice for you too, Aileen. Being Nicho's and Suzanne's—well—sort of representative. It would give you a nice social position, darling. Think of that. You could meet some interesting people—like an eligible man or two. Worse things could happen."

"But that's not a job. I don't have to work for you, Suzanne, in order to put a book in the mail—"

"But I want you to. And you'll have to come back here in a few months for the babies' christening. Then we could go to Paris together. Nicho wants me to get the apartment in order there. And he has a country house in England, I think. I suppose I'll have to do something about that. You know I can't do junk like that myself."

"Aileen, you're so efficient and organized. You know Suzanne's taste. So you'll help her. It's perfect," Aunt Bea said.

From cousin to confidante to paid companion. I felt a lump rising in my throat.

"You can charge us whatever you want. Nicho agrees. It was Nicho's idea, really—and Mama's. I don't want you to waste your time on some stupid job, Aileen. Besides, I know I'll need you more and more."

"Aileen, you're such a sensible girl. And what a golden opportunity!"

"I'll think about it," I said. "Let me think about it."

"You can't say no," Suzanne said, smiling at me, certain she had solved all my problems, as well as a few of her own.

"I'll think about it," I repeated.

"There's nothing to think about," said Aunt Bea, a little sharply.

And so I am packing. Tomorrow morning Aunt Bea and I are flying off first class on one of Nicho's 747's. He has already told his New York staff to prepare an office for me, a corner office. I am not to be called a social secretary, not that, but a "special, private, personal assistant." And my salary is to be generous, more generous than anything I could earn even if I were a successful magazine's editor-in-chief. Nicho also wants me to move out of my West Side slum to something more suitable, closer to the co-op he wants me to buy for Suzanne on Beekman Place. He wants me close at hand when Suzanne visits, to chat with her, go shopping, visit the hairdresser (a new hairdresser, of course), to keep her away from old friends, and perhaps even babysit for the twins, I suspect.

To all these plans I have not said yes, exactly, but then again, I have not said no. I am being paid off, Nicho knows it; Suzanne knows it but will not admit it to herself, *especially* to herself. Maybe even Aunt Bea somehow understands, even though she does not know the details. It is my payoff for helping Suzanne through her pregnancy, those last few weeks, those last unpleasant oh-so-difficult moments.

Outside Suzanne, Nicho and Aunt Bea are sitting on the beach, with the babies. It is warm again today. Suzanne is wearing an old bikini. Her stomach is almost flat again, but there are pale stretch marks on her hips and a dark-brown line bisects her stomach, running down from her navel. Her breasts are huge. The bikini bra just covers her large brown nipples.

Suzanne is digging in her beach bag, looking for a mirror. "Shit, maybe I better start dieting a little. Shit," she says, "look at my hair." She is frowning for the first time in weeks. I walk away. I don't want to hear. I have to pack.

My dresser drawers are all empty. I double-check them, just to make sure. And the medicine chest is empty, too. Always careful, I don't want to leave anything behind. Idly, I open the night table drawer, expecting nothing. But there is a letter in the corner. A CBS envelope. Goddamn it! Michael's letter. I had forgotten.

I hold it in my hand, examining it. Then I tear it open. It is typed perfectly, without an error. I wonder if his secretary typed it up for him.

Dear Aileen:

I was very much surprised to receive your note which said you were going away. I must point out, you neglected to give the address where you are going. I very much wanted to talk to you this week so this set of circumstances has greatly disturbed me. I decided to write to your office which I assumed would have your forwarding address. Incidentally, when I phoned the office, someone there said you had resigned. I find this all very strange. I repeat, I wish I had the opportunity to talk with you before your departure.

But to the crux of the matter: Aileen, all I can say is, I find myself in a rather incredible situation. I know what I'm going to tell you will be hard for you to believe. In some ways, it's hard for me to believe. But to put it bluntly: on next

Sunday morning I am marrying a girl named Mary Katherine Gallagher at the Church of The Resurrection in Astoria, Queens.

Surprised? I thought you would be.

Mary Kay is a secretary in the Programming department. She's a Katharine Gibbs graduate. She is only twenty-two, has red hair, and was the second runner-up in the Miss New York State contest last year.

Frankly, I wish you could meet her. I have always thought you were a very astute judge of character and might have possibly made a damn good lawyer. I'd like your honest appraisal of Mary Kay.

I must confess that while I was dating you, I was also dating M.K. I know you must think I am a crumb for doing such a thing. And I probably am.

Mary Kay isn't like you. She isn't well-read or ambitious. She is what I call an old-fashioned type girl. She is also an excellent gourmet cook. But more than that, there is something about her that appeals to me deeply. Such things just happen, I guess.

Aileen, dear, I just want to tell you that I like you. I have enjoyed our evenings together very much. I always thought your comments on books and movies were particularly incisive.

I felt I had to write and say, well, I'm sorry. I hope you can understand.

Best wishes to you always.

                                        Michael

P.S.: Can you imagine my parents' reaction to all this? It's no joke. My sister is especially upset and sends you her regards. I wouldn't be surprised if she calls you.

P.P.S.: Aileen, I just want to tell you, you will always have my greatest respect.

I throw myself back on the bed and laugh until I
begin to cry.

Even the heart I thought I might have broken, I
didn't break. Even the heart he thought he definitely
broke, he didn't break. The story of my life: no
dramas, no climaxes. Maybe a few pratfalls. Like lovers in a comedy routine who with arms outstretched
walk right past each other.

After about ten minutes I stop crying and laughing, laughing and crying. I stop doing everything but
thinking, thinking for and about myself. And I suddenly know for certain I am not going home to be
Suzanne's high-priced lady-in-waiting.

I pull my bathing suit out of the top of my suitcase
and put it on. I run down the path to the beach.
Suzanne sits cross-legged on her haunches, her back
to the sun. Her mane looks golden-fiery in the sunlight. She is very still, watching over the babies. Nicho is reading a report. Aunt Bea is dozing, her
mouth open, a French fashion magazine spread out on
her lap.

"I'm sorry," I began, but why apologize? "Listen," I
say instead, "listen to me—I've changed my mind. I
don't want to go home yet. But I don't want to stay
here either."

"Then what do you want to do, Aileen?" Aunt Bea
is wide awake and alert, looking at me through her
sunglasses.

"Go away. Travel. Places where I've never been."

"But you've been here for so long. Don't you want
to go home for a little while?"

"And you'll come back for the christening. We'll go
to Paris afterward. You said you would."

"Where do you want to go?" Nicho asks quietly.

"I'm not sure. I just want to see things. Deserts, jungles, oceans—"

"Oh, God, you're too old for that stage," says Aunt Bea.

"I just want to look around," I finish lamely.

"This doesn't sound like you," says Suzanne.

"Come home for a while. You'll be busy. Then in a few months, if you want to take a little trip—"

"No," I say firmly. "I'm sorry, but I'm not going home tomorrow. I am just going—" When in doubt, run like hell.

"I can write some letters of introduction for you, of course," Nicho says. "And if you need some money—"

"I think I can manage."

"It would be my pleasure," he says. He doesn't want me to go without that payoff.

Suzanne says nothing but gives me a look: speculative, appraising, almost, well, envious. No, no, it can't be.

"Crazy," says Aunt Bea. "Absolutely crazy. And you're usually such a sensible girl, Aileen."

"Look," Suzanne says, "just look—" One of the twins is asleep but the other, lying on his stomach, has picked his head up, higher and higher, looking around. Suddenly the weight of that great bobbing head is too much. He is off balance, pulled over onto his back. He gives a terrific squawk.

"He turned over! He turned over! They're not supposed to do that for months—"

She picks him up, cuddles him, lays him down again. A moment later, his tears forgotten, he raises his head like a turtle coming out of his shell, a sea creature crawling onto the land, a glorious achievement. He flips over.

The other twin, awakened by the noise, raises his

wobbly head to look around. He arches his neck higher and higher and turns.

"Not for three months at least," says Suzanne, bending and kissing and comforting. Nicho looks at her tenderly and takes her hand. Aunt Bea looks at the babies and beams with pride. We spend the rest of the afternoon in the warm sun, sitting close together on the blanket. The four of us, for once, are filled with contentment and expectation, watching the babies turn over and over, revolving like small worlds.

Now it is very late and I am leaving in the morning. Tomorrow I will say good-by to Cousin Suzanne, wish her well, and step center stage into my own life. Any story I tell in the future is going to be my own. For, fellow groupies, I've decided that in life, like in books, the problems of the heroine are always resolved. It's the minor characters who have to look after themselves.

Sally Says

Who is that enchanting young woman currently charming Kuwait's gilded-with-oil Sheik Abdhul Hassam Al Yamani (or your life) known to his intimates as Al-Saqer, the Hawk of the Harem. Friends say the mystery lady is a relative of Nicho "Big Daddy" Anapoulis, whose adorable wife Suzanne, the recent mother of two bouncing baby boys, is already pregnant again. Oh, you naughty Nichol As for the Sheik whose ancestral Bedouin tents are pitched on practically a sea of black gold, all he'll say about his fetching inamorata is: "Her? She makes me laugh." And the lady in question isn't talking at all but smiles a lot. Isn't that sweet! Now don't you just love unexpected romances? Don't you just love happy endings? Who else tells you these things?